Praise for Be My Valentino

"I adored *Be My Valentino*! Sandra D. Bricker has such a knack for dialogue that I felt as if I were watching a movie. And I fell in love with her characters—Grampy is especially charming! The epilogue is perfect (as is the sneak peek at the next book). Sandra D. Bricker has a new fan, and I can't *wait* for the next Jessie Stanton novel!"
—Deborah Raney, author of *The Face of the Earth* and the Chicory Inn Novels series

"Get swept into the glamorous world of Jessie Stanton! Set against the dazzling backdrop of Los Angeles, *Be My Valentino* follows Jessie as she struggles to hold her new life together while her ex-husband does his best to tear it apart. With an uplifting faith message, a fun cast, a hunky boyfriend, and sweet Grampy, this book will leave you panting for the final installment of Jessie's adventures!"
—Jill Kemerer, Harlequin Love Inspired author

"From light-hearted, breezy romance to stomach-churning intrigue, *Be My Valentino* has a little something for everyone. I particularly enjoyed the exquisite narrative and the sweet chapter openings. Kudos to Sandra D. Bricker for another five-star story."
—Janice Thompson, author of the Weddings by Bella series

"Dramatic, engaging, romantic—*Be My Valentino* is all that and so much more. The newest Jessie Stanton novel by Sandra D. Bricker will leave you wanting the next book from this talented author. Novel Rocket and I give it a high recommendation. It's a must read."
—Ane Mulligan, President of Novel Rocket and author of *Chapel Springs Revival*

Other Books by Sandra D. Bricker

The Jessie Stanton Series
On a Ring and a Prayer
Be My Valentino
From Bags to Riches

The Big Five-OH!

The Love Finds You Series
Love Finds You in Snowball, Arkansas
Love Finds You in Holiday, Florida
Love Finds You in Carmel-by-the-Sea, California

Another Emma Rae Creation Series
Always the Baker, Never the Bride
Always the Wedding Planner, Never the Bride
Always the Designer, Never the Bride
Always the Baker, Finally the Bride

The Quilts of Love Series
Raw Edges

The Contemporary Fairy Tales Series
If the Shoe Fits
Rise & Shine

SANDRA D. BRICKER

BE MY

Valentino

A JESSIE STANTON NOVEL

Abingdon Press
Nashville

Be My Valentino

The persons and events portrayed in this work of fiction are the creations of the author, and any resemblance to persons living or dead is purely coincidental.

Macro Editor: Ramona Richards

Published in association with Books & Such Literary Agency

Library of Congress Cataloging-in-Publication Data

Bricker, Sandra D., 1958-
  Be my Valentino / Sandra D. Bricker.
     pages ; cm. — (A Jessie Stanton novel ; book 2)
  ISBN 978-1-4267-1161-9 (binding: soft back) 1. Chick lit. I. Title.
  PS3602.R53B4 2015
  813'.6—dc23

                                                                    2015010424

All scripture quotations unless noted otherwise are taken from the Common English Bible. Copyright © 2011 by the Common English Bible. All rights reserved. Used by permission. www.CommonEnglish Bible.com.

15 16 17 18 19 20 21 22 23 24—10 9 8 7 6 5 4 3 2 1

MANUFACTURED IN THE UNITED STATES OF AMERICA

For Eva.
Jessie, Danny, and I are so much better
for knowing you.
Thank you for hanging in there with us.

Acknowledgments

Many thanks to my editor, Ramona Richards;
to my Launchies;
and to my head cheerleader, Marian Miller.

Prologue

Ain't nothin' on God's green earth more satisfyin' than answered prayer. That's what I got when my Jessie called home to catch me up on the things happenin' in her life out there in LaLa Land. That counterfeit husband o' hers might just meet Brother Justice and—if that ain't enough—Jessie done met the man I been prayin' fer all these years.

"He's like no one I've ever known, Grampy," she told me.

But if she hadn'ta said it, I'da known anyways. The good Lord changed my Jessie in her troubles, no doubt about it. I knew them blinders would drop off her eyes eventually if I just took enough blood pressure medicine to keep me prayin' fer my girl.

"He's a God-loving man like you, Grampy."

Course he is.

"He makes me want to be better. And stronger."

Course he does.

Comes a time in everybody's life when the prayers of the people that came before 'em start to get answered. And the Lord 'n me been chattin' for years upon years. All that other stuff was just bumps in the road that took my Jessie to use the good sense the good Lord gave 'er. Set her priorities right. Drop the blinders on her eyes and see things how they really are.

No, ain't nothin' in the world like answered prayers, and the Lord's got a way of whisperin' in a sack of ears when somebody needs the fervent prayers of righteous men. And women. Jessie says a new friend, an elder like me named Marjorie, been prayin' for her too. Lotta others besides, no doubt. Yeah. Tonight I'll be thankin' God for the prayers He answers as well as for the ones He don't.

Jessie's old grandpa is gonna sleep sound tonight.

1

Jessie gazed at the people gathered around the warm and beautiful table near the hearth on the back wall of Tuscan Son. Beneath the yellow glow of the chandelier overhead, she tallied the ways that each and every one of them had played a part in getting her to this place. To the top of the insurmountable mountain, where she could finally look down at the path she'd taken and see it for what it was. The road toward her destiny.

Piper—her beautiful friend. Jessie wondered what she'd ever done to earn a friendship like that one. Piper had carried her to the bottom of the mountain that Jessie felt sure would be the end of her, and Piper looked up and saw only possibilities.

"Your confidence has taken a very hard blow. I get that," she had said with confidence after Jack disappeared. "But it doesn't change who you are, Jess. You can do this. You're going to pick yourself up, dust yourself off, and you're going to start a whole new life."

Like in most things, Piper had been right. Against all those horrifying odds.

Beside her sat Amber. If Piper was the driving force to begin the climb up the mountain, Amber was the pickax that helped clear away the clutter.

"I'm your girl," Amber had said to her when they met for the first time to talk about the future. "I'm available today. Do you want to take me home with you and show me your closet?"

What if she hadn't gone into the ladies room that night, at the precise moment that she did? She might never have crossed paths with Amber Davidson, Force of Nature.

Next to Amber sat Courtney Alexis, the raven-haired angel who had taken a turn at carrying Jessie's backpack up the side of the treacherous mountain when it became too heavy to bear. Jessie's first guest blog for Courtney had garnered more than 200,000 views . . . and roughly 87 new Adornments customers. After Amber's first blog and Jessie's second, six designers had sent inventory to the store in the hope that Adornments' new stylist might introduce them to a demographic they might never have known otherwise. Just a few weeks from the adoption of her bouncing baby girl, Courtney's gut feeling about Jessie had changed the course of her life . . . and taught her what it meant to renew a dream.

After a full day of painting the nursery and laughing over trying to assemble a Bellini crib on their own—and finally summoning the big guns with a call to Danny—Courtney had reached across the floor and jiggled Jessie's hand. "You're going to be doing this for your own nursery, Jessie. I just know God's heard your secret dreams and will bring you the babies you yearn for."

Far too soon in her relationship with Danny to start talking about babies, but still . . . the hope of becoming a mother had been rekindled in her, and she felt a joyous assurance in Courtney's words that day.

Jessie continued her survey of the table. Next to Courtney, Antonio—the owner of Tuscan Son—smiled and gave Jessie a little wink.

"Okay, the truth is," he'd told her that very afternoon when she'd arrived, "I have been blessed beyond measure in my life. This kind of blessing is not meant to be hoarded. I may have encouraged Piper to help out with the furnishings and a couple new appliances. Just to give you solid footing to make your leap to the next phase of your life. Did I tie a big red ribbon on a used car for you? Yes. I admit it, *carissima*. I've been found out, and Danny insists that I tell you. But you needed transportation. You are *famiglia* to Piper and me, Jessie. This is what we do for *famiglia*, for the ones we love."

Next to Antonio sat Aaron Riggs. She'd had no idea when he offered one of the vacant apartments in the building he owned that he would become the rope-and-pulley for this climbing expedition her life had become. As she watched him, Riggs leaned into his chair, tossed back his head, and unabashedly laughed. That was something she'd come to love about Riggs. There wasn't a false bone in the guy's body. He lived in a van, for crying out loud; and made no excuses about it either. He did whatever he had to do in order to provide everything his daughter needed in life; lending a helping hand to others came second on the list; he was a distant third.

And Danny.

Jessie's heart melted a little as she looked at him. If life had moved a mountain before her, Danny was the summit she had finally reached. When he glanced up and met her gaze, he narrowed his steel eyes and smiled at her . . . and the world stopped rotating in that moment; everything in it fell away. There was only Jessie and Danny, and her chest squeezed with heartfelt emotion.

How did this happen? she asked herself in wonder. *How did this man happen to me?*

She'd found so many things to love about Danny, so many qualities that made him the most unique person she'd ever met. Laid-back and cool, sweet and funny, a warm and golden heart encased by a Christian faith that she both admired and feared, wondering if she might find something like it for herself one day. Her Grampy had faith like that—completely confident and utterly submissive at the same time—but for some reason, she'd largely dismissed it in younger days. But now . . . after everything . . . it tugged at her from somewhere deep inside.

Nearly everyone at that table with her had a deeper faith and followed some invisible guide; a guide that had somehow led them straight to her, equipped them with the net she would so desperately need, and the tools to make them ready to catch her when the moment arose. Even while chastising herself for the cheesy sentiment, Jessie suddenly imagined that back room of Tuscan Son restaurant—filled with the helpmates without whom she might never have triumphed—as some consecrated place and moment where everything she needed had intersected sublimely.

She almost laughed out loud at her own dramatic emotion. Instead, however, she picked up the Toscana glass tumbler of tea sitting in front of her and stood. "I need to say something to you all."

The various pops of chatter faded away, and all eyes nestled sweetly on Jessie.

"When the tsunami came and washed me out of the life I had known," she began, pausing for a moment to form the words. "Well, I didn't think there was anything left for me. But what I've learned because of each and every one of you at this table is that . . . new beginnings aren't possible until old obstructions are destroyed. Bit by bit, every one of you has helped me stand up again and move forward, and because of you I've found something I never thought was possible for me. I'm not sure there are words adequate enough to thank you."

Danny stood and rounded the table, finding a place beside her. He kissed the side of her head and placed his arm loosely around her shoulder. When she looked up into his eyes, Jessie evaporated a bit under his warmth.

"Raise your glasses," he told them all. "Let's drink to the new future of Jessie Hart."

Glasses of wine, tea, and club soda were lifted all around the table. Jessie felt as if a shower of joy had begun to rain down on them as she raised her own glass.

"A new future," she repeated. "I love that."

And just as the last clink of glasses was heard, another voice chimed in.

"Hello, Jessie."

As she turned and looked into the familiar gray eyes of Jack Stanton, a horrified Jessie dropped her glass and it crashed on the floor.

She'd seen it in the movies, but never felt it for herself. That moment where the live wire of horrified shock meets the damp floor of reality and the sizzling begins. The background moves toward a person until it becomes more sharp and clear than the foreground, and something far behind begins to swirl—around and around until they can't stand to focus on it any more. The eyes of the movie character usually rolled back in their heads about then, and a slow-motion shot dollied along with them as they fell to the ground, unconscious.

"What are you thinking?" Piper exclaimed as she jumped to her feet and blocked the way between Jack and the table. "You have no right to come here. Not after all you've done."

Jack had long ago dubbed Piper as a "mama bear," and Jessie could see from the somewhat amused expression in his eyes that he remembered why.

Raising both his hands in a mock surrender, he told her, "I just came to talk to Jessie for a minute."

Jessie's dinner rose halfway to her throat on a wave of burning acid.

"I don't think so," Piper said. "Do the police know you're here? Maybe we should call them and let them know where to find you."

Jack lifted his pant leg to reveal what looked like a large, square-faced watch strapped around his ankle. "As you can see, the authorities know where I am every minute."

"And yet you're roaming around anyway."

He shifted his eyes from Piper to Jessie as he said, "You have nothing to worry about here."

Jessie jerked toward Danny, looking up at him with panic and churning emotion. "Did you know about this?"

"I didn't," he muttered, just to her. "Steph called earlier and left a message, short and sweet. But I didn't have time to call her back."

Danny's friend Steph worked for the FBI as an intelligence analyst, and she'd utilized her handy connections to help them in their quest to find Jack. She'd revealed to Danny that, along with rolling Jessie's life up into a tidy little rug and leaving town with it under his arm, Jack had also absconded with a fortune exploited from the accounts of his financial clients. She'd unknowingly shared more than a decade with a younger, more stylish version of Bernie Madoff.

Jessie groaned under her breath and turned her focus back on Jack, who didn't look any worse for wear now that she took a moment to notice. He wore a casual black blazer over a black sport shirt and jeans. If you could even call what looked to be never-washed, still-creased dark gray denim trousers "jeans." Apparently, he'd had time to go wardrobe shopping before popping in to ruin her evening with friends.

"Jessie?" he inquired. "Can we talk, please? For just a minute?"

A minute? That's all you think it will take to explain yourself? Sixty seconds?

She swallowed around the acid that had pooled at the base of her throat. "I can't imagine that you could have anything worthwhile to say to me, Jack. I think surrendering my car, selling the house, and leaving me nothing but some cheese puff snacks in the cupboard kind of said it all for you."

He hesitated, taking a few seconds to glance down at his shoes. "Jessie, please," he finally piped up. Holding up one hand, fingers splayed, he added, "Five minutes."

"You haven't even earned five *seconds* of her attention," Piper snapped. And with that, Antonio squeezed his wife's arm and made his way toward Jack.

With a nod from Danny, Riggs got up too, and the two of them rounded opposite sides of the large table and followed Antonio as he escorted Jack to the door. Jessie exhaled the breath she hadn't known she'd been holding and deflated into her chair. An instant later, Piper was on one side and Amber on the other.

"Are you okay? What can I get you?" Piper asked.

"Do you want me to drive you home?" Amber chimed in. "Danny can follow after he takes care of this."

"I'm okay. I just need to"—she rolled her hand as if to push oxygen into her nose as she breathed in deeply—"recover."

"It's a shock. Anyone would be shocked," Piper said, and she grabbed Jessie's hand and held it for a moment. As Antonio and Riggs walked back to the table, she gave a sigh of relief. "Look. He's gone now. It's okay."

"Where's Danny?" Jessie asked them, rising to her feet.

"He said he had to make a call."

"And Jack?" Piper inquired.

"In his car and on his way," Antonio replied.

"What did he say?" Jessie said, reeling. "What did he want?"

"He's under the delusion that he can make things right with you in a few words," Riggs cracked, sinking back into the chair he'd occupied throughout dinner. "I think we set him straight."

Jessie craned her neck to get a glimpse of Danny when he stepped into view, then stopped again, his cell phone pressed to his ear. The instant their eyes met, she hurried across the restaurant toward him, touching his arm when she reached his side.

"Is that Steph?" she asked quietly, and he nodded.

"Thanks, Steph. I'll check in with you tomorrow."

She waited until Danny tucked the phone into his pocket. "What's going on? He's been arrested?"

"They apparently got a tip that the alias he might have been using was flagged on a flight out of Indonesia and into Australia, which is where the authorities caught up with him."

"Why didn't someone let me know?" she whimpered. "Instead of letting me be blindsided like that. And how did he know where to find me?"

"It all happened pretty quickly, and Steph didn't hear about it until after he'd already been extradited. He was only just brought to the States and arraigned last night, and he had to surrender both passports and wear the jewelry provided by the feds."

"Is Patty with him?"

"I don't know. Steph is going to gather whatever information she's free to share, and we'll meet up tomorrow."

"I want to be there."

"Okay," he said with a nod. "I get it."

"But if he could find me here at the restaurant, does he know where I live too? Will he just walk up to my front door later?"

"It won't matter," Piper said as she joined them. "You're coming home with us tonight."

"Oh, Piper," she replied, "I can't. I have a blog due to Courtney tomorrow, and I've got to finish it up tonight. All my notes are at home and—"

"Danny, will you talk some sense into her?"

"No need to worry," he reassured her. "Riggs and I are swapping rides. He'll go back to my place for the night, and I'll park his van on the street outside her door and keep watch."

Piper sighed, her relief showing in her smile. "That's great."

"Danny, you don't have to—"

"I am aware. But stakeouts are old hat to me. It's a piece of cake. Now I'm going outside for a minute to make another call."

"Who?" Jessie asked, wide-eyed.

"Rafe. He can help grease the wheels to get us started on an order of protection. A restraining order."

"Good thinking," Piper said. "Let's go back inside and relax for a few minutes while Danny does his thing, yes?"

Jessie nodded and followed, stopping halfway across the restaurant to cast a look back to Danny for one comforting moment.

"I really do think I'm falling in love with him," Piper muttered softly, and they exchanged a grin.

"Yeah," she replied with a sigh. "Me, too."

Danny swiped the page on his tablet, then swiped it back again when he realized he hadn't retained a single word he'd just read. Despite his anticipation for the release of this third book in a popular series of suspense fiction, he just couldn't seem to concentrate on anything except the unexpected and jarring resurgence of Jack Stanton.

The guy turned out to be more imposing than Danny had imagined. Tall, muscular, a little chiseled in the jaw line. And far more suntanned than any of the pictures he'd seen. Apparently, Stanton had been enjoying his exile to the fullest. Maybe those visions Danny had of him on a Bali beach sipping exotic drinks weren't so far off after all.

It wasn't hard to picture Jack standing on top of a high-end wedding cake with Jessie at his side, or sauntering about that 3,000-square foot Malibu rug he'd pulled out from under his wife. *Wife.*

The reference left a bitter taste at the back of his throat. More than just the simple aversion to thinking of Jessie as anyone else's wife, Danny found it particularly repugnant to envision this particular person tied to her until death they did part. Or until abandonment and possible divorce.

He reminded himself as he gave up and switched off the tablet that there was always the possibility that they'd never been legally married in the first place. He couldn't gauge how detestable it made him that he found a strange degree of comfort in that painful scenario, but he harbored the secret notion that it should be a relief to Jessie as well.

His startled reaction to the sudden rap on the window sent the tablet flying out of his hand to the floor on the passenger side. He looked up to see Jessie's face beaming at him from the other side of the glass.

Man oh man, she's beautiful.

He reached across the seat and pushed the stubborn door of Riggs's old van until it creaked open. "You scared the living breath out of me."

"I'm sorry. I thought maybe you'd like some coffee," she said, lifting a travel mug with a ribbon of steam emerging from the opening on top of it.

"Thank you."

He reached across the seat to take it from her, but she slipped into the van instead and yanked the door shut behind her before handing him the cup.

"I couldn't sleep," she told him, her eyes trained on the deserted, dimly lit street. "My mind is just racing with . . . all sorts of thoughts."

Danny inched over to the edge of the driver's seat and angled toward her. The instant he stretched out his arms, she did the same on the passenger seat and fell into his embrace.

"I'm so glad you're here," she whispered.

"Not going anywhere," he returned, and he planted a kiss on the top of her head as he held her.

"Danny, can I ask you something?"

"Always."

"Do you think Jack is . . ."

He waited, but she didn't complete the thought. "Do I think he's what?"

Her voice was raspy and emotional as she finally said, "Dangerous?"

Where had that come from? He'd scammed clients, jilted Jessie, absconded with every cent they'd had, but *dangerous*?

"Why do you ask that?" he inquired, nudging her away slightly so he could get a good look into those crystal blue eyes of hers. "Has he ever hurt you?"

"No," she answered then shrugged. "Not physically."

"What makes you worry about your safety?" He twisted a lock of hair near her face around his finger and moved it back.

"I guess I just realized everything I thought I knew about us— Jack and me—was a lie. It wasn't real. So how do I really know what kind of man he's become?"

"I can tell you this," Danny reassured her. "You know what kind of man I am. Would I ever let him hurt you again?"

Her smile appeared edged with timid confidence. "No."

"We'll get to the bottom of all of this," he promised. "And you're going to be free of Jack Stanton sooner rather than later."

She wriggled toward him and planted her head underneath his chin with a sigh. "When you say it, I almost believe you. You're good at that."

"Yes, I am," he teased.

After a few minutes of comforting silence, Jessie tilted her head upward and stared into his eyes.

"What?" he asked, and she smiled.

"You know what else you're good at?"

"So many things," he replied.

"Yes. But would you kiss me? I feel safe when you kiss me."

Without another random word, Danny leaned down and placed his lips on Jessie's. A muffled sigh came from deep within her throat, and he raked his fingers through the silky hair at the side of her head. When their lips parted, she snuggled beneath his chin again and softly moaned.

"Thank you, Danny."

"For?"

"All of it. Every bit of being you. Thank you."

He chuckled. "Glad I could be me for you."

"Me too," she said, sincerity apparent in the expression. "I've never had a Danny Callahan in my corner before. It's startling . . . and a relief, really."

"Yeah. I get that all the time."

The two of them sat there together in Riggs's questionable-smelling van for an hour or so as Danny sipped his coffee and Jessie talked through the details of the blog post she'd just completed. He didn't have a clue what it all meant in the great scheme of the world of fashion, of course, but she seemed adequately distracted by it, and that was all he really cared about.

"Do you want me to walk you to the door?" he asked her.

"No. I thought I'd dazzle you by making the journey all by myself. Want to watch me?"

"Sure. Make it entertaining for me?"

"Sure thing," she chirped, and she quickly pecked his lips before pushing out of the van.

At the edge of the sidewalk, Jessie raised her arms to an imaginary partner and gave him a comical glance before she waltzed up the middle of the driveway toward her apartment door. Danny's laughter followed her, and he watched closely until he felt certain she was tucked safely inside.

Two very round headlights appeared at the corner a short time later, and the sedan-shaped car moved slowly up the street toward him. When it passed the apartment building without altering speed, Danny leaned down and watched the car's retreat in his side mirror before dialing Rafe on his cell.

"Hey, Detective," he said when Padillo answered, the familiar hum of the precinct behind him.

"Hey, Callahan, where you at?"

"You wouldn't believe me if I told you."

"What's up?"

"Jessie Stanton's husband—I mean, *Jessie Hart's* husband—is back in town," Danny advised. "Anything you can do to help us hurry along a restraining order?"

"I thought he was living high in Costa Rica."

"Bali. It's a long story, but he's back in the States, modeling some ankle armor courtesy of Uncle Sam."

"But you're still worried he'll try to make contact?" Rafe asked.

"He already has. Walked right into a public restaurant and tried to have a chat with her. Fortunately, we were able to dissuade him, but only for the time being. Can you help lead the way toward an order of protection?"

"Text me his details and I'll make a call. Hang in there, and I'll try to get back to you tonight."

"Good deal. Thanks, Rafe."

Danny keyed in the vitals the second they ended the call.

John Fitzgerald Stanton. Driving late model green hybrid Accord. Picked up by feds for fraud, embezzlement, possible bigamy. Ankle bracelet while pending prosecution.

An odd-shaped car turned the corner and cruised up the street. It bore no resemblance to the Accord he'd seen Stanton drive away earlier in the evening, so Danny barely gave it a glance. He bent down and retrieved the tablet Jessie had picked up and stowed under the dash. Just as he started to take a second stab at reading, another set of headlights rounded the corner of Pinafore Street. The form could possibly be an Accord, but he couldn't be sure. He tossed the tablet to the passenger seat and slouched down anyway.

The car swerved into the driveway to Jessie's apartment building and cut the lights before the engine. Danny's pulse went from a soft drum to urgent pounding as the dark shape of a man emerged from what could definitely be an Accord. Tall . . . broad-shouldered.

Yep. That's Stanton.

Danny pushed open the door and it cracked, metal against metal, drawing the attention of the unwelcome visitor. As he turned toward the sound, Jack stepped into the yellowish bath of light from the street lamp. Danny closed the distance between them and stood face-to-face with Jack Stanton for the second time that day.

"What are you doing here?"

"I came to speak to Jessie."

"I thought we covered this at the restaurant," he said evenly. "What could you possibly have to say to her at this late date?"

Stanton sighed and, shaking his head, peered down at the uneven concrete driveway. "That's between me and my wife."

There was that word again.

"You sure do toss that wife label around lightly, don't you?"

"Look," he said, slamming the car door shut, "this is really none of your business. What are you, the new boyfriend? That's . . . well, it's adorable."

Stanton's sarcastic lilt set acid to churning in Danny's gut, lifting a foamy fire into his throat. "Almost as adorable as you leaving one wife to flop on a beach with another. Grow tired of the little umbrella drinks, did you? Oh, wait, no. Once you were stupid enough to try and vacation in a country with an extradition treaty, you probably didn't have much choice in the matter. You received your return flight ticket courtesy of the FBI, I believe."

As Stanton turned away from him, Danny quickly patted every pocket with open palms in search of his cell phone. When he finally found it tucked into the front of his shirt, he grabbed it and redialed Rafe. Just as he answered, Danny spotted Stanton already at Jessie's door.

"Rafe!" he exclaimed, sprinting up the driveway. "We need some help over at Jessie's apartment on Pinafore. Stanton is—" His words came to a grinding halt as Jessie opened her door. "No! Jessie, go back inside."

"Callahan?" Rafe bellowed over the line. "What's going on?"

"Go back inside and bolt the door."

He watched helplessly as Jessie's terror-ridden face curled up and she pushed the door shut; but his insides flopped with a thud as Stanton pushed it open again, charged inside and closed it behind him.

⤝⤞

Jessie backed away from Jack in three enormous steps, grabbing the first thing her hand touched and whipped it in front of her. The large candle fell to the floor as she wielded the holder like a sword.

"Are you serious?" Jack asked her, one corner of his mouth twitching in amusement.

"Get out of here now, Jack, or I'll show you how serious I am."

Danny's thunderous pounding on the front door let her know Jack had locked it behind him. She scanned the bolts and realized it was just the doorknob latch he'd secured, and she almost

22

laughed out loud. That flimsy thing wouldn't keep Danny out for long.

"What do you want, Jack?"

"I just want to talk to you—"

"I'm guessing you've got about thirty seconds, so you'd better be succinct."

"—make sure you understand."

"Understand which part? There are so many facets to my confusion."

Jack darted toward her and grabbed her by the wrist, twisting until the candle holder fell to the floor, bounced twice, and rolled away.

"Let go of me!"

"It wasn't supposed to go the way it did," he blurted, sparks of desperation flickering in his eyes. "I didn't mean to let it get so out of hand. I need you to know that, Jessie. I always loved you."

She tried to wriggle out of his grasp, but couldn't manage it. She winced in pain.

"I need you to back me up. I need you in my corner, or they're going to put me away."

Not that she found anything about the current situation the least bit funny, but for some reason, she chuckled. "Are we even married, Jack? I need to know because there seems to be some confusion about whether you and Patty ever even divorced."

"I . . ."

With that, the front door flew open and Danny stormed in.

"I really need to know," she cried as Danny pried Jack's grip loose. "Jack, you owe me the truth. Were we ever married?"

Before he could answer, Danny sent him flying backward with one punch to his midsection, and he crumpled like a wadded piece of paper on the floor. While he groaned, Danny stepped in front of Jessie, acting as a barrier between them, leaving Jessie to peer around the slope of his muscular shoulder.

"Please," she appealed to him. "Just tell me."

Jack raked back his hair with both hands as he glared up at them. Just when she thought she might have to give up on getting a straight answer out of the complete stranger on her floor, he let out a grumbly sort of sigh.

"No," he stated. "I never divorced Patty."

Those four words swirled around in her ears until she could hardly stand them anymore.

"Thirteen years," she muttered. "You let me believe we were married for thirteen years."

She collapsed to the arm of the slightly used charcoal chenille sofa that had replaced the pale sage Tommy Bahama in their sham of a dream house, and she rubbed her forehead until it ached.

She hadn't realized Jack made it to his feet again until he spoke. "I'm so sorry. I never wanted to hurt you. I really need you to understa—"

"That's enough," Danny declared as he stomped toward Jack and grabbed his arm. "You need to leave."

"So this is the new one, Jessie?"

She jerked her attention to Jack and dropped her hands to her lap. What did he mean? The new *what*?

"He's not doing a very good job taking care of you. I mean, look around at this place. It's a dump."

"But it's my dump," she muttered. An assertive wave washed over her as she added, "And I don't need anyone *taking care of me*. I can do that all by myself."

"Oh, come on. You've been wobbling around on those two feet for . . . I've known you for how many years?"

"Zero," she replied, popping up off the sofa and planting herself next to it. "You don't know me at all. And heaven knows I've never really known you either."

"Jessie, listen—"

"I'm through listening to you, Jack."

"On your way," she barely heard Danny tell him.

"Jessie, listen. They're going to be hauling you in to talk to you about—"

"Am I not speaking English?" Danny chided. "Move it. Let's go."

Jessie didn't turn around until she heard Danny struggling with the door and turn the deadbolts, one by one.

"We've got to get you a new door," he said. "I'll take care of that tomorrow."

"No," she blurted, rigid as she yelled at him. "I'm not your project, Danny. You don't have to replace my door . . . or even break it down when the big, bad wolf comes knocking. Although in this case, I didn't entirely mind that you did."

He moved cautiously toward her and touched her arm, speaking in the softest, sweetest voice. "You're okay, angel. He's gone now."

For some odd reason, it galled her that he seemed to know her so well. She wasn't angry at him at all, and he instinctively knew it. She wondered if he also discerned the direction of her anger; toward Jack and the words he'd so callously spoken. She despised the truth lingering in what he'd said, hovering over the accusations of frailty and weakness like a pregnant storm cloud. Frowning, she turned away from Danny and sighed.

"You can go now," she somehow managed to say without whimpering.

"Jessie . . ."

"Please go."

With her back to him and her ears perked, she listened as he considered her words and sighed. His footsteps creaked over the floorboards—those dumb laminate floorboards—and he released a soft groan as he wrestled with the door.

"Lock this behind me."

Several seconds ticked past, the high-pitched silence of her apartment screaming in Jessie's ears. She finally fell limply into the corner of the sofa and brought her knees upward and hugged them. Just before the emotional tsunami crested.

Jessie never did take kindly to a light shinin' up on her shortcomin's. One of her school chums called her a "messy bess" one day, and the next afternoon she shows up at her grandpa's place and tells me, "I can't stay around today, Grampy. I have to go home and clean my bedroom." Her mama said that little girl organized and dusted and cleaned her room spic 'n span that day. Re-shelved and alphabetized her Nancy Drew mystery books too. Her mama wanted to know what'd got into 'er. Even skipped supper to get 'er done. Just to prove that school chum wrong, I'm guessin'.

Since she popped outta her mama's womb, my Jessie's been fightin' the odds against her. Most times, that's a good thing. Gives her a target to aim her efforts t'ward. Other times though, I seen her rebel hard in the altogether wrong direction, just for the sake of goin' agin the grain. Sure can make for a lotta unnecessary thrashin' around. But my Jessie ain't learned that lesson yet.

Hope she will someday.

2

I can't even believe you came in today." Amber gingerly set down a cup of coffee on the desk in front of Jessie. "I'd still be reeling. Are you reeling?"

"A bit," Jessie admitted with a sigh.

"I don't blame you. What can I do? Can I get you something?"

Before Jessie had a chance to consider the offer—although she had no idea what she could request that little five-foot-four Amber could get for her—Piper stormed through the door to the miniscule office and crowded in with them.

"How did you know?" Jessie asked the instant she spotted the look of terror/concern on Piper's face.

"Danny called me."

"Of course he did."

She knew it made little sense to anyone but herself; however, the lingering fuel of her resistance to his role as her protector hadn't quite burned off yet. She swallowed to keep from screaming at the very idea that she might even need one.

"He's concerned about you. And so am I." Piper looked at Amber pointedly. "Did she tell you Jack forced himself into her apartment last night?"

Jessie stood and gripped the edges of the desk with both hands. "Enough. This is my place of business, and business is the only thing that's going to keep me sane today. It is officially declared a No Drama Zone for the rest of the day."

Piper chuckled. "Does that work? Just declaring it?"

"Yes." She pondered the absurdity for a moment before adding, "I need it to work. I have things to do."

"What things?"

"We have new inventory to sort through, and . . . and *if I could concentrate*, I could probably tell you what else."

"You've got Francesca Dutton at three o'clock," Amber prompted.

Jessie scratched her head. "Who?"

"She's the daughter of Stella Dutton. The woman who passed away? She invited you to come and look through her closet?"

"Oh. Of course."

Francesca had called the store and described a wonderland of designer labels left behind by her mother, inquiring about whether Jessie might be interested in choosing a few things to sell on consignment. She'd refrained from explaining that Adornments was a rental boutique and that, despite her eventual hope of expanding into retail consignments, she wanted to wait until the store gained momentum. Perhaps in a year or so. But the opportunity had presented itself to dip a toe in those waters with Stella Dutton's enviable closet, and she decided not to look a gift horse in the wide-open mouth.

"Every designer from A to Z," Francesca had stated. When she added, "Armani to Zac Posen," Jessie was sold. But with everything going on since, she hadn't given it another thought.

When the phone buzzed, Amber snatched it up from Jessie's desk. "Thank you for calling Adornments. This is Amber." Jessie massaged her throbbing forehead until: "Sure, Danny. She's right here. Hang on."

She stared at the phone Amber pushed toward her, making no move to take it.

"Jessie," Piper chastised in a whisper.

She clicked her tongue and surrendered. "Hello?"

"I won't keep you," he stated in that matter-of-fact monotone she hadn't heard in quite a while. "I wanted to quickly tell you that Rafe made a couple of calls on your behalf, and an attorney named Tina LaBianco will finalize a restraining order against Jack for you this afternoon." A pregnant pause left her wondering if he'd hung up. Then: "If that's what you still want."

"Yes, of course it is." She scribbled the lawyer's name on the pad in front of her and added, "I'll call her right away."

"Good."

"Good. Well. Thank you, Danny."

"Have a good day, Jessie."

And with that, the line went cold.

"That was short and sweet," Piper commented.

Jessie looked down at the unruly desktop in front of her. *Just keep your eye on the ball.*

"Are you ready to get to that inventory?" Jessie asked Amber as she returned the handset.

"Sure." The jingle of the front door announced a more immediate need. "As soon as I tend to some customers."

Amber hurried out front and, instead of following, Piper sat in the chair across the desk from Jessie and smiled. "Let's talk about it," she urged. "You start."

Danny grabbed Carmen, his favorite of the three surfboards hanging on the rack, and stowed her under his arm. Zipping the wetsuit, he made his way across the sand. Frank galloped ahead of him, the Great Dane's shiny harlequin coat glistening under the late morning sun. Riggs hadn't waited on him, and Danny could see him bobbing atop his bright coral board a hundred yards out. They'd probably missed the best of the swells, but he'd take whatever wave therapy he could get.

Frank barked twice and followed him into the first few feet of foamy surf until Danny hopped to his stomach on the board and paddled through the channel to the outside. By the time he reached the lineup, Riggs had already caught his ideal wave and ridden it out so Danny didn't have to concern himself with avoiding a drop-in. He simply headed for an ideal spot, sat upright, and watched over his shoulder for a rideable wave. One came along in no time at all, and Danny caught it just before the break. Anchor-heavy thoughts of Jack Stanton, restraining orders—and even Jessie herself—sank into the water behind him as he angled his board across the wave and rode it home.

Riggs had flopped on his longboard in the sand, face up to the clouds as he ripped a bite out of a massive sandwich. Danny laughed at Frank. The dog looked like a drooling soldier standing guard over Riggs. Instead of turning out for another ride, Danny grabbed his board.

"Let's go in, Carmen."

Just as he dropped the board, parallel to Riggs's larger one, and sat down on it, Riggs extended the sandwich to Frank and let him take a huge, unruly bite out of it before taking another of his own. Danny winced slightly at the act.

"Don't get me wrong," he remarked to Riggs as he focused on another surfer riding just inside the curl, "I love my dog and all, but you're not ever gonna see us swapping spit."

"Eh," Riggs replied with a wave of his hand, "it's all the same to me. And if Frankenstein minds, he's never mentioned it."

Danny chuckled and shook his head.

"Hey, listen, my kid wants to go paddleboarding this weekend. Any chance at snagging the keys to your family's mountain casa?"

"The last time you used my folks' place in Big Bear Lake, you left without closing up the windows," Danny reminded him.

"Yeah, but who knew that freak snowstorm was headed in?"

"Uh, anybody who turned on the news?"

"I'll do better this time. So can we use the place?"

Danny glanced over at Riggs, still flat on his back, now cradling Frank's head as the dog lay on his back as well, paws pointed skyward.

"Hey, you could come with," Riggs exclaimed.

"Make sure the windows get closed?"

"That, and drive your old man's boat."

"Chop some wood, make sure there's food in the house, that kind of thing?" Danny teased.

"Not a single one of those is a bad idea. What do you say?" With a second thought, he added, "Why not invite Jessie along?"

Danny blew out a sigh that mixed with a groan. "Yeah. Jessie's not feeling me so much at the moment."

Riggs twisted out from beneath Frank and propped up on his elbow. "What'd you do?"

"Nice. Assuming I did something."

"Well, didn't you?"

Danny fell backward on the board and stretched out. "I guess I'm just an inconvenient truth."

"Like global warming."

"Yeah. Like global warming. Jessie's the globe, and I'm the warming." He closed one eye against the rays of the sun. "And by warming, I mean me being one more guy she's not sure she can trust."

Riggs dug his fingers into the fur at the back of Frank's neck and clicked his tongue. "Man, if she can't trust you, I don't know who the guy is that she can." He thumped a couple of pats to Frank's large back. "So we on for this weekend, or what?"

Danny thought it over. "Yeah. I guess so. Yeah, sounds like a plan. I'll call my folks in a bit."

"All right then. When will you call and invite *her*?"

"Sometime next month?"

"C'mon. The place is a monster. Jessie and Allie can take the big room. With you and me up in the loft on the other side of the place, she'll never know you're there."

Danny looked out into the horizon. "I'll sell it to her just like that."

"Mother liked to organize her closet according to designer," Francesca announced as she tugged open the double doors to a massive walk-in closet and flipped on the light, drenching them in opulent elegance.

Amber and Jessie exchanged fleeting wide-eyed glances before Amber dug her fingers into Jessie's arm until she winced.

"Probably my imagination," she whispered, "but do you hear angels singing?"

"Mm-hmm," Jessie muttered before addressing Francesca. "This is really amazing."

The woman placed a hand on one bony hip and looked around as if seeing the closet for the first time. "I suppose it's a little ostentatious, isn't it? But then Mother was an extravagant person by nature."

Jessie had met Stella Dutton a time or two before her death. She wouldn't really categorize her as extravagant as much as . . . impeccable. The first time they met was the Women of Excellence in the Arts benefit tea at the Marina del Rey Ritz-Carlton. Piper had chaired the event planning committee, and Jessie had volunteered to staff the registration table as a courtesy to her friend. She'd noticed Stella the instant she stepped into line at her table in a vintage Chanel suit, a double strand of pearls, and two-toned slingback pumps. In a different time, she might have been mistaken for Jacqueline Kennedy.

"The first time I met your mother," she commented, "she was wearing the most exquisite Chanel—"

"Double-breasted?" Francesca interrupted.

"No. No, it was an off-white wool with black seam detailing and gold-tone buttons."

"Yes, of course," she said, heading to the far end of the closet. She unzipped one of the clear garment bags. "This one."

Jessie's hand flew to her heart, and she and Amber released appreciative sighs in perfect harmony.

"She did look lovely in this, didn't she?"

Jessie nodded. "I remember thinking she eclipsed every other woman in the room just by wearing that suit."

"Mother loved Coco Chanel. She said the designer wasn't just stylish; she also created the very concept of personal style."

"I'd have to agree."

"What do you suppose you could get for something like this?"

Jessie stepped forward to examine it more closely. "The logo buttons are still pristine and the stitching is unblemished. We could easily put a price tag on it for, say, nineteen hundred."

"And for consignment, the store takes twenty-five percent when it sells?"

Jessie discerned a sense of desperation in the question that their surroundings didn't convey. "Yes, twenty-five percent."

"All right. Put that one aside. I'll have Elyse bring up a garment rack for us while you take a look to see what else you might like. Let's start with maybe ten or twelve primary items and another dozen from the shoes and handbags, shall we?"

"That's more than generous," Jessie told her. "It will give us a solid look at whether my customers will be interested in purchasing as well as lease options."

Once Francesca's Prada heels clopped down the hall and to the stairs, Amber and Jessie shared muted squeals from inside the closet.

"Do you believe this closet?" Amber squawked.

From the elaborate crystal chandelier to the subtle lavender fragrance enveloping them to the three inches of thick white carpet Jessie smoothed with the toe of her shoe, the term *closet* seemed slightly . . . *inadequate* to describe their surroundings.

"It's bigger than my whole apartment."

"Never mind the size of the closet," Jessie whimpered as she floated toward a section of floor-length gowns. "May I escort you to the *bling* section?"

Amber gasped as Jessie removed an ethereal strapless evening gown with a sweetheart neckline, banded waist, and draped ruffle skirt. A stunning blue-and-grey print seemed to flutter over layers of airy, semi-sheer silk organza.

"Is that—" Amber breathed.

Together, they confirmed the label. "Badgley Mischka."

"We've got to have this one," Jessie declared.

"We can't leave here without it."

Over the next ten minutes, they found about twenty different garments they couldn't leave without and, while Amber joined Francesca in the sitting room to fill out the consignment paper-work, Jessie arranged each one on the crystal hook on the back of the closet door and shot a digital record with Amber's small camera of the four dresses, two jackets, six suits, and three gowns they'd agreed upon.

Elyse helped by enclosing each article in its own garment bag and hanging them on a wheeled rack while Jessie took addi-tional pictures of the six immaculate pairs of shoes, seven like-new handbags and two exquisite wraps Francesca had agreed to include. After the accessories had been packaged and stacked, it took the both of them to roll the cart out of the closet into the sitting room where Amber and Francesca sat at a carved walnut table.

"You know," Jessie said, pausing to consider how best to broach the subject tactfully. "I have a deal in place with several benefac-tors where they've given me items to lease out and collect a sort of royalty on each rental. If you'd like me to take more from the closet for that purpose, we'd be happy to do that."

"How exactly would that work?" Francesca asked, and Jessie noted a mist of grief in her mahogany eyes.

Jessie sat on the quilted Parson's chair adjacent to Francesca. Touching her hand gently, she said, "This can't be easy. Is there anything I do for you?"

"Return my mother to me?"

Jessie's heart seized. "I understand. I can't tell you what I'd give for just one more day with my mother."

A single blink, and the tears tumbled out of Francesca's eyes and streamed down the slopes of her cheeks.

"Things weren't right between Mother and me at the end," she admitted. "I wasn't the best daughter to her that I could have been. My only consolation, really, is that she had a very strong faith that allowed her a certain fearlessness at the end."

Amber scraped her chair closer to the opposite side of Francesca. "Would you like us to pray for you?" she asked, and Jessie's heart immediately pounded. "Right now?"

"Would you?" she asked, and Jessie's breath caught in her throat at the unexpected reply.

<hr />

After my April passed, little Jessie come to live with me a few blocks over from her homestead on Eaton Street. 'Bout a week in, after April was snug and buried, Jessie and me got done sayin' our nighttime prayers, and Jessie looks up at me and says, "Grampy? Whatcha s'pose Mama's doin' tonight?"

The old ticker just 'bout gave way at the hope in those eyes o' that young'un.

"Can't know for sure," I tells her. "But I guess she's probly takin' it easy, restin' up."

"Yeah, she musta been purdy tired, dontcha think?"

"I do."

I could see her wheels a-turnin' as I tucked in the covers around her and kissed her on the head.

"If I talk to her, do you s'pose she might hear me?"

"Could be," I says.

"Do you wanna talk to Mama with me, Grampy?"

I thought it over a quick second before I says, "Why don't we talk to the Father instead 'n He can relate the message when she's rested up."

"Okay. I guess that'd be all right."

Three-quarters of an hour ticked by whiles Jessie talked to Jesus about all the things her mama had missed since she'd gone away. She covered the spelling bee at school, the supper she liked best of all—stew 'n biscuits with the short carrots—and the orange cones up on the corner of the main road where somebody'd knocked down a phone pole.

"I hope you'll tell Mama about the flowers too, Jesus. She got so many of 'em that Grampy donated some to the hospital up the highway so's some people who didn't get no flowers when they was sick might wake up and see somethin' purdy in their room. But we kept the ones that were Mama's favorites. She liked the daisies and the long purple ones—"

"Iris," I told 'er.

"Yeah. Irises. I like those too."

"You think we might want to wrap this up, girl?" I threw in.

"Okay. Grampy says I need to wrap up," she continued, her eyes clamped shut tight. "On account o' you're probly pretty busy and all. But if you wouldn't mind, give Mama a kiss goodnight for me? On the cheek 'cause she likes that."

My thoughts made it hard to sleep that night. A lotta nights after too. A girl without a mama needs a lotta things an old geezer like me didn't know how to give.

Did my best, though, in the years that followed April up to heaven. Owed her that. Owed Jessie too.

3

Jessie pulled the door open and stared into the face of a cardboard box bearing the logo of Granny's Pizza on Broadway. Best pizza in Southern California, she and Danny had determined when they had lunch there together a couple weeks back.

He slowly lowered the box. "I come bearing pizza."

She resisted the urge to return his charming smile. "Granny's?"

"You said it was your favorite," he replied. With a lilt to his voice, he added, "Grandma's secret sauce, fresh mozzarella, and parmesan reggiano with sprigs of baby basil."

"Now you're just mocking me."

"I'm not," he teased. "I'm emulating your passion for the cuisine."

She purposefully cocked one brow. "Toppings?"

"Pepperoni and onion. Mushrooms on your half."

Her rebellious stomach growled in reply. *Traitor.*

"So can I come in?" Danny asked.

She took a moment, pretending to think it over. "Or you could just leave the pie and call me tomorrow."

"Nothing doing. I had to smell this baby all the way over here."

"Fine." She stepped back and tugged the door the rest of the way open. "But only because I'm really, really hungry."

The orange sun dipped low behind him, nearly finished with its day's work. The sunglasses on his head held back normally straight hair that had dried in an unruly, wavy mop, and the faintest traces of saltwater tickled Jessie's nostrils as he slipped past her.

"I'll get some plates."

Jessie heard Danny fiddling with the locks on the front door as she produced a couple of plates, some flowered paper napkins, and two bottles of water from the kitchen. When she returned, he'd made himself at home on the sofa.

She sat on the floor on the opposite side of the coffee table while Danny loaded two slices on a plate and handed it to her.

"I assume this pizza comes at a cost?" she inquired.

"Indeed it does." He grinned, sliding two more slices to his plate before dropping to the floor, folding his legs, and propping his arms on the coffee table in front of him.

"Do tell."

He took a huge bite from one of the slices. "The price is conversation," he said over a full mouth.

"About?"

A haze of serious concern transformed his expression, and he wiped his mouth with a napkin he already had wadded in one fist. "You have to ask?"

Her heart palpitated sharply. "Well, I can't read your mind." She ignored his pointed gaze long enough to bite into her pizza. "Mm, this is so good." But the deliberate weight of his glare pressed in without wavering. When she lifted her eyes to meet it, in fact, she buckled under its intensity. "Thanks for bringing this."

"Look, I know Jack's return has thrown you."

"You think?" she muttered, dropping her line of sight to the meal before her.

"I don't know what all he said the other night, but I could see it rocked you. In turn, you pushed me away."

She didn't respond with anything more than the twitch of her shoulder.

"You want to talk to me, Jessie?"

"Not particularly."

"About anything? Or just not about Jack."

Her pulse thrummed in her ears. She'd been avoiding his calls, putting off this moment for just this reason. She had no idea what to say to him. Did she know how unfair it was to let their new relationship suffer from the war wounds Jack had left behind? Of course she did. But could she do anything about the way she felt?

No.

Danny reached across the table and touched her hand. "I'm not just another Jack Stanton in your life, Jess."

Her reply came out in a hoarse whisper. "I know."

"Then why did you throw me out along with him the other night?" he asked. "And why have I not heard from you since?"

Tears rose in her eyes and stood there, hot and stinging, as she looked up at him. She owed him an explanation; and she wished she had one.

"What did he say to you when he was in here alone with you?"

Sometimes it felt like Danny could read her thoughts. Why did she feel like she couldn't hide anything from him?

"Did he hurt you?"

"Only in here," she said, tapping her balled fist against the sore place where her heart rested.

"What did he say?"

"Nothing." Okay, that was a lie. "Nothing I didn't already know."

"Like what?" he pressed.

"Like how I always seem to have some guy taking care of me. First, my grandfather. Then him. Now you."

"Really?" he said, dropping the balled napkin onto the pizza still sitting on his plate. "You moved away from Louisiana to stand on your own and make a life here in L.A. No one was taking care of you then. You met and married someone who left you high and dry, and how did you respond? You picked yourself up and made a business out of nothing, all on your own."

"Hardly on my own."

"Jessie. I'm not here to take care of you," he stated. "I'm here because you're a part of me now. A part that—without it—I feel hollow. And I've never said that to another human being before in my life. Did you ever think . . . maybe . . . you're the one taking care of me?"

A spike of emotion pierced her, dead center in the chest, and she narrowed her eyes just enough for the pool of tears to spill over and stream down her cheeks.

"I'm sorry," she managed, and she wiped her eyes with a napkin with a large blue flower stamped on the corner. "That's a really nice thing for you to say."

"It's not just words, Jessie. Not just something I said."

"I know."

"Do you?" he asked, a question mark curving in his voice. "How do you know that?"

"Because you're not the kind of man who just says what someone wants to hear."

"That's right."

Danny pushed himself up from the floor and rounded the table. He eased himself down next to her and wrapped his arm around her shoulder, pulling her close.

"You and I started because of Jack," he said softly. "But he has nothing to do with who we became."

She dropped her head to Danny's shoulder and sighed. She wanted to believe him, she really did. But something deep within Jessie made her feel like a foolish young girl again. The kind of girl she used to be. The kind of girl who could believe the pretty words of a pretty man, just because she wanted to believe them.

─────

Danny hadn't made the trip up the mountain at this time of year in a long time. He'd nearly forgotten what a beautiful drive it could be until that afternoon as they chugged up the snake-like road. But here they now were—he and Jessie—enjoying a leisurely pace in his open Jeep so that Riggs and Allie, following behind them in his clunker of a van, could manage to keep up.

"What are those pale yellow flowers along the side of the road?" Jessie asked him. "They smell like heaven."

"Wild honeysuckle. My mom loves it too," he told her. "She used to nag my dad until he pulled over and let her pick some on the way up, and she'd put them in those . . . you know, the jars?"

"Mason jars?"

"Right. She had them all over the cabin."

"Ooh, that sounds really nice. Can we?"

Danny grinned. "There's a turnout a few miles ahead." He produced his cell phone from the pocket of his shirt and handed it to her. "Number three on the speed dial. Give Riggs a heads up that we're about to make a stop."

Allie apparently answered her father's phone. The lilt in Jessie's voice told him so. He couldn't help sneaking one lingering glance at her—so relaxed, so different from the woman who could hardly look him square in the eye just a few nights prior over pizza. It did Danny's heart good to see the change in her once the restraining order against Stanton had been issued and a little time and space had come between the two of them.

Jessie had put up a fuss when he'd asked her to come along on this weekend getaway, but enlisting Piper's considerable influence had helped. And even Riggs had contributed to putting her mind at ease about the trip.

"I dropped by to replace her front door," he'd confessed to Danny after a morning of surfing. "She offered me some coffee and I just told her casually that she could bunk with Allie. She's into all that fashion stuff, and it's not like there's anybody like Jessie she can talk to about it, right? I didn't tell her how, when she heard about the trip, Allie immediately asked if Amber was coming along. I just said she'd be doing me a solid by spending a little girl time with my kid."

"And that worked," Danny had marveled.

"Yeah, I guess. She said she's going, didn't she?"

"That she did."

Every now and then, *Aaron* Riggs popped up and shocked him. This was one of those times.

Danny lowered the volume on the radio as he angled into the turnout. The tires on the two vehicles pushed crushing sounds out of the gravel as they came to a stop, side by side. Allie thrust open the passenger door on the van and jogged toward them.

"Isn't it something up here, Jessie?" she exclaimed. "Beautiful, right?"

"Very." Jessie swiveled out of the Jeep and they walked toward the border of wildflowers on the edge of the mountain. "Let's pick some for the cabin."

"Okay, cool." Allie's voice carried across the slope of the mountain. "One time when we came up here, we went to this ski place and took the lift all the way up the mountain. You can have a picnic up there on account of it's not winter and they're not using the mountain for anything else, and then we rode our mountain bikes back down again. Maybe we could do that this time, if you like riding bikes."

Danny got out of the Jeep and stretched. He looked over in time to see Riggs doing the same next to the open door of his van.

"What do you figure," he asked Danny as he approached, "another ten, fifteen minutes?"

"A little more than that. Maybe twenty to get as far as town. Another ten to the cabin."

Riggs looked after the girls and one corner of his mouth lifted into a fragmented smile. "She can hardly wait to get out on the lake. She's been chattering about it all the way up the mountain. You think Jessie will give it a try?"

"No idea."

"Anything else from the scumbag?" As long as Danny had known Riggs, he switched gears like that. Still, even after so many years, the change in conversation tripped him up at times.

"Stanton? Not that I know of. Rafe helped push through a restraining order."

"Those things never really stop someone intent on harassment."

"No. But it gives him something else to lose." Danny pinned his hope on that. "Might make him think twice."

Allie's laughter jingled like silver bells on Christmas morning, drawing Danny's attention to the inside of the turnout where she and Jessie had stopped; Allie on a large boulder, and Jessie standing behind her. A large bouquet of cuttings—honeysuckle stems mixed in with bluish-purple lupine—lay casually on the ground next to them while Jessie braided the girl's glossy dark hair, inserting tiny yellow blossoms as she went.

The afternoon sun peeked through the branches of trees behind them, and one long-armed beam reached straight through shimmying leaves and landed on the slope of Jessie's shoulder, igniting her dark hair with gold and copper. She glanced at Danny just then and smiled—seemingly so carefree and happy. A sharp jolt of electricity ran straight through him. He couldn't help hoping that it lasted, that it wasn't just a fleeting moment of peace for her.

"Do you like my hair?" Allie asked as she ran toward her father.

"It suits you," he said, kissing the top of her head. "You've always been my little flower child. Jessie, can you do mine next?"

"Don't mind him, Jessie," Allie said over a rolling giggle. "He just likes to be silly. Can we get something to eat soon? I'm hungry."

"Let's get on our way up the mountain then," Danny suggested. "Jessie, you want to ride with us? Ooh, or I could ride with—"

"Jessie's going to ride with Danny," Riggs interrupted with a quick wink. "C'mon. Keep me company the rest of the way."

"But we'll get something to eat soon, right?"

"We'll stop in town," Danny promised.

Once they buckled into the Jeep, Danny circled around and pulled out onto the mountain road behind Riggs's van.

"Mind if I put on some music?" Jessie asked.

"Sure."

She chuckled as she seemed to decide on one of the CDs in the case, and he waited to hear what she'd chosen. On the first few notes, he recognized James Taylor.

"What's this remind you of?" she asked, cranking up "Shower the People." He didn't need time to think it over, but she didn't wait to find that out. "It played that afternoon when my car broke down and you picked me up. Remember, I met Steph for the first time that day."

"I do remember."

"Speaking of . . . She sent me an invitation to her wedding."

"You mentioned. That's good."

"So you still don't mind if I go."

"Mind?" he said with a grimace. "Why would I mind?"

"I don't want you to feel like I'm intruding."

"Jessie." He sighed. Didn't she know by now that she hadn't insinuated herself into his life? He'd drawn her there with ease and enthusiasm. There was only one individual in that Jeep with any reservations about the future at all, and he wasn't that person.

"Okay. Well, I'd like to go," she said.

He'd thought it had been established the day she told him she received the invitation, but he asked her anyway. "Do you want to go together?"

She hesitated before replying, "Sure. That might be fun."

Jessie softly sang along with the music for the next few minutes up the mountain, and Danny lounged in the sound of it. When "Carolina on My Mind" came up on the queue, he grinned, remembering what she'd once told him about that song.

She sang along a few moments, then she glanced over at him and giggled. He allowed the recollection of their time together that afternoon to skitter through his mind. The way she'd accepted the band for her hair and joked about their "matching ponies," and how she told him about her love for James Taylor's music, and especially how she'd taken to changing his *Carolina* lyric to *California* instead.

"I always knew I wanted to get out of Slidell, and Southern California was just this pie-in-the-sky sort of Nirvana of glitz and movie stars, so I started dreaming about coming here long before it was even a real possibility. So I had California on my mind."

Danny sighed. "So how do you feel about it now? Cali still on your mind?"

"Well. My personal glitz is now otherwise engaged," she joked.

More and more all the time, he reckoned.

For him, though, it was another song that had taken root in his memory since that day. Every word, every note of one old song by James Taylor whispered Jessie's name every time he happened upon it, transporting him back to that very afternoon when, for possibly the first time, he'd realized he'd found the other part of himself. A part that had been missing or damaged—or broken entirely—until she happened upon his door.

Something in the Way She Moves. And at that very moment, there went Taylor on the Jeep's sound system again, digging it all up in him one more time.

"She has the power to go where no one else can find me . . ."

"Such a pretty song," Jessie commented, and Danny nodded. "Very."

My little Jessie growed up so fast after her Mama left us. She went from checkered dresses with petticoats and frilly little socks to skirts so short I near 'bout had a heart attack. For a few years there, I became like one o' them guards with the big hats standin' watch at the gate to the Queen's palace overseas. Pointin' my finger at her like a musket. She knew just by lookin' at me to go back to her bedroom closet and try again.

"Grampy, you have no fashion sense a-tall," she used to tell me.

"Maybe so," come my reply. "But I'll find some way to o'ercome."

Thank the Lord, when she growed into her own style, brought with it a degree o' modesty that put an old man's heart to ease after a lotta years o' standin' at the back door, finger ready to point the way back around.

Then come that husband o' hers, and he did the finger waggin' fer me. Didn't have much use for that stuffed shirt, but I sure didn't mind him takin' the reins of watchdog at the door.

"Jack likes everything just so," Jessie told me when they come to visit.

Next thing, I figured I'd see her with a little pill box hat 'n some o' them white gloves, like Jackie Kennedy. Yeah, he liked everything just so, all right.

Too bad my Jessie weren't a just-so kinda girl at the heart of her.

4

This is your *little vacation home*?"

She thought Danny snickered, and she peeled her eyes off the front of the enormous wood and stone house before them.

"Danny," Jessie told him with a sigh. "You really should have told me."

He threw the gear into neutral and turned off the ignition. "Told you what?"

She waved her arm through the open roof with a flourish. "Told me . . . *this*. You let me think we were going camping or something."

"It's kind of like that. But the tent is really nice."

Jessie let him climb out of the Jeep alone. She needed an extra few seconds to process what she saw in front of her.

"C'mon, Jessie," Allie exclaimed as she trotted toward her. "I'll show you where we'll be."

When Danny had said he and Riggs would sleep in the loft, leaving the master bedroom to her and Allie, she'd imagined a small staircase between them. Maybe a miniscule hallway or something. From the look of things, they were entering the equivalent to a couple of separate residences. A quaint little A-frame and a sprawling ranch pushed together to make one immaculate, inviting mountain retreat. For a dozen or more of the Callahan family's closest friends.

Before she could tug on the door handle, Danny opened it from the other side. Jessie unbuckled the seat belt and swung her legs out, her feet landing on a sand-colored stamped concrete driveway bordered on both sides by slightly darker stones. The curved path led to massive double doors boasting large beveled glass windows that caught the afternoon light and reflected it back in colorful bursts.

Danny led the way, lugging his overstuffed duffle bag behind one shoulder while dragging Jessie's wheeled Louis Vuitton close to his heels. She grabbed her handbag and the white leather hat box case from the backseat and flipped the handle over her wrist as she hurried to follow them.

"You're going to love this place," Allie told her. "Wait until you see the view from the loft."

"The loft is off-limits," Riggs exclaimed as he passed them.

"Oh, come on . . ."

"You girls have the whole rest of the house. The loft is The Man Zone."

"The Man Zone," Allie muttered to Jessie with a dramatic roll of her eyes. "Please."

Jessie couldn't help chuckling at the teen's dramatic flair.

She came to a wobbly stop just inside the front door, clutching her bags, mouth gaping. From the large planks of distressed maple on the floors to the rough beams across the twenty feet of ceiling—and everything in between—the home broadcast an unmistakably advanced design aesthetic she never would have associated with Danny. His laid-back Santa Monica surfer persona hardly fit with the picture before her.

"Yeah, I know," he said, and she snapped to attention, surprised to find him standing next to her. "It's pretty great, right?"

Jessie turned her head and gazed at him for a moment. "Great?" she repeated with the shake of her head. "Yeah. It's pretty great."

"Hey, Danny," Allie called out.

Jessie spotted her on the other side of an oversized rustic table centered beneath a rubbed bronze oval chandelier.

"I'm gonna make a sandwich, okay?"

"Sometimes I forget," he muttered as if he hadn't heard Allie.

Jessie watched after him as he wandered away, leaving her standing there alone.

"Hey, Callahan." Riggs thundered down the circular staircase in the corner of the great room. "Our bags are stowed upstairs. What did Brunswick bring us to eat?"

Jessie inched past two light-green leather sofas, which faced each other over a low, square coffee table like a couple of amiable visitors. The high hearth of the stacked stone fireplace balanced one pristine pile of chopped wood with a display of heavy iron utensils beneath a mantle that matched the overhead beams. She left her handbag and cosmetics case on the table before rounding the corner and stopping, breathless, beneath the wide arched entrance to the kitchen.

Oversized squares of Mediterranean travertine led the way into the most magnificent and inviting kitchen Jessie thought she had ever seen. Stainless steel appliances and brushed nickel accents and fixtures set off two walls of cabinetry, light beige and green granite counters, and an enormous farmhouse sink. By the time Jessie found her breath again, her three companions had kicked into full gear handing off packages of cold cuts, cheese, sandwich rolls, condiments, bottled drinks . . .

"What can I do to help?" she asked.

"You can grab plates and stuff," Riggs said. He headed through the open glass French doors that led to a massive redwood deck overlooking a large blue lake and surrounded on three sides by a bench broken up at each corner with planters of colorful flowers.

"Over there," Allie said on her way out the door behind him.

Jessie headed toward where Danny stood at the counter slicing tomatoes. "Here?" she asked him.

He tugged open the cabinet door to his left. "Plates up here. Glasses to the right. Silverware is in the drawer on the other side of me."

As she navigated about collecting four of everything, she nudged him with her elbow. "Danny, did you grow up spending time here?"

"Yeah, my folks bought the place when I was about ten."

She smiled, trying to imagine her grandfather standing in the middle of the cavernous kitchen, "stirrin' up slop," as he used to call dinner preparation.

Jessie gazed at the stretch of blue beyond the trees. "Is that Big Bear Lake out there?"

"Our little piece of it, yes." He picked up the plate he'd pre-pared and nodded toward the door. "Let's eat outside."

She followed him. "Where did all this food come from?"

"Brunswick," Riggs chimed in as they reached the outdoor dining table at the edge of the deck. "He's the all-knowing Giles."

"The what?" she asked with a chuckle.

"Len Brunswick," Danny clarified. "He opens and closes the place for us, stocks the fridge, that kind of thing."

"All-knowing Giles?"

"Ah." Danny waved his hand in dismissal.

Allie giggled. "Dad likes to think of Mr. Brunswick like one of those English butlers on TV. He says they're always named Giles. And he's psychic because he always seems to bring our favorite foods." Without missing a beat, she turned to her father. "Did you bring out the chips?"

"Forgot 'em," Riggs said over a full mouth.

"Chew your food," she remarked, hopping up and heading inside. "Were you raised in a barn?"

Riggs cackled and shook his head at Jessie. "She's a clone of her mother."

Allie reappeared with two bags of chips, and she tossed one to her father before taking her place at the table. "Can we go paddle-boarding after supper?"

"Let's save all that rigamarole for tomorrow. We'll get an early start."

"Early, as in early for you? Or early for the rest of the world?" his daughter teased.

"Hilarious."

"Then can we go swimming?"

Riggs took another large bite from his sandwich before nodding and talking over it. "Yeah. I guess."

Riggs and Allie raced down the dock and, without even the slightest hesitation, both of them catapulted off the end of it into the water. Danny shook his head and chuckled.

"Two pieces of the same cloth," he remarked. "He thinks she's just like Charlotte, but Allie's so much like him it scares me a little."

"She's beautiful," Jessie commented.

Danny held back from returning that observation back to her. She looked almost ethereal sitting there, sideways on the bench, in cropped cotton pants and a short, loose gauze blouse, the breeze from the lake toying with her hair. As she leaned against the planter, she raised her knees and wrapped her arms around them. The afternoon sun illuminated her, gave her hair the appearance of spun glass. When she lowered her sunglasses on the bridge of her nose and looked at him over top of them, his heartbeat picked up the pace to a full-on hammering against his chest.

"I'm glad you invited me along, Danny. And I especially appreciate you all shifting things to Sunday."

"I knew you couldn't be away from the store on a Saturday. It worked out fine. I'm just glad you wanted to come. I wasn't sure."

"No?"

"No," he admitted. "The air between us has gotten a little thick since that night at your place."

"I know." She sighed. "I'm sorry."

"Do you feel like telling me what that's about?" he broached. "What is it about him and what *he's done* that makes you think you can't trust *me*?"

She clucked out a chuckle and pushed her sunglasses back into place. "I have no doubts about whether or not I can trust you, Danny Callahan."

"No?"

"No," she assured him. "I just became painfully aware of my history of leaning on the men in my life, and I don't want you to become one of them. I need to stand on my own. I'm not sure I've ever done that."

At first, he thought she must be joking. When he noted the seriousness shadowing her expression, he told her, "You're the strongest woman I know."

"I'm not."

"You are." He wasn't about to back down. Not on this. "Everything you've been through in the last few months would have done most women in, Jess. But look what you did—"

"Oh, Danny," she said softly. "You don't understand."

He stood and crossed the deck toward her. She reached up and took his hand, squeezing it, and Danny sat on the redwood bench beside her feet before she released him.

"Don't shut me out, Jessie."

The words seemed to stroke her. She removed her sunglasses entirely and balanced them on her knee. "I might have to," she said, her voice like warm velvet. "Just for a little while."

He wanted to argue, to plead his case and tell her how important she'd become to him. But something stopped him from doing it. Good sense, he figured. But before he could question it any further, he noticed someone walking up the stairs from the dock.

"Danny," the older woman called out to him. "Danny Callahan."

He stood up and waved to her. "Mrs. Slaughter, how are you?"

"Can I stop up?"

"Of course." Danny nodded at Jessie. "Our neighbor, Kaye Slaughter."

She turned and planted her feet on the ground, combing through her hair with both hands.

"Danny, how are you, honey?" the woman said as she reached the top of the stairs. "I hope I'm not intruding."

"Of course not," he said, taking her hand. "Let me pour you something to drink. Is tea all right?"

"That would be just fine." She brushed Jessie with a warm smile before stating, "Hello. I'm Kaye Slaughter."

"This is Jessie Hart. Jessie, Mrs. Slaughter owns the place right down the dock."

The woman reached out and shook Jessie's hand. "I don't know how many times I've told this boy to call me Kaye, but he insists on formalities. I don't know whether to feel insulted or respect his upbringing."

Jessie chuckled. "I wouldn't be insulted."

"Pleasure to meet you, dear."

"You, too."

She sat down on the bench next to Jessie and accepted the glass of tea from Danny. "Thank you. I saw your friend Aaron swimming out there with his young daughter. My, she's grown up, hasn't she?"

Danny grinned. "She has."

"I was so glad to see you were here, Danny. I thought perhaps we could have a chat."

"Anytime. You know that."

Kaye fidgeted with a lock of short silver hair. She ran her finger around the rim of the glass and stared down into it for another long moment before speaking. "I have a situation, Danny."

"A situation."

"And I thought of you right away because of your being . . . you know, an investigator."

Danny dragged one of the chairs away from the table and sat down on it across from her. Kaye Slaughter had been a friend of his family for more than a decade. The only time he remembered her breaking her game face was that week in the summer of 2009 when her husband Burt had suddenly passed away. Until now, anyway. He spotted a sense of panic mixed with confusion churning in her gray-blue eyes, and an array of possible sources ricocheted in soft pings through his thoughts.

Danny reached over and touched her hand. "Take your time and tell me what's going on."

"Thank you, dear." She dabbed the tip of her nose with a tissue he hadn't noticed she held wadded in her fist. "It could be I'm just being silly. I don't know."

He caught Jessie's eye just quickly enough for an exchange of shared concern, and he nearly loved her for it.

"I know I'm getting on in years, so it could just be . . ." Her words trailed away, and she sighed. "I've tried to convince myself it's my imagination, but I know it's not, Danny. I know something strange is going on over there."

He wanted to clarify her quick nod toward the docks. "At your place?"

"Yes. Something isn't right."

Jessie touched the woman's arm. "I find it's better not to over-think things. Our instincts are pretty much dead on."

Kaye smiled at her. "I'm not getting any younger, so when I first noticed it . . . I started to wonder if it wasn't a warning sign of things to come. But it's happening more and more, so . . ."

"What's happening more and more, Kaye?" Danny interjected.

"Oh, I'm sorry. In the beginning, I noticed things seemed to have been moved around. The spatula in the drawer instead of hanging on the rack over the stove, that kind of thing. I never keep the spatula in the drawer."

"How long has it been happening?" Jessie asked.

"A month or so, I think. Every time I drove up from Pasadena, it seemed like something else was out of place. Then a couple of weeks ago, I noticed the key to the storage cabinet in the garage was missing from the hook in the kitchen. And you'll never guess where I found it. Right there in the lock."

"In the garage?" Danny asked.

"That's right. Hanging right out of the cabinet lock."

"Have you ever left it there before?"

"Danny, I don't think I've gotten into that storage cabinet since Burt passed."

"Well, that doesn't sound like your imagination," Jessie said.

"I don't think so either. And that made me more keenly aware, and I went looking for things that might be moved or missing." She pulled a folded sheet of paper from the pocket of her trousers and ironed it open with her palm before handing it to Danny. "I made a list."

He took it from her and skimmed the page.

Only 5 wine glasses—should be 6

Bottle of merlot

Bathroom drawer standing open

Green pillowcase

Danny glanced up at her. "You're missing a green pillowcase?"

"Oh. No. The green pillowcase is supposed to be on the square pillow. But two weekends ago, it was on the rectangle, and the lilac case was on the square."

The corner of his mouth twitched, but he reeled in the chuckle that simmered at the base of his throat.

Next to the *TV Remote* notation, Kaye had scribbled, "Still missing."

½ laundry detergent gone

Wet towels in dryer—2 bath, 1 kitchen

Red comb out of the drawer—sitting in the shower

Anniversary necklace missing

"Anniversary necklace?" he asked her.

"Burt bought me a lovely amethyst necklace that we saw in one of those little shops in town."

"Amethyst," he repeated. "Is that valuable?"

"It was just a hundred dollars, I think. But the setting was very unique, and . . ." She swallowed before turning toward Jessie. "It was our last anniversary together before he went home."

"I'm so sorry."

Danny turned his attention back to the unexpectedly lengthy list.

Oatmeal cookies from the freezer
Neck roll missing from the guest room
Riley and Duncan's bags

"Riley and Duncan's bags?"

"When the grandchildren come up in the summer, they enjoy camping out on the deck," she explained. "We keep their sleeping bags on the shelf in the garage. I mightn't have noticed they were missing except that I thought to wash them before they're out for the summer."

"What are you thinking?" Jessie asked him.

Danny cocked a brow. "I'm thinking this has gone beyond coincidence or forgetfulness."

"Really?" Kaye's timid smile oozed grateful relief.

"I remember your schedule being fairly regimented. Is that still the case? Do you normally arrive and leave on the same day of the week?"

She nodded. "I volunteer at Huntington Memorial Hospital Tuesday through Thursday, and I generally make the drive up the mountain late Thursday afternoon and stay through most of the day on Sunday."

"So you would normally leave tonight."

"Around five."

"I think you should go ahead and do that, just like always," Danny advised. "Then I'll do some surveillance and see if there's anything going on. Do you have an extra set of keys to the house?"

"I can drop them by on my way down the hill," she told him. "Thank you so much, Danny."

"Don't thank me yet. Let's see what I can find out."

Kaye stood up and smiled at him. "Oh, and it was a pleasure meeting you, Jessie."

"Same here. And don't worry. If there's anything to find out, Danny's the one to do it."

Danny took the woman by the arm. "I'll be back in a minute," he told Jessie. "I'm just going to walk Kaye down the dock."

"Take your time. I'll clean up the rest of the dishes."

Although she was a little slow going down the wooden plank stairs, Kaye still held herself with the posture of her younger days. He recalled a barbecue she'd attended right there on the deck the summer of his sixteenth birthday, wearing a flowing blue dress. To a typical sixteen-year-old, the beautiful and regal Kaye Slaughter looked like a member of the royal family on holiday. Truth told, he'd had a bit of a crush on her back then. Now, many years later, infatuation had evolved into deep affection.

When he left her at the base of the stairs leading to her own vacation home, Kaye kissed his cheek and squeezed his hand.

"I'm so grateful," she said.

"I'll give you a call."

On the walk back, he slowed at the dock where Riggs and Allie lounged side by side, feet dangling over the side as they chatted sweetly. Danny envied the easy relationship between father and daughter, and he wondered whether he might ever be so blessed. As he took the stairs up toward the deck—and before he could stop the train of thought barreling down the track—he tried to imagine a sweet little girl with Jessie's glossy dark hair and crystal blue eyes simmering with fascination for the world around her, blended with his mother's single-dimpled smile and melodious voice.

"Oh good, you're back," Jessie exclaimed as he reached the wooden summit and stretched out on the long bench where she'd been sitting when he left. She grinned at him from the other side of the table, and leaned down to zip a small cooler. "I packed a few stakeout snacks for us. When do we leave?"

———— ✕ ————

"I thought we'd go out Picayune way today. Maybe catch us a speckled trout 'r two."

These was the words that delighted my Jessie's young soul. Not 'cause she ever took to fishin' all that much. What she did like was packin' us up a lunch to share from the bank o' that river, and pickin' a Hardy Boys book to read out loud to me while I cast a line or two.

"You sure you don't wanna bait a hook and give it a cast?"

"Nah," she'd tell me. "That's icky."

"Then why you wanna go fishin' a-tall?"

"We do our best talkin' out here, Grampy. You wanna hear what the Hardy Boys are up to next?"

5

Jessie glanced over at Danny seated next to her on the floor behind Kaye Slaughter's sofa. She could almost read his mind, and it tickled her somehow.

How did I let her talk me into this again?

As if on cue, he sighed. "I don't know why I keep letting you talk me into coming along on stakeouts."

"Uh, because I'm good company and I help you *solve cases*?" she ribbed, rolling her eyes at him dramatically. "*And* I brought snacks. What do you want? Chocolate chip cookies or corn chips?"

He tried to resist and make a point, she could tell. She giggled when he surrendered. "Corn chips."

She pulled out a snack bag and handed it over before opening the zipped plastic bag of cookies. "So what's your gut feeling?" she asked. "You think anybody's really going to show?"

Danny leaned against the back of the sofa and shrugged. "I don't know. But I have a hard time buying Kaye as a doddering old woman who doesn't remember washing a load of towels."

"Yeah. She strikes me as pretty sharp," she remarked before stuffing a whole cookie into her mouth. "Kick the cooler over here, will you?"

Danny snagged the strap of the cooler with the toe of his shoe and maneuvered it toward her.

"This floor is getting cold," she said, producing a can of root beer. When she popped the top, Danny shushed her. "Sorry."

She took a couple of chugs from the can and handed it to Danny. "Share?" He downed half the liquid inside before passing it back to her. A soft rumble drew her attention, and she nearly lost her grasp on the soda. "What is that?"

"Excuse me," he offered, tapping the center of his chest with a closed fist.

"Not that, silly. That sound. I think it's coming from the kitchen."

Danny glared a hole into her. "The garage."

"It's coming from the garage?"

"It *is* the garage. The door is going up. Stay here."

Before she could even reply, Danny shifted and popped off the floor. He disappeared around the other side of the sofa, and Jessie shimmied to her knees and peered over the back of it.

"*Get. Down.*" he whisper-yelled at her. "I mean it. Stay put."

"Okay, okay." She slowly lowered herself, but then snapped back up again. "Where are you going? Do you have a gun or a knife or something?"

At the corner near the kitchen, Danny turned back and looked at her. The odd expression he flashed elicited a snicker that she barely caught with both hands over her face.

"Well," she managed over the hushed giggles, "you have to defend yourself."

"Jessie," he hissed, slicing his hand through the air.

"Okay. Okay."

Crouched behind the sofa where she'd been relegated, Jessie only saw the reflection of the kitchen light as it turned on.

"Mind telling me what you're doing?" Danny called.

The question was immediately followed by a crash and the strange sounds of a scuffle. When someone groaned, Jessie popped to her feet in an instant. She bounced from the ball of one foot to the other, her heart racing and all the nerve endings in her body crackling with electricity. When another groan sounded—

this one definitely Danny—she grabbed a carved elephant sitting on an end table and raced into the kitchen ready to clock someone if necessary.

When she reached the doorway to the kitchen, clutching the elephant by the trunk and holding it in the air, Danny had already pinned the intruder to the marble floor, face down, and held him there with both hands.

"Who are you?" he demanded. "How did you get this?"

Jessie craned her neck until she spotted a garage door remote on the floor next to them.

"I found it." The creaky little voice of the lanky man under Danny came out in puffs.

"Try again . . ." he said, yanking the wallet out of the man's back pocket. He flipped it open and added, "Brandon Rucks."

"All right. Will you get off me so I can breathe, man? No kidding, I need some air."

"Better talk fast then. What are you doing here? And how long have you been letting yourself into a house that doesn't belong to you?"

"Th-three months," he sputtered, and Jessie inched closer.

Danny eased up on the guy and rolled him over to his back. Leaning over and glaring into his face, he asked, "Why?"

Brandon squirmed beneath him and groaned. "Let up, would you? I can't breathe."

Danny backed away and stood, extending his hand. As Brandon Rucks accepted it, allowing Danny to tug him to his feet, Jessie realized their intruder was just a string bean of a disheveled, dark-haired boy with torn jeans and well-worn tennis shoes.

"How old are you?" she asked, and Brandon jerked toward her. "You can't be more than sixteen."

"Seventeen," Danny answered for him, holding up the kid's wallet.

"Who are you people?" Brandon snapped.

"I'm in charge of the questions," Danny reminded him. "Tell us what you're doing here."

Brandon glared at the worn toe of his old shoe. "The only job I could get is part-time at one of the resorts in town. They put a roof over my head most weekends, but I don't have any place to stay during the week."

"So you thought you'd squat here."

"It's only for a few more weeks. Until I save enough for first month's rent on a studio in Fawnskin."

"Not a few more weeks, buddy," Danny said. "Not even a few more hours. You can't just break into somebody's house and make like you live there."

"And steal their jewelry," Jessie added.

"I only took the one necklace," he reasoned.

Danny lightly smacked the boy's arm. "Only?"

"I was gonna put it back in a couple of weeks."

"That necklace is very important to the owner of this home," Jessie told him. "You need to hand that over right now."

"I can't. I hocked it."

Jessie's heart dropped. She imagined some greasy guy—not unlike that Chaz Decker who bought her engagement ring— drooling over the amethyst pendant Kaye had described. The difference being it had been given to her by someone precious; not a duplicitous faux husband.

"Where?" Danny's question catapulted Jessie back to the moment.

"Valley Pawn, down the hill."

"The one in Yucaipa?"

"Yeah."

"You got a ticket on it in here?" Danny asked as he opened Brandon's wallet again. "This it?" he asked, holding up a yellow receipt.

"Yeah. I just did it so I could eat. And gas up the bike." Danny tucked the receipt into his pocket, and the kid sighed. "You gonna call the cops on me?"

Jessie expected a resounding, "Absolutely!" But Danny hesitated before answering. "No."

"No?" Brandon yelped. "Are you kidding? That's cool, man. You're really cool."

"But that courtesy is going to cost you," he qualified. "You're going to get out of here now—right now, tonight—and you're not ever coming back. Do you know how I know this? Because I've got your information and I won't hesitate for one L.A. minute to turn you in if I ever get even the slightest scent on the wind that you've been within a mile of this place. Do you read me?"

Jessie stifled the grin threatening to break into the seriousness Danny had created in the moment.

"Yes."

"Which resort are you working at?"

Brandon grimaced. "Ah, come on, man. I need that job bad. There's a chance I could go full-time when we get closer to the winter season."

"I'm not gonna mess that up for you, kid. Although I probably ought to. Just tell me where you work."

"The Summit."

Danny nodded, and Jessie wondered where he might be going with his line of questioning.

"I know somebody with cabin rentals near The Summit. I'll call him and see if I can't put a roof over your head for a month until you can get into your Fawnskin studio."

Brandon looked from Danny to Jessie and back again. "You serious?"

Danny pulled his cell phone out and gave the kid a nod. "You get this place cleaned up while I call. There's a broom and dustpan in the garage. But of course you know where everything is around here, don't you?"

Brandon lowered his head to camouflage a nervous chuckle.

Jessie watched Danny carefully as he spoke into the phone in a hushed tone, reminded again that his kindnesses to her in the beginning of their relationship hadn't just been a case of isolated pity. Danny was seemingly empathetic to everyone enduring hard times, deserving or not, who crossed his path.

When he disconnected the call and moved back toward her, she touched him on the arm, and he shot her a quick nod with a questioning cock of his eyebrow.

"Sometimes I forget how kind you are," she admitted.

He dismissed it with a sniff and a lopsided smile, then he shook his head.

"All right," he directed at Brandon as the kid swept up the last of the mess. "Finish up there and I'll drive you into town. You've got a place to stay, but in return you'll do some odd jobs that need doing around the place. Before you tell me if you have anything to say about that, let me remind you people are doing you a favor here. So . . . do you have anything to say?"

"Yes," the boy replied seriously. Jessie could hardly believe his gall.

"Then let's hear it."

He lifted his gaze to meet Danny's and murmured, "Thank you."

"Where have you guys been?" Allie exclaimed as Danny and Jessie walked through the door. "We were worried you got murdered and cut up into tiny pieces or something."

Jessie grinned at her. "Well, thanks for your concern."

"Did you at least catch the bad guy?"

"We did," Jessie replied. "And Danny rehabilitated him as well."

"What's that mean?" Allie asked, her gaze darting between the two of them.

"Long story," Danny commented. "Where's your pops?"

"He's out building up the fire in the pit while I look for the marshmallows."

Danny pointed in the direction of the kitchen. "In the pantry. Top shelf."

"You got any graham crackers? We could make s'mores."

"Also in the pantry."

Jessie waited for Allie to disappear around the corner before moving close and facing Danny. "That was really nice what you did for Brandon."

"Somebody had to. The kid was headed for lockup."

"Yeah, but . . . people are always saying somebody should do something," she told him tenderly. "You seem to be the one who actually does."

Danny's eyes turned smoky as he looked down at her and graced her with half a smile. Without thinking it through, Jessie tucked her hand around the back of his neck and pulled him close enough to plant a kiss on his warm lips.

When they parted, she smiled at him. "I just think you're . . . *extraordinary.*"

"I like you very much, too," he teased.

"Are you going to call Kaye and tell her you solved her mystery?"

"I want to stop in Yucaipa on our way back Tuesday and see if I can get her necklace first."

"That would be an added piece of good news, wouldn't it?"

"I think it would."

"Hey, you guys," Allie shouted at them from the other side of the room. "We've got everything we need for s'mores. Are you coming?"

"Wouldn't miss it," Danny told her, his eyes trained on Jessie. "I do love a good s'more."

Jessie giggled, and she slipped her hand inside his as they headed through the glass doorway to the deck.

By the time the last embers in the copper fire pit dwindled down to nothing and far too much chocolate, marshmallow, and graham crackers had been warmed and consumed, Jessie felt more than ready for her head to fall on a pillow. Unfortunately, all that sugar had other effects on Allie. The girl chattered all the way down the hall and into the bedroom, throughout their turns in front of the bathroom sink, after pajamas had been donned, lights turned off, blankets tucked under chins. Yes, Allie was still talking.

". . . and I told her it wasn't going to work like that. She had to play hard-to-get and not let him think she liked him, you know? Boys get a head full when they think a girl likes them, don't you think so?"

Jessie yawned. "I think it depends on the boy, honey."

"You think so? I never met a boy who didn't get a head full when he found out for sure."

"You know what, Allie?"

"What?"

"I'm really tired. I don't want to be rude, but I can't stay awake another minute."

"Oh. Okay."

"We'll talk more in the morning, okay?"

"Yeah, okay. You're going paddleboarding with us, aren't you?"

"Mm . . ."

The next thing Jessie knew, the sun had pushed its way through the window and flooded the whole bedroom. The bed Allie had occupied the night before sat conspicuously empty under a heap of disheveled blankets. Jessie made up both the beds before she dressed and ventured down the long hallway to the living spaces of the house. Through the glass, she spotted Danny lounging on the deck, reading a newspaper, and sipping from a cup of coffee. She stopped in the kitchen and poured herself a cup before joining him.

"Good morning."

He looked up and broke into a full grin when he saw her. "Morning. How'd you sleep?"

"Like a rock." *Once Allie quit talking, anyway.*

"Good. Interested in paddleboarding with Riggs and Al after breakfast?"

"Ha!" she croaked. "I don't think so. I have a hard enough trouble staying upright on dry land. A surfboard is so far out of my element."

"It's not like surfing. It's much calmer. I think you might enjoy it."

"How much balance do you need?"

"Well, some," he teased. "But . . . minimal in comparison to surfing." He paused while she thought it over. "I brought a nice long board that works well for beginners. Give it a try."

She nibbled the corner of her lip before shrugging one shoulder. "Okay."

Two hours later, Jessie thought better of the casual agreement as Danny fed her instructions from a board adjacent to hers.

"You're always going to grip the paddle with one hand at the end and the other holding the center of the shaft. Like this."

Her knees ached as she examined his demonstration. "When can I stand up? My knees hurt."

He chuckled. "Get up one foot at a time and stay in the middle of the board." As she pushed upright, he added, "Good. That's right. Wait!"

Too late. Her other foot slipped over the side of the paddleboard, and she fell off into the water. When she breached the surface again, Danny, Allie, and Riggs were cackling like irritating hens.

"It's all right," Danny told her. "Just climb back on and try again. Keep your feet parallel this time."

She groaned, not really wanting to try again. However, on her third attempt, she found herself standing, balanced, and paddling along next to Allie. She now felt pretty happy she'd stuck with the efforts to stand upright.

The sun's noontime rays cut through the tangle of leaves hanging from the border of trees, playing glittery tricks on the smooth surface of the water. Jessie dipped the paddle into the lake with the blade angled away from her and pushed it through the water. With her hands firmly in place, she lifted it to the other side of the board and repeated the action, not even trying to suppress the happy giggle that bubbled up from inside.

"Check you out," Riggs called to her with a nod. "Lookin' good!"

"I think I've got it, right?"

A couple of kayaks brimming with rowdy teenagers rounded the curve. The ruckus distracted Jessie for just a moment, and she nearly lost her balance before recovering.

"Hey, Dad! I'll race you," Allie called out, and she and Riggs took off across the lake as if sliding on glass.

Danny navigated his board closer to Jessie's as they moved out from under the shade of the trees. When the golden sunlight found him, the blonder sections of his multifaceted hair kindled into blazing streaks. His gray tee and long black shorts took on a silvery glint, and he lowered the sunglasses from the top of his head to the bridge of his nose.

"You know what I was thinking?" he asked, completely unaware of how weak in the knees just the sight of him left her.

"What's that?"

"During the spring and summer months, you can take the ski lift to the top of the mountain. What do you think of grabbing some lunch and taking it up?"

"Really? That sounds like fun. I should probably change clothes though—"

"Why? You look beautiful."

"Lies," she muttered with a laugh, adding, "I look like a drowned rat."

"I like the wet look."

She self-consciously ran one hand through her wet locks. "Oh, hush."

Danny cupped one hand around the side of his mouth and called out, "Riggs! . . . Hey, Riggs!" When his friend turned back toward him, he shouted, "We're heading back. See you later."

An hour later, while Jessie pushed her damp hair back into a loose ponytail and changed into dry clothes, Danny put together a quick picnic lunch in the kitchen. Just as they headed for the door, however, Jessie's cell phone buzzed from inside her handbag.

"Sorry," she said as she checked the screen. "It's Amber calling from the store. I need to take it."

"Go ahead."

Jessie pressed the talk button as she headed back into the kitchen. "Amber?"

"Hi, Jessie. I'm so sorry to bother you while you're on your getaway."

"It's fine. What's up?"

"You'll never believe who just called the store for you." Amber didn't give her time to guess. "Perry Marconi."

"The—?"

"Stylist to the Hollywood stars!" she blurted. "Yes. *That* Perry Marconi."

"He asked for me?" Jessie clarified.

"Yes. He has two clients presenting at the Legacy Awards, and another one nominated!" Jessie's mind raced with musings on what this had to do with her, but Amber ran her thoughts right off the track. "Guess who it is. The one who's nominated."

"I have no—"

"Carolyn Coleman, that's who!"

"Carolyn Coleman . . ." Jessie had seen every movie the glamorous Carolyn Coleman had ever made. From her beginnings as a teenaged starlet in black-and-white classic movies to her long-running television show in the eighties, the woman had aged with more grace than any of her counterparts. "Wait. Amber. What does this have to do with Adornments?"

"Are you sitting down?"

"Yes," she lied.

"No, you're not. Sit down."

"Okay." Still standing. "Tell me."

"Perry Marconi wants to work with you to style all three of them."

Jessie backed up to the counter and leaned on it. "He . . . I'm sorry. What?"

"It turns out he's a friend of Courtney's," Amber exclaimed. "Since Courtney's already off to London to pick up her new little girl, he said she told him you're the only one he should work with!"

Since the day tiny Courtney Alexis with the contradictory deep, raspy voice walked into Adornments on the day of the opening, she'd been changing Jessie's life, one opportunity at a time. They'd collaborated on offering styling sessions at the store; then she brought Jessie and Amber onboard to write guest columns for her fashion mega-blog. The two had become great friends, bonding even beyond their love of fashion and the pending adoption of Courtney's beautiful baby girl. And now this.

"I'm so glad you called and told me, Amber. This is such great news."

"It's epic," she shouted. "The only thing is . . . he wants to meet with you tomorrow."

"*Tomorrow?*"

"I told him you were away and could meet with him midweek, but I could hear him waning, and I was afraid we'd lose him. So I said I'd call you and—"

"You did the right thing. Hang on." Jessie hurried out of the kitchen and into the living room just as Danny came through the front door. Covering the mic with her hand, she winced and tried to convert it to a smile. "Danny? Would you hate me if I asked you to take me home tonight?"

"What happened?"

The alarm crackling in his eyes incited her immediate reaction. "Oh. No. Nothing's wrong. In fact, something could be very right. A great opportunity for me, but I have to take a meeting tomorrow."

He smiled. "We can leave within the hour."

She hurried toward him and kissed his cheek. "Thank you."

"I still need to stop in Yucaipa to get Kaye's necklace."

"Yes, of course."

"But you'll be back in Santa Monica in time to get a good night's sleep."

Jessie squeezed his wrist and shook it. "Thank you!" Before he could reply, she turned her attention back to Amber. "Call him back right away. Ask him to meet me at the store at noon tomorrow. That will you give you and me the morning to strategize. I'll be there by nine."

"I'll bring the coffee."

"I feel sick at my stomach every time I think about it, Grampy."

I was crawled under the kitchen sink workin' on the pipe, and Jessie got herself up on the counter, sendin' her words down the drain t'ward me.

"Why you botherin' with that, girl?" I ask her. "Ain't nothin' you kin do 'til tomorrow anyhow."

"Yeah, I guess so. But I can't help myself. Can't think o' nothin' else but that dumb old book report I gotta give in front of the whole entire class."

"You read the book?"

"Yeah."

"You write up the report?"

"Well, yeah, Grampy, but—"

"But nothin'," I tells her. "You done all you kin. Now you just wait 'til the time comes, and you stand up there and tell 'em what they need to know. What's so complicated 'bout it, girl?"

She set there quiet fer a time 'fore she says, "Why you gotta go bein' all logical 'bout everything anyway?"

"And why you gotta be a worrywart?"

"'Cause, Grampy. That's how I was made, I guess."

Sure enough, she had a point there. The girl'd been worryin' 'bout things she couldn't change her whole young life. Her mama used to say sometimes she thought if Jessie was an automobile, worry were the gas that made 'er get up 'n go.

6

Danny had packed up the Jeep, left a note with instructions about closing up the house for Riggs and Allie, and got them on their way without delay. He navigated the winding mountain road as he called Mr. Brunswick, the caretaker of his own family home, to enlist his aid in changing the locks and garage door opener at Kaye Slaughter's house.

"And if you could also follow after my friends when they're gone, just to make sure our family home is still standing? . . . Thanks so much. Talk to you soon."

When they reached Yucaipa, the town tucked into the base of the mountain, the temperature had risen considerably and Jessie had to remove the light jacket she'd found necessary at Big Bear's cooler elevation of nearly seven thousand feet. They made a fast stop at Valley Pawn to retrieve the stunning amethyst pendant Kaye had called her "anniversary necklace"—there and waiting on the other side of the collateral receipt, just as Brandon Rucks had said it would be.

"Yeah, I remember that kid," the thick-necked proprietor told them. "Said he'd be back to get it in thirty days. You know, they all think their luck's gonna change and they'll be back. Ain't too often things go as they plan. But that's how we stay in business, right?"

It took no more than ten minutes for them to admire the stunning necklace and for Danny to pay the hefty ransom to take it with him. They sidetracked to a fast food drive-thru for something cold to drink before migrating onto the 10, heading west to Santa Monica. The diverse soundtrack of the next ninety-some minutes of their journey ran the gamut from Casting Crowns to Sweet Baby James, The Beach Boys to Mandisa, and conversation went smooth and easy as well.

"So explain what this all means in non-fashionista language that I can understand," Danny said after she told him the reason for her hasty return to the real world.

Jessie giggled. "Well, Perry Marconi was a stylist to C- and D-listers in Hollywood for years. Then a couple of seasons back, one of his no-name clients gets nominated for an Academy Award with no real chance of winning—but she does, against all odds—and she's suddenly the next Lupita Nyong'o with Perry hailed as the genius who dressed and accessorized her straight out of the depths of obscurity. And now he's showing me a little glimpse of his coattail."

Danny grinned at her. "Yeah, I still don't entirely get it. But . . . this meeting with Perry Somebody is a very good thing for you, yes?"

"Yes," she said on a rolling chuckle.

"And there are potential coattails to be ridden."

"Yes."

"Then you shall ride them," he declared with a nod. "Straight out of the depths of obscurity."

"Here's hoping."

As they took the Lincoln exit off the expressway, Jessie lowered the volume on the music. "You know, I've been meaning to ask you . . . Who's taking care of Frank this weekend?"

"Oh, he's on a three-day playdate with my folks out in Newport. But I think I'll go pick him up after I drop you at your place."

"Don't want to spend a night without him unnecessarily, Papa?"

Danny chuckled. "Although the way my mom babies him, he might not want to come back with me."

"Like that could ever happen."

He cocked an eyebrow and tilted his head slightly toward her. "She cooks him a breakfast of chicken, rice, and eggs every morning when he's with her. I try to bring him home and give him a bowl full of his regular kibbles, and he looks at me like he's nailed me trying to pull one over on him."

Somehow, Jessie could see that so clearly. Danny's extra-large dog had quite an expressive face—albeit a really large one—with two cropped ears, one of which always seemed to be folded over at the tip.

"How much does he weigh?" she asked.

"Frankenstein comes in just under one-twenty-five."

"A hundred twenty-five pounds," she said, shaking her head. "I only have a few pounds on him!"

"He'd be happy to hear that comparison," Danny commented. "It'd make him feel quite svelte, I'm sure."

She laughed at that. *Frank* and *svelte* in the same sentence. "Indeed."

Danny pulled into the driveway in front of Jessie's apartment building and turned off the engine, and the music along with it. The sweet quiet enveloped her in arms of peace, and she decided to enjoy it for a minute or two. She sighed and closed her eyes, tilting her head to rest on the seat back. The fragrance of a distant outdoor barbecue wafted sheepishly by, tickling Jessie's nose and inciting a growl of hunger from deep in her stomach.

"Mm," she moaned. "Do you smell that? Somebody's grilling out."

"We should have stopped to grab a bite," he said. "Do you want to run downtown?"

"I'd love to, but I have so much prep work to do before tomorrow's meeting."

"How about I haul your bags in, and you get settled," he suggested. "Start doing what you need to do. I'll pick something up and bring it back for you and get out of your hair."

"You wouldn't mind?" she asked. "I'm sorry to be such a dud. My head is just somewhere else. If I wasn't so hungry right now—"

"You have to eat something. Riggs told me about a new Italian place they just opened around the corner. I'll grab you some pasta and a salad. How's that sound?"

"So great, Danny. Thank you."

He hopped out of the Jeep and yanked Jessie's bags from the back while she dug into her purse to find the apartment keys. Danny took them from her as he passed and, by the time she climbed out and followed, he'd opened the front door and stepped inside.

"Jessie."

The sound of Jack's voice cut straight through her, slicing her straight in half. Jessie reeled around to confirm. Jack stood at the rear bumper of Danny's Jeep, and dread crept over the top of her head and dripped downward in a thick, molasses-like consistency.

"What are you doing here, Jack? You're not allowed within—"

"A hundred yards," he cut in. "I know."

"Then why are you here?"

Danny passed through the apartment door and bellowed, "Stanton." He punched in numbers on his cell phone as he stalked toward them. "Are you learning impaired, man?"

"No," he stated, stone-faced before he softened and shot a glance at Jessie. She'd never seen Jack's bravado crumple like that. He looked almost sad to her. For a fleeting moment, she remembered the man she'd once known, the fraud who left her weak in the knees.

Stop it, she warned herself. *That man died the instant he cleared out your life and disappeared with his actual wife.*

He directed his focus back to Jessie. "I just needed to talk to you, and you weren't at the store—"

"You went to my store?"

"Relax. I just wanted to speak to you for five minutes."

"No, Jack." Her emotions softened and she sighed. "The time for us talking is long gone."

"They're going to serve you with papers early in the week, Jessie."

"What kind of papers?" she asked, and Danny stepped close enough to her that their arms pressed together. His cell phone remained at his ear.

"They're going to have you come in for a deposition, and I just wanted to talk to you about it before you—"

"Rafe," Danny said into his phone. "Listen, man. We have a problem here at Jessie's again. Stanton just showed up on her door."

"Jessie," her faux husband pleaded. "I know I don't deserve any mercy from you, but . . . they want you to help bury me."

"You did that yourself without any help from me."

"How long until you can get someone out here?" Danny asked, and Jack's eyes ignited with panic.

"They'll arrest me, you know. Do you want that to happen just because you wouldn't hear me out?"

"Jack," she said, and before she knew it she'd reached out and touched his arm. "Get out of here before you make things worse for yourself. No matter what we talk or don't talk about, I'm going to tell the simple truth to whatever questions they ask."

He looked so pained, almost broken, and Jessie found it odd that her heart swelled up with sympathy the way it did. She nearly hurt *for him*, this man who had lit the fuse to the dynamite that exploded her life. It made no sense, yet there it was. She felt sorry for him.

"Thanks, buddy," she heard Danny speak to Rafe.

"Jack," she urged. "Go now. And don't come back."

With that, he turned and walked away from her. Again.

"He didn't even look like the same man," Jessie told Piper. "Just completely . . . I don't know what . . . broken."

"Good."

Jessie knew her friend didn't mean such a thing. Piper was the most compassionate woman she knew. But she appreciated the support just the same.

"Okay," Amber declared as she rushed toward them with Jessie's open laptop in her arms. She plopped down to the floor across the coffee table from them both and turned the screen so that they could see it. "I found some pictures of Carolyn Coleman, and I know we can find something great for her out of the new inventory we scored from Francesca Dutton. And I did some research to find out who these other two clients of Perry's might be, and I think I have it narrowed down." She took a much-needed breath. "I hope I do anyway. How cool would it be . . ." She added as she tabbed to another screen ". . . if we get to dress Misha Koskov?"

Piper moved closer to the laptop for a better look. "Who is she?"

Amber shot her a frown. "Really?" she teased. "She's that Russian ballet dancer who was all over the news a couple years ago when she wanted to become an American citizen."

"Oh, that's right. And now she's an actress?"

"She got a couple of parts in some indie films," Jessie contributed.

"And she's dating Corbin Marchant," Amber added.

"The director? He's old enough to be her grandfather," Piper exclaimed.

"Anyway," Amber said with a grin, "Perry Marconi styles all of Corbin's up-and-comers. Misha's got a very unique style. Goth meets ballerina. She'd be a ton of fun to dress, don't you think?"

"Yes, but do we have anything right for her? I guess we could pull that Betsey Johnson—the one with the burst of colors."

"I was thinking the Riccardo Tisci gown that just came in."

"Oh. That's perfect."

"Who's Riccardo Tisci?" Piper interjected.

"Haute couture for Givenchy," Jessie said. "Very dark and *avant garde.*"

Piper chuckled. "How do you two know all this? You're like evil geniuses of fashion."

"I like to think of us," Amber said with a lopsided grin, "as a match made in heaven." With a sudden gear shift, she added, "I'm starving. Are you guys hungry? We can order something."

"There's a ton of baked rigatoni in the fridge," Jessie told them, her focus set keenly on the laptop screen. "Danny brought me a bite earlier that, as it turned out, could feed a small village."

"Is it any good?" Piper asked.

"Well, it's no Tuscan Son dish," she replied. "But it's pretty good."

"I'll heat it up," Amber said, popping to her feet and disappearing into the kitchen.

Once she had moved out of earshot, Piper leaned closer to Jessie and smiled. "You doing okay? Really?"

"I think so," she replied with a tired smile. "I have so much going on, and now this stuff with Jack. It's exhausting. Right before you got here, I was served with a summons to appear at a deposition on Friday."

"What? *Tonight?* Why? I mean, what could you possibly tell them about Jack? He kept you as much in the dark as they are. Maybe more."

She sighed and tilted her head backward until it came to rest on the sofa seat cushion. "I don't know. But Danny says I don't have any choice. I have to go and answer their questions the best I can."

"Do you want me to go with you?"

Jessie hadn't considered having anyone with her. "I don't think they'd let you in the room."

"I don't care. I can sit in the lobby and wait for you. And we'll go have something delicious after to make it all go away."

"You know, I'd love that," she said with a sigh. "Thank you."

Piper beamed. "That's what we do, right?"

Danny downed the last of the tea in his glass and returned it to the redwood tabletop with a thud.

"Refill?" his mother asked.

"Nah, I have to be on my way." He scanned the deck until he spotted Frank stretched out in the corner, on his back with all four paws upright. "He'll be heartbroken to leave."

"Oh, we had such a nice time. I love it when you bring the granddog for a visit."

Danny chuckled. "The *granddog*," he repeated. "Only you, Mom."

"Look, if a mother's son won't do his part to make her a grand-mother, she finds solace wherever she can."

He shook his head and smiled. "You do know Frank's been neutered, right? The family tree stops with him."

"Daniel Ryan Callahan," she murmured as she stood up and cleared the glasses from the table.

"Ooh, all three names. That's not a good sign."

Beyond the deck, cream-colored velvet sand led the way to breaking waves and a dark azure sky. Several mornings had passed since he and Carmen had hit the waves, and he missed them both; the waves *and* his faithful board.

Danny's mother resumed her spot on the other side of the table. "So you and Aaron had a nice time up at the cabin?"

It amused him the way she always referred to a four-bedroom home with a loft and a boat dock as "a cabin." As if it was little more than a place to camp out in the mountains.

"Yeah, I love it up there. We took his daughter paddleboarding on the lake before I had to come back early."

"Oh? Why?"

"Business commitment."

Okay, so it was Jessie's business commitment and not his. But the mere mention of Jessie going along would have only opened the floodgates for the inevitable questions and assumptions, and perhaps return the topic of conversation to those grandchildren she wanted so much.

"And Jessie?" she asked out of the blue. "Did she have a nice time?"

Danny nearly swallowed his tongue. Once he recovered, he asked, "How did you know about Jessie? Do you have spies up the mountain?"

"Certainly not," she said with a chuckle. "Didn't I mention Stephanie stopped by for a visit?"

Ah, Steph! For crying out loud.

He'd made the mistake of giving his old friend a call on his way to pick up Jessie before they left the city. An ordinary chat, just checking in, from her last-minute wedding plans to the sudden appearance of Jack Stanton to the need to get Jessie out of town to breathe in some fresh air. Who knew someone as smart as Steph Regnier could work for the FBI and not know any better than to share everything she knew about a guy with his mother?

"Are you going to tell me about her—this Jessie—or are you intent on keeping her a secret?"

"I thought I might."

"Which? Tell me or keep the secret?"

"The latter."

"Well, Stephanie tells me your Jessie is a lovely girl . . . with husband trouble."

"She's not married, Mom," he assured her.

"I know. She told me that too."

"Did she leave anything out?" he teased. "Or are all the gaps filled in nice and tight with information?"

"Don't be smart." She sighed and tucked a lock of short blonde hair behind her ear. "Are you bringing her to the wedding?"

Again, Danny had lost track of Steph's wedding that weekend. "I might not even go," he joked. "That'll teach her to spill my secrets to my nosey mother."

"Nosey. Well, when you have a son who never shares his personal life, a woman has to get a little bit nosey. She has no choice."

"There's always a choice, Mother."

"*Mother*," she repeated. "The equivalent to my calling you by all three names."

Danny chuckled as he stood up and rounded the table. Leaning over her shoulder, he planted an enthusiastic and sincere kiss on her taut cheek.

"You still love me then," she stated.

"I have no choice. You're just lovable."

———⊶⊷———

Myths of a monster catfish roaming 'round Lake Pontchartrain used to bring anglers in from far 'way as Texas and Oklahomie. The legend only grew bigger when the local news would air an interview with some guy who said he spotted it, hooked it, and lost it, felt it lift up his fool boat.

"Grampy, you need to do what I do when I got a oral report to give or somethin'. I just take a deep breath of air—like this," and she demonstrated. "Then you gotta let it out real slow-like. Like this."

"Makes you feel better, does it?"

"Well, not better really. But it helps me from pukin' anyhow. And why do you care about them fishers sayin' Catfish Joe exists anyways?"

"Because it's just gonna drive up the traffic 'round these parts with fools 'n idiots lookin' for notoriety 'steada the pure love o' throwin' a line."

"You shouldn't let it getcher goat, Grampy."

"If it don't getcher goat," I says to her, "then you ain't got a goat to be got."

Jessie'd cackle like a hyena ever' time I said that. She liked that sayin' o' mine. Once she growed into havin' her goat got on a regular basis anyhow.

7

When Amber burst into her office, Jessie kept her eyes clamped shut tight and raised one rigid index finger into the air. "Sh. I'm finding my mellow."

"Well, you better find it quick. Perry Marconi just pulled up outside. And get this. He drives *a Bentley*!"

Jessie inhaled deeply and held the air in her lungs until they started to sting. After slowly releasing her breath, she did the same thing over again.

"Okay," she finally said. "I'm ready."

She followed Amber out into the store, but never had the chance to step behind the counter before the front door jingled out the announcement of Perry Marconi's arrival. The moment her eyes landed on him, Jessie dug her fingernails into the palm of her hand in an effort to keep from laughing. The man looked like a cartoon character with his teal, flowered jacket, long scarf of mixed metallics, and dark pink skinny jeans. The toes of his crocodile shoes squared off harshly, and he slid expensive sunglasses upward like a headband to hold back his long and unruly black hair.

"Mr. Marconi," she said—once she gathered her senses about her. "Welcome to Adornments. I'm Jessie Hart."

"Amber Davidson," Amber said with outstretched hand.

"My friend Courtney Alexis gives you the highest recommendation, Miss Hart," he said with a high-brow and unidentifiable accent. "Let's see if you can live up to it."

"I'll do my best. Why don't we step into my office and talk about your clients."

———

"Oh, Danny, I just can't tell you how grateful I am," Kaye Slaughter gushed for the third or fourth time since he'd arrived at her home in Pasadena. "I didn't think I'd see my anniversary necklace again."

"Happy to do it."

"Will you help me put it on?"

Danny stood behind her chair, gingerly took the necklace, and clasped the chain at the back of her neck. When he sat down again, he noticed Kaye's hand over the pendant, sweet nostalgia coloring her expression.

"I'm glad you told me the boy's story," she said. "I can't recall. What was his name?"

"Brandon."

"I'm ashamed to say I might not have been so forgiving right off the bat," she admitted. "But I think you made the right choices about him. I hope you'll include the expense of relocating him in my bill."

"Your bill," he said on a chuckle. "There will be no bill, Kaye."

"Of course there will. I didn't expect you to extend charity to me, dear boy."

"It's never charity when it's family. And you may as well be part of our family."

Her hand still over the pendant, she tapped it and smiled. "We have known one another a long time, haven't we?"

He nodded. "Many years."

"Well, perhaps I can repay your kindness by bringing a new client into your life?"

He cocked a brow and grinned at her. "I'm listening."

"I have a dear friend living out in the Palisades. Her husband, John, is a television producer, and he served on the AFTRA board of trustees for—"

"AFTRA?" he interjected and shook his head.

"American Federation of Television and Radio Artists," she clarified. "Like SAG for film actors."

He decided not to ask.

"Rochelle is in the market for someone with your considerable skill set to help her get to the bottom of a mystery."

He resisted the nerd-like urge to prematurely divulge Colonel Mustard as the culprit . . . in the billiard room . . . with the candlestick.

"Do you have any of the details?"

"I'll let her explain. I just know there is a security breach within their planning for the awards ceremony coming up next month." She slid a folded slip of paper toward him. "This is the number to her cell if you decide to inquire further."

Danny tucked it into the pocket of his denim shirt. "Thank you, Kaye. I'll give her a call first thing."

Danny reported to her about the change of locks and new garage door opener Brunswick would deliver into her hands on her next trip up the mountain as Kaye walked him outside to the Jeep. She hugged him good-bye with astonishing force.

"I'm so grateful," she whispered.

"No need. Anything for you," he stated, and he kissed her cheek.

Once she walked away, he plucked the phone number from his pocket and programmed it into his phone. He'd barely merged onto the 110 before pressing the call button.

"I'm a family friend of Kaye Slaughter's," he told Rochelle Silverstein when she answered the phone. Trying—and failing—to remember the acronym Kaye had used, he simply stated, "She asked me to call you to discuss a security issue you're having."

"Yes, Danny Callahan. I'm so glad you phoned. Is there any possibility of you coming out to our house to discuss this in person?"

"I'm on my way to Santa Monica right now," he said. "You're in Pacific Palisades?"

"Yes. We're on Via La Costa in The Enclave. Do you know it?"

Danny held back the chuckle. The gated community at the top of Palisades Boulevard boasted spectacular ocean views and hundred million-dollar-plus homes. His folks had friends who lived there, and they'd attended a Christmas extravaganza there his senior year of high school. He couldn't remember their names, but that massive Mediterranean home on the hill with the infinity pool and swim-up tiki bar—and, of course, the mountain of shrimp and crab legs on the buffet table—he recalled very well. He didn't guess Rochelle Silverstein would greet him at the door with the offer of a few pounds of peel-and-eat shrimp, but he could hope.

Mrs. Silverstein had already cleared him at the security gate when he arrived, and Danny was sent on through to the elegant two-story at the end of a cul-de-sac. A uniformed housekeeper greeted him at the door and pointed him past the grand staircase, over polished marble floors, and outside to some of the most stunning scenery he'd ever encountered.

Rochelle Silverstein looked like a character in a movie as she sipped lemonade at an umbrella-draped table overlooking a sparkling blue pool with a waterfall at one end. She looked up as he approached and removed her sunglasses.

"You must be Danny Callahan."

"Pleased to meet you, Mrs. Silverstein."

"Call me Rochelle. Come and have some of my cook's special lemonade while we chat."

Danny wondered what constituted *special* lemonade, but he accepted the invitation intent on finding out. When she looked away for an instant, he sniffed the glass she'd presented to him. No sign of alcohol. At least he hoped not. He'd managed to abstain since Rebecca's death in September 2006. Not that he had a choice for those first fourteen months, of course. They generally frowned on drunk-and-disorderly while incarcerated. But when he had a choice to make on the outside, the grief and regret over what he'd done made it for him. It would be quite a shame to disregard all that tragedy and hard work entirely by accident now, so he decided to come out and ask.

"You said it was special lemonade," he said. "What's the special part?"

"That's a secret," she replied with the hint of a smile.

"As long as that secret doesn't contain alcohol . . ."

"Oh, I see. No, it does not. There is a secret ingredient, but it's of the herbal variety." She leaned forward and whispered, "Sugared lemon rinds with fresh mint and basil."

Danny raised an eyebrow. "I'm intrigued."

"You don't drink, Danny?"

"No, ma'am."

"Now *I'm* intrigued."

"It was a life choice I made nine or ten years ago," he explained, pausing to take a sip from the frosted crystal glass. The cook's interesting secret ingredients turned out to be the revelation his or her employer had declared. "This is amazing."

"Refreshing," she said, as if correcting him.

"It is." He set the glass on the table and pushed his sunglasses up to the top of his head and nodded. "Why don't you tell me about this security issue you have."

"I don't know how much Kaye told you—"

"Not much at all."

"My husband produces several network and cable television shows, and I'm a sometimes scriptwriter, so we have some pretty strong roots in the entertainment community. I was asked to head up the planning committee for the FiFis."

When she paused, Danny choked back the chuckle moving up the back of his throat. "FiFis?"

"The FiFis are only in their sixth year, but they've become quite popular for honoring family-friendly entertainment."

"Ah," he said, nodding, but clearly out of his element.

"As we began putting the awards ceremony together for this year, it became apparent very early on that we have a leak within our ranks. A few days before actress Patricia Heaton signed on to host, several entertainment news programs reported on it. Not such a disaster, of course, but we did check with her publicist about the reports. Since it wasn't their camp that leaked the news, it did send up a red flag for those of us trying to keep things under wraps."

"I understand. And no idea how it happened?"

"None at all," she replied. "And to compound the mystery, our short list of nominations was leaked before the committee had even met to discuss them. With the FiFis becoming more popular, we can't have this kind of habitual breach surrounding us. In addition to informational leaks, for the last two years, we've had another kind of problem. Photos of two or more of our presenters—obviously taken without their knowledge inside the dressing rooms at the Monarch Aristocrat Hotel—have gone viral on the Internet within hours of the awards show."

"So you have a couple of different security concerns."

"We do. I'm hoping you can help us get to the bottom of it all."

He leaned back in the chair and propped his ankle on the opposite knee. "I'd need some pretty intimate access to your process," he brainstormed out loud. "Need to get to know the key players on your committee as well."

"I had an idea about that. Would you be willing to come on board as a security expert? It's a volunteer position, but I would be willing to personally pay your regular fee as well as expenses. No one else would need to know about that."

He figured these FiFis must be pretty important to her if she was willing to fork out her own cash to figure out the puzzle before her, and he liked furthering the cause of family-friendly entertainment.

"We have a meeting scheduled at the end of the week," she explained. "Just the four of us heading up the various aspects of the awards themselves. Perhaps you could join us."

"Where and when?"

"We meet right here. Friday at eleven."

The sun had long since woven its way down the span of the cloudy horizon, and a gray-blue sky only hinted at the future of a sliver of moon. Frank lumbered across the slab of concrete patio and rested his large head on Danny's knee.

He scratched the Great Dane behind one pointy ear. "Hey, buddy. How are ya?"

Frank sighed but made no move to leave until headlights separated them. The dog took off at a full trot toward Jessie's car as she parked behind the Jeep. He barked only once when she opened the door.

"Hi, Frank." Her greeting was relaxed, a far cry from those first couple of times one hundred-plus pounds of black-and-white dog barreled toward her.

The flicker of memory tickled the back of Danny's brain, and a broad smile stretched out across his face. He'd been surfing with Riggs that morning; a morning like any other until . . .

"What's a Jag doing parked at our place, boy?" he'd rhetorically asked Frank.

"Frank!" he repeated. "Get back. Now!" The dog reluctantly retreated, circling around Danny and standing behind him like a ready-and-waiting soldier. A white one. With giant black spots.

He leaned down and peered into the car. His heart bumped a little as a gorgeous brunette with wide, glistening eyes looked back at him. Through the closed window, he thought he heard a muffled version of his name.

"What? I can't hear you."

She lowered the window by no more than an inch. "Mr. Callahan?"

Is she looking for my father?

"I'm Danny Callahan. Who are you?"

The driver leaned across the blue-eyed beauty and spoke to the opening in the window. Her very short, streaked hair framed sharper features than her friend's. "I'm Piper Brunetti, Mr. Callahan. I got your name from Vicki Washington."

The name skimmed his brain before coming back around for a landing. Cheating husband. He'd provided her with visual art to support a hefty divorce settlement the previous spring.

"What can I do for you, Miss Brunetti?"

"This is my friend, Jessie Stanton."

Weepy gray-blue eyes glittered at him, and when she forced an unconvincing smile to her apple cheeks, dimples caved in at the base of them.

"She has a situation. With her husband."

As Jessie closed the gap between her car and the patio, Danny realized his life hadn't been the same since that day.

She grinned at him before leaning down and kissing his cheek. "How was *your* day?"

"Interesting," he replied. "How about yours?"

She didn't respond right away. Instead, she simply dropped to the bench next to him and leaned back against the table. "I'm . . . tired. And I'm dreading tomorrow so much."

The deposition.

Irritation climbed the back of his throat. What could she possibly have to tell them about where and how Stanton pulled off such a horrendous scam?

"Do you want me to drive you?" he asked.

"That's okay. Piper's going with me. Antonio arranged for someone at his attorney's firm to represent me as well. I don't really think it's necessary. I mean, I'm not the one being investigated, right?"

"No, but a lawyer at your side isn't a bad idea anyway."

"Really?" She sighed and tilted her head back. "I just want to put it behind me. I almost wish they hadn't found him. I was just starting to feel like . . ."

Her words trailed away on the velvety evening breeze, and Danny slipped his arm around her shoulder and pulled Jessie close to him.

"You'll get there again," he promised.

After several minutes of easy silence, she looked up at him, her head still resting on the curve of his shoulder. "I feel like her again."

"Like who?"

"Jessie Stanton."

Danny's heart dropped a little. "But you're not. You're Jessie Hart." He cupped her head with his hand and kissed the top of it. "And don't you forget it."

"Thank you, Danny," she muttered softly.

"In other news," he said. "What can you tell me about the Fru-Frus?"

Jessie lifted her head and slowly lifted her eyes. "I'm sorry?"

"These awards they give out for family values. Or something like that."

"I still don't . . ."

"I forget what they stand for. It's in my notes, up in my office."

"O-kay."

"It's a new case. There's a leak coming out of this miniscule committee that establishes the nominees for a Fru-Fru award."

She giggled. "Danny, you have to have the name wrong."

"Maybe. But I know this: They reward family-friendly entertainment in television and movies. They've only been around for five or six years and—"

"The FiFis?"

"FiFis. That's it."

Shaking her head, she touched his arm. "You really do live in your own little surfing village, don't you?"

"You sound like you think something's wrong with that."

"Do I sound like that?" she teased.

"A woman named Rochelle Silverstein heads up the committee."

"Because she's married to John Silverstein. He's a big-time producer."

"Right."

"And . . . how do you know all this?" she asked. "You're working for the Silversteins?"

"For the missus. She's asked me to establish a cover and help her figure out who's spilling FiFi secrets."

"How did she find you?"

"She's a friend of Kaye's. I guess she referred me."

"I like Kaye," she stated. With another sigh, she let her head rest on his shoulder again. After little more than a moment, she lifted it with a bounce and asked, "Will you get to attend the FiFis?"

"I don't know. I guess."

"You'll need a date."

"And you would like that distinction? My date?"

Jessie chuckled. "I'd be honored. Thank you for inviting me."

———◦⊶⊷◦———

"What'll I say, Grampy? When Principal Howard looks at me 'cross that big ole desk o' his and asks me what I was doin' there when I wasn't supposta be, what'll I say?"

The poor little thing looked like-ta she might lose her lunch as the whole ordeal churned around in her 'magination.

"Just wait 'til you hear the question, little girl. Then answer it best you know how."

"It don't work that way, Grampy," she tells the old man with the roll of them eyes like I got so much to learn 'bout life. "A person doesn't just walk in and sit down and come up with answers on the fly. Don't you know anything 'bout prep'ration?"

8

Thank you for coming in, Mrs. Stanton. Can I get you anything? Water, coffee?"

"No, I'm fine," Jessie lied. "But please don't call me that."

"Call you . . . Mrs. Stanton?"

"Yes. Since Jack and I weren't legally married, my name is still Hart."

Despite the fact that I still feel so much like Jessie Stanton, even now.

"I'm sorry," the business-suited federal agent interjected from her end of the conference table where she had already been instructed by two square-faced federal prosecutors to sit quietly and not interrupt. "You said you and Jack Stanton aren't legally married?"

"No. We're not."

"And you know this for certain?"

"I suspected it when we discovered he'd left the country with Patty, his first wife. But Jack confirmed it for me the last time I saw him."

"He . . . did," she stated, and Jessie had to work to hold back a chuckle. Jack had a way about him; an innate ability to leave women with that confused, dazed expression.

"Yes. He did."

"And when you say 'WE discovered he'd left the country,' to whom are you referring?"

"I'm sorry, I'm a little confused. Who's asking the questions here?" Charles LaHayne, the lawyer from Antonio's firm, asked. "The federal agents or the prosecutor?"

"We are," the twin Suits replied at the same time that the prosecutor took ownership of the meeting. "I am."

"That would be Danny Callahan," Jessie answered anyway.

"And he is?" the prosecutor asked.

"The private investigator I hired when Jack left me high and dry."

It seemed to Jessie that she was the only one in the room with any real insight or information to share; which, of course, struck her as particularly odd since she thought she was the one left in the dust, not them.

"Is that Callahan with two Ls?"

"Yes."

"And on what date did you hire Mr. Callahan?"

"The day after my car was repossessed and a Realtor informed me that my home had been sold." Jessie pressed her lips together firmly and inhaled sharply. "I'm trying to figure out why you're spending any time asking me for information when I was clearly the one who didn't have one clue what was going on as my life unraveled around me."

"I think that's a fair question," Mr. LaHayne announced. "I'd like an answer to it as well."

After more than ninety minutes of repeatedly circling that drain, the same questions being asked in varied and different ways, Jessie felt like sprinting through the door when it opened at last. She held it together, however, and rode the elevator down to the lobby next to Mr. LaHayne.

"Thank you for being with me," she told him at the precipice of the glass doors to freedom. "I didn't know what to expect."

"And how did it pan out in terms of expectations?" he asked with a glimmer of a smile.

"Actually . . . it was worse than I'd imagined."

"I thought so too," he remarked with a slight shrug of one shoulder. He handed her his business card. "If they contact you again, give me a ring."

"Thank you. I will."

"And when they contact your Mr. Callahan, tell him he can call me as well."

"I'm sorry. What?"

Danny had returned to the outdoor scene of his first meeting with Rochelle Silverstein. This time, he sat beside Rochelle on one side of the table, and a threesome of faces scowled at him from the other.

"What's this going to cost us, Rochelle?"

"I was just going to ask that question myself."

"Has he been properly vetted?"

Danny guessed their glares might be able to cut glass if they combined their intensity.

"It's not costing us a thing," she fibbed. *Kind of.* "Danny is volunteering his time to our cause. And he comes very highly recommended."

George Tercot adjusted his plaid bow tie and grunted out a strange "Harrumph."

"What's your background?" Darlene Burns asked, using her fingernail to trace the line of her lip gloss without benefit of a mirror.

Rochelle piped up. "He's been a private investigator in our area for—"

"Are you licensed?" Leslie McCann chimed unceremoniously.

"Yes."

It went on like that—the *rat-a-tat-tat* of questions coming at him like bullets from an automatic weapon—for another ten minutes or so before Rochelle's fist thumped the table.

"Can we just move on to the business at hand?" she suggested with a forced smile. "At our last meeting, we all said we needed a security chief to make sure there are no breaches in the private areas, and no more information leaks. Now we have one. Let's let Danny do his job and we'll do ours. What's next?"

The shots fired fell somewhat flat—at last—as the threesome exchanged questioning glances and Rochelle continued without missing a beat.

"We've had seven new confirmations for award presenters . . ."

Danny thought the way she billowed right over their objections and moved through the business at hand was a sight to behold. Less than an hour later, with a blueprint of the venue unrolled across the table, they had discussed everything from event catering and a red carpet arrival to the ideal location for a *green room*—which apparently was a term for a private room where The Special People gathered.

As everyone assembled their belongings, the bow tie man— *What was his name?*—leaned in toward Danny. "Listen. Sorry we gave you such a hard time. The reputation of the FiFis rests on security. You understand."

Danny bit down on the side of his tongue to hold back a cluck of laughter. *The reputation of the FiFis?* Those words just struck him strangely—and inappropriately—funny.

"Of course," he managed seriously. "I'll do everything I can to"—*to what?*—"keep things secure."

"Of course you will."

George Tercot, Danny recalled, and he repeated it several times so he wouldn't forget. *His name is George Tercot.*

He glanced at the lanky bleached blonde with a penchant for showy jewelry and an abundance of cosmetics and reminded himself. *Darlene Burns.*

Leslie McCann. She lifted one sausage arm and gave a corporate wave, and Danny replied with a polite smile and a nod, then he watched the plump, sixtyish woman waddle up the path toward the Silverstein house.

The last of them had barely passed through the door to the house when Rochelle tapped the tabletop. "Sit with me a few minutes, will you, Danny?"

He followed her lead and sat across from her.

"I'd like to hear your initial thoughts."

About . . . ?

As if she'd heard his thought, she added, "Do you think any of the three of *them* could be responsible?"

"That's almost impossible to say after less than two hours with them," he said. "I'm more interested to know your instincts about each of them."

Rochelle pressed her lips together as the young Hispanic woman who had served their refreshments approached the table. "Can I get you anything more, Mrs. Silverstein?"

"No, thank you. We're just summing things up."

She nodded, swiftly collected the glasses and plates scattered about, and headed back to the house.

"I think the three of them are committed to the cause," Rochelle said, barely missing a beat. "We have six others who serve on the board that I'll want you to meet. But the contingent you met today has been deeply involved. I just can't imagine . . ."

When her words trailed after her gaze into the distance, Danny changed gears. "Can I get a copy of the map of the venue? I'd like to go over it before I report back with a plan."

"Go ahead and take that one. We have a couple more copies."

He tightened the roll and slipped a rubber band around it.

"Do you have a favorite charity, Danny?"

The question caught him off guard. "Pardon?"

"A pet cause to which you donate your time and money?"

He smiled. "Several."

"What are they?" she inquired with a directness that surprised him a little.

Danny tucked the blueprint into the leather saddlebag he'd brought along and snapped the buckle shut, even though the map poked out several inches. "Are you familiar with MRF?" When she cocked her head, he grinned. "Marine Research Federation. They're based in Long Beach."

"Of course."

"I've also traveled the mission field for a few Christian organizations—"

"*Really!*" she exclaimed. "Where have you gone?"

Danny swallowed the urge to inquire about her odd interest. Instead, he told her, "Haiti and Mexico, twice each. Ecuador last year. I'm considering a trip down south with a buddy of mine."

"Oh my." She leaned back and smiled at him, seemingly drinking in everything he'd told her. "What will you do there?"

"Whatever the organization says they need. It's a rebuilding mission after so many schools and homes are still in disrepair after Katrina, so I'm sure we'll do some construction. Deliver Bibles and educational supplies. My buddy got involved first—he has a young daughter himself—and I guess his passion caught fire in me too because I'm actually really looking forward to it."

"That's very admirable, Danny. A lot of young people talk about the troubles in the world. It's nice to meet up with someone like you and your friend who actually do something about it."

He shrugged and raked his hair with both hands. "Life has to be about more than catching the next wave or . . ." Danny spotted something in Rochelle's eyes that made him fall silent for a moment. "Or whatever."

"I suppose you think we're pretty silly," she said. "Investing so much energy into an entertainment awards show."

"Not at all," he replied. "In all candor, I accepted the job for the very reason you're probably so invested. Family-friendly entertainment has been reduced to a cyclical trend, but I'm a believer in the value of it."

Rochelle beamed. "Yes. That's exactly my thinking." She seemed to gulp around a lump of emotion stuck in her throat. "Thank you, Danny."

He stood and reached across the table to shake her hand. "I'd better be going. But thanks for your hospitality. Don't hesitate to give me a call if you have any immediate concerns, and I guess I'll see you again when everyone gathers to tour the venue next week."

"Thank you again."

Danny replayed the odd turn of their conversation as he drove toward Santa Monica. He sensed there was a lot more to it than just curiosity, but he couldn't put his finger on what it could have been. His heart felt heavy on behalf of Rochelle Silverstein but, not knowing exactly why, he did the only thing he could for her. He prayed.

As he took the turn off the freeway a little while later, his cell phone buzzed. He grabbed the Bluetooth earpiece on the passenger seat and tucked it into place before answering.

"Callahan."

"Where are you?" Steph never had learned to bother with greetings.

"Heading home."

"Can I meet you there? I'll bring eats."

"Why don't we just meet at Shoop's."

Steph growled. If they had a spot that was all their own, Shoop's European Deli on Main Street had surely become theirs. "A salmon BLT," she whimpered. "I am so there."

"Thirty minutes?"

"Done. See you then."

Steph and Danny had grown up together, and she often categorized their relationship when introducing him to others by declaring, "I'm his sister from another mister." It described their relationship perfectly. Steph was the sister he'd never had.

Growing up as an only child hadn't been quite so daunting after the Regnier kids moved in just down the beach. Steph's two older brothers had often included Danny in activities out of default, but it was their kid sister—the same age as Danny—with whom he really bonded.

At twelve, they'd smoked a cigarette together, and Steph had nearly choked to death. When she phoned him the next morning, he'd barely pressed the phone to his ear before she exclaimed, "I stink of smoke, and I've showered twice."

"Don't you ever start a conversation with a 'Hello, how are ya'?" he'd asked her.

She didn't then, and she didn't now.

Together, they'd learned to surf, to love and respect the Pacific Ocean and everything in it, and they'd worked out the considerable kinks of learning to slow dance before the high school prom they attended with partners he couldn't even recall now.

Steph stood at the counter when he arrived at Shoop's, looking every bit the part of an FBI intelligence analyst with her impeccable charcoal blazer and trousers, sensible black shoes, and no-nonsense ponytail.

"I ordered," she announced. "Grab a table."

He didn't bother asking about the details of their meal. She would have a salmon BLT, no doubt, and a raspberry iced tea. On his behalf, she would surely have ordered The Jason, a roast beef extravaganza with roasted peppers, onions, and horseradish. And an Arnold Palmer to drink. Half tea, half lemonade.

"Did you remember extra provolone?" he asked when she carried the tray to their table and sat down across from him.

"Please."

He lifted the crispy baguette and took a look. He didn't know what had made him doubt.

"So what's with the call?" he asked before taking a large first bite of the sandwich. "Calling off the wedding?"

"Mm," she replied, and her gray-blue eyes sparkled. "I think I'll go ahead and marry him. I mean, we've made all the plans, and I've paid for the bridal *ensemble*."

Danny pointed both thumbs at himself and grinned. "And you have the ideal Guy of Honor."

Steph smiled. "I heard Jessie had a chat with my people."

"Your people." He chuckled. "I thought I was your people."

"My other people."

"Yeah, she got a summons for a deposition with the guy prosecuting Stanton. Were there feds there too?"

She set down her sandwich and nodded. "I just wanted to give you a heads up. She apparently told them you had information that might pertain to the case. I'm pretty sure they're going to haul you in for a chat too."

Danny folded his hands in front of him and froze. "You're . . . *pretty sure.*"

"Yeah. I'm definitely sure."

Something thudded inside him. "Great."

A few seconds had barely ticked by before his cell phone buzzed, Jessie's pretty face on the screen. He mouthed her name to Steph before answering.

"Hi, Jessie. How'd it go?"

"Oh, Danny. I don't think you're going to be very happy with me."

He smiled. "Let me stop you right there. I'm sitting here with Steph, and I know they're coming for me. It's not a big deal, so stop worrying about it."

"Really?"

"Really."

"Can I talk to Steph?"

The corner of his mouth twitched with amusement. "Sure. Hang on."

He handed the phone to Steph.

"Hi, Jessie. How are you?" After a long pause, she reassured Jessie. "Danny's a big boy, and he's been an investigator for a long time. He's had to testify about cases dozens of times. . . . Oh yeah. Nothing to worry about." Danny could hear the distant hum of Jessie's speedy chatter before Steph finally chuckled. "No, I think my mom has everything on track at this point. But thanks for the offer. All Vince and I really need you to do is come and celebrate with us."

Danny wiggled his fingers toward her, reaching for the phone.

"Danny wants to talk to you. I'll see you next weekend, okay? . . . You too, Jessie."

He took the phone again. "Listen, I'm here at Shoop's grabbing a bite. How about I bring you some takeout after?"

"That would be so great."

"You at the store?"

"Yes."

"Okay. What's your fancy?"

"I forget what it's called. The grilled sandwich with shrimp and boiled egg and cucumbers. Do you know the one I mean?"

"Yep," he said.

"But I don't like it open-faced. I prefer when they make it into a sandwich. Oh, and I don't like the dill so much."

"Bread?"

"Multigrain?"

"I'll be there in an hour."

Danny disconnected the call and set his phone, screen down, on the table. When he looked up at her, the grin on Steph's face stretched from one ear to the other and reached her eyes with a glitter of mischief.

"What?" he asked her.

"You."

"What about me?"

"And Jessie."

"And?" he said, rolling his hand to urge her along to the point.

"I think you really do love her."

"Is that a question?"

"Nope," she said, turning her attention back to her sandwich. "Don't need to ask."

"No?"

She chuckled. "You probably don't even know *yourself* yet."

"You know the interesting thing about people right before their weddings?" he observed. "They always want to inflict commitment on those around them. What is that? Just a little something to make you feel better about your own choices? Or a sucker punch to punish those of us who haven't joined you?"

"You think of Jessie as punishment?" she teased. "I'll be sure and tell her that next weekend. Maybe right before we cut the wedding cake."

He stood without ceremony. "I need to order some takeout."

Steph's howling laughter followed him to the counter, and Danny didn't even glance back in her direction before greeting the girl in the pristine apron behind the counter.

"I'd like the shrimp sandwich to go. On multigrain rather than open-faced. Hold the dill."

<hr>

Slidell, Luziann. It's pretty much always been my home. Knee-high to a grasshopper when our pappy moved us to this place. All us kids sweared we'd move out soon's we could manage it, and my three brothers and two sisters made good on that promise before they ever started havin' kids o' their own. Not me though. I never saw no sense in leavin' a place where your roots planted ya. Fer a while, I was lonely as a pine tree in a parkin' lot. Then I met my wife, and we begat April. April begat little Jessie.

Jessie liked me to tell her all my Slidell stories when she was a little one. She specially liked to hear about how the city weren't even on no map 'til somebody sent the railroad through in the late 1800s. A buildin' camp cropped up on Lake Pontchartrain, 'n Slidell growed outta it. Jessie liked knowin' how it sprouted from a seedling when she was a young'un. But as she growed, her sight started reachin' beyond, just like my other kin. Yeah, didn't take me long to realize she was gonna be a hard hound to keep on the porch.

"Grampy, I'm 'onna live in a big city one day, just you wait 'n see," she says.

Fat lotta good big-city livin' did fer my girl once she made good on that'n.

"*Some crazy people waitin' to see if you'll come to the big city,*" I'd tell 'er. And that devil spawn she married proved me right.

Once I knowed she was really goin', I didn't wanna be proved right. I wanted to keep my Jessie far way from trouble as I could. But sometime wantin' don't stop nothin'.

9

Jessie stared at the lineup of photographs on her computer screen. She knew she should get down to the business of making some choices for her morning meeting with Perry Marconi and two out of the three celebrity clients he planned to bring with him, but she couldn't seem to drag her thoughts away from the shrimp sandwich on its way to her desk. The deep rumble in her stomach punctuated her preoccupation.

For Misha Koskov, the young Goth ballerina, she and Amber had agreed that the choices were no-brainers. Adornments only had three possibilities for someone with such a distinct style. She dragged and dropped the three pictures into the subfile inside the Perry Marconi folder: the chocolate Riccardo Tisci with the harness-like top and ruched skirt; the high-necked black Missoni; and a more subdued Betsey Johnson A-line with ruffles and an above-the-knee hem.

She blew out a sigh. One down, two more to go.

The empty subfile labeled with the name of Marianna Wetherly sat on her desktop beneath a series of nearly a dozen images. The young twenty-something ingenue had been cast in a new original series for the USA Network, and Perry had used words like *unpretentious*, *approachable*, and *girly* to describe her. Amber had compiled an e-mail loaded with notes on the girl's style, and had attached ten possibilities for Jessie's consideration. She looked them over again beneath the weight of anticipation for Danny's arrival.

The ivory Lauren Conrad she'd taken from her own closet—a lace dress with cap sleeves tied with ribbons—seemed like a good choice, and she dragged it to the Marianna file. The pale pink Jill Stuart wedding-inspired gown with layers of chiffon billowing from the empire line pinched Jessie's heart. She'd purchased the gown for the vow renewal she and Jack had been discussing . . . back in her *other life*. Useless as it was to Jessie, she knew Marianna would look stunning in that one. For her third option, she landed on the label-less pink and white brocade with rosettes around the pleated waist of the petticoat. Piper had picked it up at one of the vintage stores down on Melrose, she recalled. For someone with as tailored and pristine a style as Piper, the purchase surprised Jessie, despite her gratitude that it landed in the consignment box when she started the store.

Amber peered around the open door of the office. "Danny just pulled up outside. Thought I'd give you a heads up."

"Thank you. He's bringing me some lunch."

"You haven't had lunch yet? It's time for dinner."

Jessie shrugged. "It's been one of those days." Closing the laptop, she slid it across the desk toward Amber. "Why don't you take this. I've settled on the choices for Marianna and Misha. Go ahead and pull shoes and bags for them, and I'll decide on the Carolyn Coleman choices post-sustenance."

"Sounds like a plan." She picked up the laptop and passed Danny as she left the office. "Hey, Danny. Good to see you."

"You too, Amber."

Just the sound of his voice dredged up a sense of relief in Jessie that went far beyond a shrimp sandwich from Shoop's.

"Keep me company while I inhale that?"

"Happy to," he answered. The fragrance of her lunch/dinner reached her before Danny had a chance to sit in the chair across the desk.

Jessie peered at him over the top of her sandwich after the second bite and moaned softly. "Thank you so much. This is delish."

"I'm glad."

When he smiled, she spotted one of those deep dimples usually fairly well hidden beneath the shadow of dark blond stubble. His steely blue eyes seemed less steely than blue on this particular day, and she attributed the intensity to the ride over in an open Jeep on such a sunny day.

"What?" he asked, and she realized he'd noticed her staring.

"Oh. It's just really good to see you."

He tipped his head down slightly and narrowed his eyes, a crooked potential grin twitching on one side. "Good to be seen."

She took another bite of the sandwich and wiped the corner of her mouth with a paper napkin from the bag. "Sorry again about name-dropping you with the feds."

"No worry."

"Really? Because I find any contact with them a little distressing. I sure didn't mean to inflict it on you."

"Comes with the dinner," he remarked.

She glanced at the empty paper bag on the desk and giggled. "Really? I didn't see them in there."

"The dinner of being a PI. Law enforcement always wants to know how we get our information. It's just a formality."

She took a moment to process that thought before digging back into her sandwich.

"So tell me about your day. Have you unraveled any mysteries to speak of?"

"Working on it."

The pensive haze in his eyes prompted Jessie to set down her sandwich again. "Want to talk it through? I've been told I'm pretty good at solving a mystery." She wiped the corner of her mouth and chuckled. "Other people's mysteries anyway. Give me one in my own life and I'm apparently clueless."

"It's all still percolating, but I got two strange phone calls on the way over here. One from a new client who sees me as some sort of messenger of guilt for not leading a more charitable life. And one from Riggs that—if it's possible—was even more astounding. What about you? What are you working on?"

"Oh, very important things," she joked. "Life-and-death stuff."

"Do tell," he said. A sparkle of amusement glistened as he leaned back in the chair and crossed his arms over his broad chest.

"Courtney's in London to pick up her new little girl, and—as you know—she gave me a referral to a very well-known stylist who has three clients going to the Legacy Awards." She leaned forward and lowered her voice as if sharing a national secret. "Now bear in mind that it is imperative to each of them that we find the perfect look. Their very careers are in my hands."

Dry as sand, he remarked, "Whatever will you do?"

She giggled, then finished her sandwich and wiped its remnants from her mouth and chin. "Well, that's my dilemma. It's the mystery to somehow solve."

"I have every confidence in you."

"That makes one of us."

"Certainly fashion and style aren't areas where you question yourself."

"Not normally," she replied candidly. "But this is my first chance going solo with one of Courtney's clients. I just really want to get it right. They're coming in tomorrow morning, and I just want to . . . be ready."

"And you will."

She swallowed around the sudden lump of doubt in her throat. "Promise?"

"Absolutely." He slanted forward and leaned both elbows on the edge of her desk. "How would you like to make plans to celebrate your success tomorrow night?"

"How overly confident of you," she teased.

"I gave you my word, didn't I? You're going to blow their minds."

She chuckled, shaking her head. "What did you have in mind, oh wise one?"

"A dinner at Tuscan Son. Tomorrow night. Eight o'clock."

"Tuscan Son? Really?"

He nodded. "Ask me why."

"Why," she stated rather than questioned.

"Because my man Aaron Riggs has actually scored a date with the ex-wife he still adores. And once that happened this afternoon, his self-confidence—not unlike yours, I might point out—took an unnecessary nosedive straight into the ground."

"Ah," she sympathized. "That's kind of adorable, isn't it?"

"While I've never thought of Riggs as even remotely adorable, I do see your point. Anyway, he wants to take her somewhere familiar but high-quality, and he wants you and me to sit across the table from them to pick up the slack when the conversation lulls."

"I don't know," she joked. "That's a lot of pressure. What if it goes south with us at the wheel? He'll always blame us for missing out on that one lone second chance."

"I think we can do it."

"Do you? Then I guess I'm in." She grinned at him. "I'd love to be one of Aaron's wing men."

"I'll let him know. Pick you up at seven thirty. Here or at home?"

"Home. I'll want to look extra special for this momentous occasion. I'll even call Antonio and ask for one of the loft tables."

"There's a loft?"

"Very exclusive. You'll love it. So do you want to help me choose a gown for Carolyn Coleman?"

Danny snickered as he stood. "I think I'll leave that kind of thing to the professionals."

"Be that way."

"See you tomorrow night."

"I'm looking forward to it. Thanks for including me, Danny."

"That thanks goes to Riggs. He requested you especially."

"That's baffling," she said on a chuckle. "The pressure's on."

She wiggled her fingers at him as he left, adding a giddiness to her wave good-bye that she didn't really feel.

"Hey, Danny," she heard Amber call out. "Before you go . . ."

Jessie perked her ears in an effort to hear the rest, but Amber had apparently turned away from the direction of her office door. After a moment, she stood and walked out to the front of the store.

"Jessie," came the greeting. "How are you?"

She spotted Francesca Dutton standing at the counter. "Francesca, good to see you. I'm doing well. How about you?"

"I brought another carton of things from Mother's closet," she said, uncertainty weighing down her voice. "I thought you might like to add them to your inventory."

"That's wonderful."

"I'm afraid I was a bit tightfisted on what I was willing to give up. Frankly," she said softly, leaning in, "Mother's financials weren't what everyone believed them to be when she passed away."

Jessie had suspected as much when they met. Francesca had expressed so much concern about what she might be able to get for some of the garments.

"I'm sorry."

"It's not easy for me to admit that I can really use the extra revenue you might be able to generate by selling or leasing a few more items."

"Your mother's taste was impeccable," Jessie reassured her. "We'll do everything we can to make it beneficial for us both."

"Thank you." Francesca gazed at her with a tentative spark. "I started feeling a little . . . Well, the thing is . . ."

She stopped abruptly when the front door jingled and Danny came in with a large cardboard box. Amber held the door open before rushing around him. "Right back here in the storeroom will be fine. Just follow me."

Francesca waited for them to pass before continuing. "The loss of my mother has been the catalyst for a lot of soul-searching, as I'm sure you can imagine."

"I can," she said with a nod. "I lost my own mom when I was pretty young, but I remember the way it upset the balance of the world."

"Exactly. And the thing is . . . Mother was a very frugal woman. Some might have said chintzy. But what did it get her? She died surrounded in luxury all around her, but with barely five figures in all her accounts combined." She paused, rubbing her forehead with the tips of her boney fingers. "I've got an estate specialist coming in to liquidate the house and furnishings, which should cover the outstanding debt. But it occurred to me that I would like to do something . . . in her name."

"Like a charitable donation?"

"No. Not exactly."

Jessie caught sight of Danny beyond the slope of Francesca's shoulder, helping Amber move the swiveling rack they'd discussed relocating to the front of the store. He cast her the flicker of a smile before his focus shifted back to Amber.

"As I was going through Mother's closet, I noticed she has an abundance of business attire. Suits, shoes, and handbags; that kind of thing. And . . . I can't seem to escape the thought of starting some sort of charity where women starting over, trying to make a go of it in the business world might benefit from Mother's plenitude."

"Like *Dress for Success*," Jessie commented. "I'm sure they'd love to see a donation of—"

"Yes. But I like the idea of starting something fresh, something that bears Mother's name."

"Oh," she exclaimed. "You want to start a new charity?"

"I thought I'd run the idea past you to see if you had any knowledge about such things."

"I . . . really don't." Disappointment pushed Francesca's hopeful half-smile down her face like a canyon mudslide. "But I think it's a lovely idea," she added.

"What is?" Amber asked as she and Danny joined them at the counter.

"Francesca is thinking of starting a nonprofit, possibly something like *Dress for Success*, to make maximum use of some of her mother's business attire."

"A truly great idea," Amber declared.

"Well," Francesca said with a sigh, "at this point it's nothing more than just that. An idea. I don't know the first thing about a start-up like this. I was kind of hoping to partner with someone."

Danny stepped forward and offered his hand. "I'm sorry to interrupt you ladies, but I thought I'd introduce myself."

"Oh, I'm sorry," Jessie cut in. "That was rude. Francesca, meet our friend, Danny Callahan."

"Pleased to meet you, Mr. Callahan."

"Danny."

"Danny," she repeated with an attempt at a smile. "Francesca Dutton."

"Pleasure. I overheard your plans, and I hope you won't mind me stepping into your conversation? I might have something to offer that might help."

"Certainly."

He looked at Jessie. "Remember I told you I had a phone conversation on the way over here with a new client?"

She nodded.

"Rochelle Silverstein," he said, and Francesca perked.

"I know Rochelle. She's lovely."

"Well, one of our recent conversations leaned toward some charity work I'd done, and she called me just today to say that she wanted to get involved in something new. She asked if I had any suggestions, and I told her I'd give it some thought and we'd talk about it soon." He cocked a brow at Jessie and lifted one shoulder in a slight shrug. "Maybe the two of you together would make a good connection."

"Danny, what a great idea," Jessie exclaimed, tamping down the swell of pride.

"Why don't you give her a call?" he said, transferring her number from his phone to a slip of paper Jessie handed over. "I didn't

111

really think I'd have much to offer her by way of advice. I mean, I can't really see her financing one of the mission trips like the one I'm making soon, but this seems like a pretty good fit for Rochelle."

Jessie bit down on the corner of her lip before blurting, "You're going . . . *away?*"

Danny met her frown with an annoyingly serene smile. "I'll tell you all about it later."

Later?

"You look so beautiful," Jessie told Courtney while smiling at her through the Skype screen on her laptop.

"Don't lie. I look like a rhinoceros. I'm a stress eater." She sighed and blew a puff of air upward, propelling her messy hair away from her face. "But look what I got for my trouble," she sang, brightening.

Courtney moved back so that the webcam included a look at her long-awaited nine-month-old Moldavian daughter bouncing happily on her knee. Jessie's heart squeezed at the sight of the baby's chubby, red face and the patch of black hair standing straight up on the top of her head.

"Court, she's gorgeous."

"She is, isn't she?" she replied, staring down at the child swaddled in a pale green hoodie covered with yellow ducks wearing top hats and tangerine bow ties. "Katharine Alexis," she said. "I call her Katie. And she behaves like an angel, but we probably need to get the business out of the way before she makes a liar of me. Don't be afraid of meeting Perry. At first look, he can come off a little . . ."

Cartoonish? Jessie thought, but didn't dare say out loud.

". . . strange."

"He stopped by the store already, so I've met him. He's bringing Misha and Marianna by in the morning for the actual consult, and we'll show him a few alternatives for Carolyn Coleman as well."

"Carolyn Coleman," Courtney repeated. "I'd love to be there to style her. She's a classic, and such a lovely woman."

Jessie smiled. "Thank you so much for entrusting such a big client to me, Courtney. I'm going to really try not to let you down."

"Let me down," she dismissed with a noisy puff. "You were born for this. I don't have a single doubt you can handle this and make Perry and his clients question how they ever existed without you. I'm just relieved I have someone to cover me while I get to know this little pumpkin seed."

The joy in her friend's eyes as she gazed down at her baby choked Jessie's throat with emotion.

"You're next for one of these, you know," Courtney said as if she'd read Jessie's mind. "I just know you'll see that dream realized one day, and you'll be the most wonderful mother."

She hesitated, not sure how to respond to such a declaration. "Listen," she said, switching gears, "how long before you and Katie can travel? Any idea when you might get back to the States?"

"Another few weeks, I'd guess. I want to spend some more time here with my folks. But I'll let you know when I book our flight."

"I can't wait to get my hands on her," Jessie admitted with a wide grin.

"Mom says she should come with a warning label. CAUTION: HEART-STEALER."

"I've been warned. You have a lovely time getting to know your daughter. And I'll be in touch after the meet with Perry."

"Sounds good."

After their Skype call ended, Jessie closed her laptop and leaned back into her desk chair with a trembling sigh. As happy as she felt for Courtney, she couldn't escape the heaviness on her heart at the sight of mother and child. Nor could she escape the wonderings that still plagued her so often.

It was always moments like this one, right out of nowhere, when the shadowy memory of the baby she and Jack had lost so long ago stood up and demanded notice. What might Bella have looked like had Jessie not miscarried? Would her cheeks have been chubby like little Katie's? Perhaps she'd have had a tiny patch of dark hair the color of her mother's, or a full head of wavy locks like her father.

Jessie shook thoughts of Jack and their past together out of her head before packing up the laptop, grabbing the garment bag hanging on the back of her office door, and setting out for home.

Enough time's passed by that thoughts of Jessie's tragedy don't consume me anymore. Not like at the beginnin' when the pain o' her torment like to killed me.

But ever' now and agin, I wake up thinkin' 'bout how she wailed when she tried to tell her old Grampy 'bout the death of the daughter growin' inside her belly. It was the kinda cry that comes straight up from the gut of the one doin' the wailin' while tearin' up the gut of the one doin' the hearin'.

Always figgered only a woman could understand the wrenchin' pain of such a thing. But hearin' my Jessie wail like that, I figger I got a world o' hurt and understandin' too.

10

Danny passed a small grouping of colorful mats topped with yoga lovers in various stages of downward-facing dog. Frank, on the other hand, took the stance of *upward*-facing dog as the Great Dane tugged at the end of the leash and led the way up the slight incline of the concrete pathway toward the finest stretch of azure scenery Ocean View Park had to offer. Danny's old Reeboks thumped out a rhythmic soundtrack to his sunset run while brushstrokes of pink, purple, and dark blue burnished the horizon awaiting them.

He felt uncharacteristically short-winded as he reached the top, and he paused there to lean against the fence and catch his breath. Frank took the opportunity to flop down to the ground and scratch the doggie equivalent to an armpit, growling softly in ecstasy as he did.

Jessie's face photobombed Danny's thoughts, and her pained expression at the fresh news of the mission trip left an acidic taste at the back of his throat. He'd meant to talk to her about it, but with everything else going on hadn't negotiated the opportunity.

"You're going . . . *away*?" she'd exclaimed at the mention of his trip.

He didn't know why her stunned, almost-frightened expression still haunted him more than twenty-four hours later, but it did. He resolved to tell her more about it when he picked her up for dinner in a few hours. He would reassure her that the threat Jack posed now would surely be resolved by the time they took off, and he'd remind her that he wasn't going to leave her in the lurch . . . he wouldn't be gone long . . . he would enter Rafe on her speed dial . . .

It occurred to him now to wonder whether all the reassurances were for Jessie . . . or for himself.

He had plenty of time to shower and change, but he tugged at Frank's leash and the two of them double-timed it all the way home as if running seriously late. Once inside the door, Frank lapped up nearly a whole bowl of fresh water while Danny downed a bottle of Aquafina. Peas in a pod.

After his shower, Danny wiped the steam from the bathroom mirror and studied his reflection, wondering if he should shave away the usual stubble for such an occasion. At long last, Charlotte had allowed a miniscule opening in that gargantuan wall she'd erected between herself and Riggs since their divorce. Just a simple dinner, nothing more. On the surface anyway. It only shone through as the miracle it was to those select few closest to Aaron and Charlotte Riggs. As he shaved his face clean of his trademark stubble, Danny sent a prayer of thanksgiving upward, adding a straightforward petition for God's grace on the evening as a stepping stone to the restoration of a marriage that never should have ended.

Truth told, he had mixed emotions of his own about the evening's plans. Although Tuscan Son's scintillating menu drew a wave of enthusiasm—from the overloaded bread basket with the mini focaccia broiled with gorgonzola and fresh garlic that Jessie loved so much and the salted grissini that set Danny's mouth to watering at just the memory . . . right down to the chocolate ricotta dessert cake with toasted pistachios and gelato. Beneath the culinary anticipation, something else lingered. The mindful recollection of Jack Stanton standing at the foot of their table, yanking the rug right out from underneath the new life Jessie had struggled to construct. Jessie had mentioned requesting a table in a loft Danny hadn't known about, and he hoped she remembered to do it. Perhaps a different landscape—in an entirely different part of the restaurant—might fog the memory and allow her to enjoy the evening.

Danny topped his dark jeans with a navy blue shirt and charcoal jacket. He supposed sandals or flip-flops were out of the question, so he reluctantly pulled on a pair of socks and pressed his feet into what he used to call "cement shoes." The kind that encased a foot used to the open air and a little sand. The kind that represented one of the few pitfalls of Southern California living: closed shoes.

He stopped to top off Frank's water bowl and drop a few scoops of kibbles into the empty bowl next to it before grabbing his keys and heading out the door to pick up Jessie. He'd given himself thirty minutes in case of traffic, but he made it to Pinafore Street in less than fifteen. He'd just turned off the engine and started considering whether to knock on her door a little early or just sit there for a few minutes before doing so when her front door opened and she waved.

He gave her a casual nod, but Danny couldn't peel his eyes away from her as she bolted one lock after another on her front door. Wearing a cream-colored sleeveless maxi dress with a racerback, she started down the driveway. His breath actually caught somewhere between his chest and his throat. She appeared almost ethereal as the cascading cream-colored fabric flowed gently with each stride she took toward him. When she lifted the dress slightly and climbed into the Jeep, he found himself wishing he'd cleaned the inside of the thing a little better.

The stack of silver bangle bracelets jangled when she tugged the door shut behind her. Why hadn't he gotten out to open it for her? He wanted to kick himself in the backside. At the sight of her, he'd lost all sense of courtesy like some sort of caveman.

"I saw you pull up," she said. "This is going to be fun tonight, huh?"

She crossed her legs and shifted, smiling at him. He caught a glimpse of flat sandals embellished with clear stones beneath a peek of suntanned leg.

"Yeah," he replied, turning the key and backing out of the drive. "Hey, how did your meeting go today?"

"Oh. Yeah." Her entire face seemed to cave in for a split second before she shrugged. "It was fine, I guess. Nothing more than a blip. Two of the three clients came in with Perry Marconi, flew through the choices we pulled for them, made final decisions in a flash of lightning, and they were out the door. I have no idea if they were actually pleased."

"I'm sure it wasn't that bad."

"It is what it is," she said with another shrug. "But I've decided we did our best, and I can't change anything by fretting over it. I just have to wait to hear back from Perry or Courtney."

"Very professional."

She surprised him by grazing his cheek with her fingers. He paused in the middle of the street, shifting into gear without going anywhere.

"I don't think I've ever seen your face clean-shaven," she remarked.

"No?"

"No. Why did you do that?"

A melody of different answers came to mind—from pointing out it was their first date in a while and he wanted to look good for her . . . to admitting that he thought it seemed a little more civilized and a better fit for a guy with a woman like her on his arm. But he landed on a simple shrug.

"Just felt like a change."

She leaned forward and gave him a once-over. "Did you get your hair cut, Danny?"

"This morning. Just a trim. I do that sometimes."

She curled up her mouth into a pout that nearly did him in right then and there.

"Don't like it?"

"You look yummy," she said. "I just like it better when you look . . . *like you.*"

"Stubbled and grungy."

"Yeah," she replied with a broad smile. "It's the Danny I fe—"

Well, there was no mistaking that. The Danny she thought she fell in love with.

But maybe doesn't love still?

"Well, you know," she tried to recover. "I think you're most attractive when you're just being yourself."

He swallowed a hard gulp of nothing. "Speaking of attractive," he managed. "You look pretty in that dress."

"Thanks. You want to know a secret?"

He shifted and headed down Pinafore. "Sure."

"I bogarted it from the store. I couldn't resist."

"You're entitled."

"That's right," she said with an amusing little attitude. "I'm the boss. I can borrow a dress if I want to." After a moment's thought, she added, "I wonder where that term came from. I'll have to ask my Grampy."

"What term?"

"Bogarting. I mean, I know it probably has to do with Humphrey Bogart, right? But . . ."

"*Treasure of Sierra Madre.*"

"Pardon?"

The corner of his mouth twitched before he finally gave into the smile. "Have you ever seen the movie?" She shook her head, and Danny sighed. "You really need to see it. From the forties. Bogie and two other guys go prospecting for gold, and Bogie's character gets greedy and tries to keep it all for himself."

"So he was actually the first hoarder. I hate those shows about hoarders. Have you ever seen them? So depressing."

As they pulled up in front of Tuscan Son, Heath—the kid with the perfect hair—met them at the curb out front and pulled open Jessie's door. "Mrs. Stanton," he greeted her.

"Hart," she corrected him. "I'm just Jessie Hart now, Heath."

"Oh. Congratulations."

Danny snickered as he opened his own door and climbed out of the Jeep.

"You look really pretty."

"Thank you," she replied with a wide, white smile.

"When's graduation, Heath?" Danny asked as he handed over the keys. "Can't be long now."

"Finishing up the semester," he beamed.

Danny smacked the kid gently on the shoulder and smiled. "Take care of her," he said with a nod back at the Jeep. "She's a gem."

"Yes, sir. She sure is."

Jessie twirled the large crystal flower ring on her index finger as she waited for him at the door, and Danny placed his hand on the small of her back to lead her through the arched wood and beveled glass entrance. The fragrance of garlic and basil accosted them at the door, and Jessie moaned softly.

"I can't wait for the bread," she muttered.

She'd called the bread at Tuscan Son "life-changing" when they'd come to Antonio's restaurant the first time, and Danny had dismissed the reference as one made by a rich, entitled trophy wife who'd been abandoned as trophies usually are. As they passed the colorful hand-painted tiles of the entry and crossed the vibrant sunflower they formed on the floor, Danny grinned at the sudden notion that he'd somehow managed to score a season with that exquisite so-called trophy Jack Stanton had tossed aside. He didn't know quite how or why it had happened, but he thanked God for Stanton's stupidity and his own unlikely good fortune.

He touched the arm of this woman, so much more than some guy's arm candy, and a question formed in her glittering blue eyes.

"Did I tell you how stunning you look tonight?" he asked her.

A simple nod preceded the grin that spread across her face like warm olive oil. "But feel free to tell me again at short intervals throughout dinner."

"Will do," he replied with a chuckle.

"Your party is waiting for you in the loft," the sharply dressed host told them as he led the way toward the wide spiral of wrought iron at the back of the restaurant.

"I wore flats," she whispered as they reached it, "in the hope that the loft was available tonight."

Danny followed her up the stairs and spotted Riggs and Charlotte seated on one side of a large rectangular table of natural wood. Overhead, a chandelier nearly as large and the same shape of the table held more than a dozen flickering candles, each beneath square glass hurricanes; below them, the restaurant formed a carpet of humming conversations and clinking glasses. Strings of small white lights twinkled from inside the vines of ivy on the walls, and Charlotte lit up like one of them when she spotted Danny.

He rounded her chair and kissed her cheek. "Hi, Char. Good to see you. You remember Jessie Hart?"

"Hi, Jessie," Charlotte beamed, tucking a lock of shiny dark auburn hair behind her ear.

"I'm so happy to see you again." Danny pulled out the chair across from Charlotte for Jessie to sit. As she did, she smiled at Riggs. "Thanks for inviting us along. You know how I love the food here."

Riggs placed his arm loosely around the back of Charlotte's chair. "The owners are close friends of Jessie's."

"How else would we have scored a table up here?" Danny joked.

"Friends in *lofty* places," Jessie chimed in.

"It's just beautiful," Charlotte said.

Jessie leaned forward and grinned. "Wait until they bring the bread. It's a basket of carbohydrates from heaven."

Amiable laughter floated above an exquisite dinner and surprisingly great company. Jessie felt relieved, relaxed, and at home as she and Danny sat across the table from Aaron Riggs and his ex-wife, Charlotte. Conversation hadn't lulled once throughout the meal, and they'd lingered over empty dessert plates and coffee for nearly an hour.

"I'm going to excuse myself to make a trip to the ladies' room," Charlotte said, slipping her chair away from the table. Aaron and Danny both stood.

"Mind some company?" Jessie asked, and her new friend grinned.

"I was hoping."

The first face Jessie saw once she and Charlotte descended the stairs into the main part of the restaurant was Antonio's, smiling at her from where he stood at the foot of a table of patrons seated in front of the fireplace. He excused himself from them immediately and headed straight for her.

"*Carissima*," he said as he enveloped her with an enthusiastic embrace. "I wondered if you all were still here. How was your meal?"

"Fantastic, as always," she replied, one arm still on his shoulder. "Antonio Brunetti, meet my new friend Charlotte Riggs."

"Riggs," he repeated. "You're Danny's friends."

"Charlotte, this is Antonio's restaurant. And he's married to Piper, my closest friend."

"Of course," she said with a wide smile. "Aaron gave me all the background, but I don't think he did the food here justice. What an amazing meal!"

"*Grazie*," he said as he shook her hand. "Happy you enjoyed it."

"Antonio is a vintner from Italy," Jessie told her. "Fortunately, he followed Piper to the States and started the restaurant."

"Not fortune," he remarked through the Italian accent he still had. "*Destino*. Was destiny."

Jessie's heart fluttered a bit. This man loved Piper in the most exquisite and authentic way. "You don't have to convince me," she said with a nod. "We're headed to the ladies' room, Antonio. Why don't you go up and say hello to Aaron and Danny."

"I'll do that. Charlotte Riggs, it was a pleasure to meet you. I hope you'll return often."

"Well, I have no choice now that I've tasted the linguini."

He leaned toward her and grinned. "This is our master plan."

"He lures you in with linguini and captures you with the bread and dessert."

Antonio chuckled as he kissed Jessie's hand. "See you soon."

Charlotte followed Jessie around the curve of the tiled floor and through the ladies' room door labeled *Donne*.

"Your friend is charming," Charlotte commented.

Jessie smiled. "He's lovely. And he treats my best friend like she's made of china and gold."

With a subtle shake of her head, she remarked, "What every woman dreams about."

The two of them stood side-by-side at the mirror. Charlotte repaired a slight smear of liner underneath her eye with the corner of a tissue while Jessie reapplied a coat of Tickled Pink lip gloss.

"I'm really happy you and Danny came along tonight."

She'd said it so softly, and Jessie turned toward her and smiled. "I am too. I think it went pretty well, don't you?"

The corner of Charlotte's mouth twitched as she answered. "I didn't know what to expect, really. I don't think I even meant to accept when he invited me to dinner, but it just came out."

"You've been apart for quite a while."

"Yes. And I'm very concerned about getting Allison's hopes up that her father and I are getting back together. She adores him."

"She certainly does," Jessie said. "And she's the apple of his eye. He lights up at even just the mention of her name."

"Yes." Charlotte hesitated thoughtfully. "Our split was so difficult. And we've somehow finally made it work for all three of us. I just . . . don't want to make any mistakes to lose that ground, you know?"

"I understand."

"I'll always love Aaron." A spark of pain flashed in Charlotte's eyes. "There's no doubt about that. I just don't know if we were . . . you know . . . meant to be *together*."

Jessie weighed her words carefully. "Well, you thought so once upon a time, yes?"

"Yes." A smile spread across Charlotte's pretty face with a strong, steady progression until it reached her greenish eyes and spilled over like rays of light searching for a means of escape. "We were so happy for a while. But Aaron . . . Well, he's not like most husbands. He didn't fit into the idea I'd always had of what a marriage and a happy family would be."

An awkward tension tightened Jessie's heart as she formed her response. "But it's different for every couple, isn't it? My grandfather once told me a marriage is like a tightrope where the couple just tries to navigate, making up the balance and next steps as they go along."

Charlotte chuckled. "I suppose that's true."

"And from my own experience, I can tell you for absolute certain that loyalty and trust are the most important thing. You won't ever have to wonder about Aaron's loyalty."

"This is true."

"I'm not trying to talk you into anything here," Jessie said with a sigh. "But I've come to really love Aaron as I've gotten to know him. And now, getting to know you, I can see it."

"See . . . what?"

"How you fit together."

Charlotte crossed her arms over her stomach and shook her head. "It's the strangest and most unexpected fit I could ever have imagined."

Jessie touched her arm and waited for eye contact before she reassured her. "And maybe that's all you need to know for tonight."

Charlotte sighed. "Maybe you're right." After a moment of deep thought, she turned to Jessie and smiled. "I'm really glad I got to know you better. Allie came back from the paddleboarding trip talking a mile a minute about how much she likes you."

Jessie chuckled. *Talking a mile a minute* described Allie to a tee. "She's a wonderful girl," she said.

Charlotte squeezed Jessie's hand. "Thank you, Jessie."

"Hey, you know what?" she exclaimed. "I met Amber right here in front of this mirror. She's the—"

"Yes, Amber. She works with you at your store. Allie loves her too."

"So I'm thinking this bathroom sink is unbelievably good luck. You're the second important friendship forged in front of it."

Before she saw it coming, Charlotte pivoted toward her and pulled Jessie into a somewhat awkward embrace.

"Thank you, Jessie."

⸺∞⸺

Shy as Jessie was, people never know'd it. She saw somebody who needed somethin' or another kiddo left alone at the jungle gym, my Jessie was the first one to try'n do somethin' 'bout it. Saw her leave a boy hangin' many a time to go mop up a girlfriend who got her heart broke. It was that kinda treatment of people that made the ring of friends 'round her all through school. Fact, it weren't 'til she married that Stanton fella that the transformin' begun.

"Grampy, he's a very important man," she says to me. "Lotta responsibilities and places to be. Sometimes I find myself feelin' so lonesome."

Girlfriends moved on to boys with places o' their own to be, and new friends the likes of people congregatin' 'round a fella like Stanton ain't the kind who stick around. Just 'bout the time Jessie started feelin' like she mighta made a mistake alienatin' herself to just Stanton and nobody else, that little Piper come along.

"You did a good job raisin' Jessie," she tells me when we met up that first time she come with Jessie for a visit. "I think she's the best friend I ever had."

Little elf nose and oversize lips, a redhead with all kinda colors shootin' through it. "Highlights," Jessie called 'em. "Isn't she beautiful, Grampy?"

Sure 'nough, her friend Piper was a pretty 'un all right. Married some Italian boy who cooks suppers for a livin'.

"You take good care o' my Jessie," I tells Piper when she gave me a hug good-bye.

"Promise," she whispers in my ear.

Gave me a few good nights o' sleep, that 'un.

11

Charles LaHayne struck Danny as one of those men who didn't know when to give up the ghost of their folliclely challenged dreams. He'd combed several thin clusters of what was left of his hair over the top of his bald scalp, presumably in the hope that it resembled an actual mane. It did not.

"I'm glad you called," LaHayne commented, and Danny straightened his back against the uncomfortable chair.

"I appreciate you coming in with me," he replied as they sat alone on one side of the over-glossed table centered in the small, glass-enclosed conference room. "I think Jessie feels better knowing you're in on both of the interviews."

"She's been through a lot."

Captain Understatement.

"She has."

"Just remember to only answer questions that you're asked," he said, sounding every bit the lawyer that he was. "Don't expound on anything or add any details they haven't inquired about. Remember, this is a fact-finding mission about Jack Stanton. It has nothing to do with you beyond the scope of what you've discovered since Mrs. Stanton hired you."

"Hart."

"Pardon?"

"Well, her name is officially Jessie Hart. Not Stanton."

"Yes. They'll ask you about that as well. They'll want to know how you uncovered the deception. Just explain, step by step."

The glass door whooshed open, and two fraternal twins entered. First, a man. Second, a rather manly woman. Both of them wearing gray suits and starched white shirts, he with an added dark tie, and both with polished yet sensible black shoes. The feds had arrived. Danny stood, more out of habit than courtesy.

"Have a seat," the woman said with a strange little smile.

"Mr. Callahan," her male counterpart said without looking at him. "Thank you for coming in." He fidgeted with some files jammed with paperwork. "Let's start with your relationship to Mrs. Stanton."

Hart.

"Can you recount your first meeting for us?"

"Sure, but I'd just like to make it clear at the top that Jessie Hart had no knowledge of Jack Stanton's activities. She was as much in the dark as anyone I've ever seen when she came to ask for my help."

"And when was that, exactly?" Guy Suit kept his focus fixed on the paperwork before him. "The date."

"I think this will save a lot of time." Danny slipped the flash drive he'd prepared from his pocket and slapped it on the table between them. "Here are copies of all our meeting notes, documents I uncovered, dates and times, everything you'll need."

The suits looked at each other, bewildered. He had to work at suppressing a smile.

Danny realized they'd never even given him their names. He found himself wondering if Steph adopted this same all-business, no-frills company line in her nine-to-five. He had a hard time picturing it.

Girl Suit placed her hand over the flash drive and slid it in her own direction. "Thank you."

Guy Suit had found his game face again. "Stanton had in his employ an executive assistant by the name of Claudia Stern."

Was that a question?

"Yes, that's right."

"How did you become acquainted with Ms. Stern?"

Danny folded his arms across his chest and thought back to the day Jessie phoned and asked him to turn around and return to her apartment. He arrived to find the raven-haired, middle-aged woman seated on the couch.

"She contacted Jessie," he explained, "after Stanton had called to ask her to retrieve an envelope he'd left for her in his safety deposit box. He also asked her to destroy the rest of the contents of the box."

"And did she comply?"

"She did not. She brought them to Jessie who, in turn, handed them over to me."

The Suits folded their arms in unison, and Guy Suit clarified, "And you've been holding on to this evidence ever since."

"I have."

"The moment Mr. Callahan was contacted about your interest," LaHayne cut in, "he scanned everything in his files and loaded it on the flash drive for you. He's been more than cooperative, and I believe you will find his case notes extremely detailed."

The agent narrowed his dark eyes and stared at Danny for several moments. "Can you summarize the contents and your conversation with Ms. Stern for us now?"

"Certainly," Danny agreed, and he inhaled sharply in preparation for laying it all out for them. "We met for under an hour, and she presented Jessie with several documents, which included a note from Stanton to Claudia and an envelope of cash. She asked me if she could legally keep the money, and I suggested she contact an attorney. Also in the envelope were two marriage licenses—one for Stanton and his first wife, and another for him and Jessie. There was also a letter from Patty—somewhat romantic in nature—as well as some correspondence from Stanton's personal attorney at Spence & Spence."

Girl Suit spoke next. "What was the nature of that correspondence?"

"Informing Stanton that his divorce from Patty had not been finalized in time for his marriage to Jessie."

"Mrs. Stanton mentioned in her interview that John Fitzgerald Stanton had confirmed to her in their last meeting that he had never, in fact, dissolved his first marriage. Were you present for that conversation?"

"Yes."

He remembered the pain on Jessie's face when Jack had given her the truth she thought she wanted so badly. It pinched Danny's heart.

"Will you recount that for us?"

"The notes are all on the drive," he reminded them. "But in my research, I wasn't able to locate a certificate of divorce between Stanton and his first wife, Patty. A while after I'd shared that with Jessie and continued to search for the data, Stanton showed up, and she asked him outright."

"On what date was this?"

"You'll have to check the notes for the date. But it was on the evening when he forced his way into her apartment. It took me a few minutes to get inside. When I did, there was an altercation and, while he was still spread out on the floor, Jessie asked him if they were ever even legally married."

"And he told her—"

"He said he'd never divorced Patty."

"And you heard him admit to that fact."

"I did. Yes."

"You've included notes on the altercation as well?"

"Yes." Danny waited a few beats before asking, "Are you going to prosecute him for bigamy? What kind of time will that add to his sentence?"

Girl Suit looked up seriously. "Bigamy alone isn't going to make a significant difference, but it is a felony in most states. The existence of a valid divorce prior to a second marriage is essential in every jurisdiction."

Danny grinned. "Yeah. So what does that mean, exactly? In this particular case, I mean."

"In California," LaHayne cut in, "bigamy is punishable by a fine not exceeding ten thousand dollars or by imprisonment of up to one year. Added to Mr. Stanton's other crimes, I think we could easily see an additional year added to his sentence once it's proven."

"Had you ever had any business dealings with Jack Stanton?" Guy Suit asked.

Danny cocked one eyebrow. "Me? No. I'd never even heard of the guy before Jessie showed up at my door asking for help."

"You never did any work for him, any investigating for his business?"

"No. Why would you ask that?"

"When he was picked up in Sydney, Stanton had your contact information in his phone, along with some photographs."

This tidbit rocked Danny's gut. "Are you sure?" Turning to LaHayne, he asked, "What kind of photos?"

LaHayne shrugged slightly, but he didn't speak until he diverted his gaze to the Suits across the table from them. "Is there anything else, or can my client be on his way?"

Jessie pulled up to the front of the restaurant and stopped. Heath jogged around to the driver's side and smiled. "Afternoon, Ms. Sta—oh, sorry. Ms. Hart. Are you going inside?"

She lowered the window. "No, I'm just picking up Mrs. Brunetti. Would you let her know I'm here?"

"Sure thing."

She watched him as he crossed to the podium and picked up a mobile phone, noting the way the California sunshine lit up his cropped blond hair into streaks of light. Heath had come to work for Antonio as a valet right around the time Jack had left, and he'd been a staple of her trips to the restaurant ever since. It seemed like, no matter what time of the day or evening she arrived at Tuscan Son, Heath greeted her with a smile and a polite word. He couldn't have been much older than twenty, but his work ethic seemed as firm and stable as someone twice his age.

"She asked if you'd wait just a couple of minutes," he said upon return to her window. "She'll be right out."

"Happy to."

"You know, Ms. Hart, I never got to tell you this, but I saw the piece that local reporter did on your store out in Santa Monica. It looked pretty cool, and I wanted to congratulate you on it."

"Thanks, Heath."

"I never would have thought of something like that. It's pretty unique. How's business?"

"It's going pretty well. We've expanded a bit on the retail side, and it's still too soon to know for sure. But I think it was a good move. Time will tell."

Piper appeared at the front door of the restaurant, waving at Jessie.

"Well, congratulations," Heath said. "Keep up the great work."

"Thank you."

Heath opened the door for Piper, and she slid into the passenger seat and buckled her seatbelt. "Hi, sweetie. You ready for this?"

"More than. I really appreciate you thinking of it."

"I wanted to do something to lift your spirits, and what lifts them faster than a spa day with your BFF, hmm?"

Nothing Jessie could think of, that was for sure.

"Did you bring your swimsuit? I booked us a few hours in a cabana by the pool after our massages."

"I brought it."

"Good. I want you to just jiggle all the bad things out of your head and enjoy today."

"I'll try."

Jessie knew it wouldn't be an easy feat to shake away the cobwebs, but if there was anywhere in Southern California that offered hope of it, Elixir could.

Located inside the prestigious Beverly Plaza Hotel, Elixir offered an upscale solution for just about anything that could possibly ail a woman of leisure—not that she could claim *that* title any more. Wonderful food, massages, facials, even spray tans.

"Would you like to get lash extensions for your big date this weekend?" Piper offered joyfully.

Jessie giggled. Until that moment, she hadn't really thought of attending Steph's wedding with Danny as a "big date." Now that the dam was left gaping open, questions about what to wear flooded her mind.

"They're on me," Piper added. "Kelly does a beautiful job."

"Kelly?"

"The lashes. She's an artiste. Do you want me to book her for you?"

"Oh. No thanks, but you go ahead."

Over the next couple of hours, Jessie slipped out to the precipice between awake and asleep, basking in the relaxation offered by Dee-Dee, the masseuse with hands as magical and skilled as they'd ever been. Following the massage, she and Piper occupied adjoining recliners and enjoyed thirty-minute facials. Afterward, they were escorted poolside to a private cabana where a light supper was served by friendly, accommodating staff.

Dungeness crab with roasted citrus and mint, Persian cucumber and avocado . . . smoked Balik salmon garnished with apples, endives, and caviar . . . strawberry salad with hearts of romaine, opal basil, and marcona almonds.

"You know," Jessie said, "I'm just happy to spend time with you."

"Same here," Piper replied sleepily, cucumber slices cooling her eyes while a quiet young Asian woman massaged her feet.

"What I mean is . . ." Jessie glanced over at her oblivious friend. "You don't need to spend a fortune on our time together."

"Jessie, that's sweet. But I have the money to spend. And I know you must have missed indulgences like this, haven't you?"

"Well, of course." She sighed. "Yes. But if I've learned anything at all, the lesson is that it's more about the person you're with than the geography of where you spend the time."

Piper moaned softly. "But if you can have both, why wouldn't you?"

That was the point. Piper could easily have both, but she knew that the expense of just that one afternoon might have kept her store running for a few months.

"Relax, sweetie. Enjoy it while you can. You can go back to reality in a few hours."

Jessie inhaled deeply and held it.

Relax. Just relax. Relax and enjoy it.

She replayed the sentiment again and again until she finally managed to follow her own advice. And just about the time that the last thread of nervous anxiety slid from her body and evaporated into the steam from the nearby Jacuzzi . . .

"Jessie Stanton? Is that you?"

Her eyes popped open wide at the sound of that familiar, grating voice.

Shea McDermott. Standing right there in the opening of their cabana, like a shark eyeing its prey.

"And Piper, you're here too. Why, the last time I saw you both, you were together then too. I believe that was the day you all had to take a taxi home because Jessie's car was locked up and toted away right out of the valet parking lot, wasn't it?"

Jessie's insides dropped so fast, she thought they might have echoed out a thud!

"Hi, Shea," Piper said, and she lowered her legs over the side of the table and slid into a thick white robe crested with the hotel's logo. "We're just having a girls' day. What are you doing here?"

"We're expanding the guest house," she seemed to drawl, despite the fact that Shea wasn't the least bit Southern. "And I simply could not abide all that construction, so Harrington and I took a suite here until they're finished."

Piper nodded Jessie over to the table, now set with beautiful china plates and tiered glass trays of delectable desserts.

Shea followed them to the table and sat without invitation. "How are you doing, Jessie? After that sordid ordeal with Jack, I mean."

Without hesitation, she replied, "I'm just dandy, Shea. Best thing that ever happened to me."

She touched Jessie's hand. "Oh, you're being so brave, aren't you, darling?"

"Not brave at all," Piper interjected. "Jack's being prosecuted, and Jessie has a whole new life. She's opened her own store, in fact. And she's writing fashion articles for one of the trendiest blog sites in the country. Oh, and Shea. She has a wonderful new man. You should see him. Danny is absolutely *delicious*."

Shea's disappointment seemed palpable, and Jessie clamped her bottom lip between her teeth to keep from laughing right out loud. This was so unlike Piper.

"Well, that's just lovely, isn't it?" Shea said, and she stood. "Nice to see you both again. We'll have to do lunch when things calm down a little."

"Take care, Shea."

Once Shea McDermott had moved out of earshot, Jessie let loose the laughter.

"What are you laughing about?"

"I seem to recall an afternoon—not so long ago, really—when I moved my hand into the sunlight in just such a way that its reflection off my ridiculous engagement ring shot over and blinded Shea McDermott."

"I know . . ."

"And you were sitting right across from me, saying something like, '*Jes-sie!* Stop that. What are you, ten years old?'"

Piper snickered. "Oh, hush. I get it now. She's horrible."

"Yes. She is. Welcome to the dark side."

"May God forgive me."

"I'm sure He will. And by the way . . . thank you. Your unchar-acteristic cattiness is much appreciated."

"Anything for you."

———

Jessie's mama know'd her way around a sewin' machine. Good thing too 'cause her girl always did like her dresses, 'n she liked 'em shiny 'n one-of-a-kind.

"Can we make it more glittery, Mama?" she'd ask 'er, and they'd pull out that big ole canister filled up with buttons and bows and sequins and beads, and they'd labor over it for hours makin' one o' Jessie's dresses into somethin' special. "I just feel so much prettier when I wear some-thin' shiny. Don't you feel that way too, Mama?"

April weren't much for shiny. She was always a simple girl. Cotton, pearls, and maybe a bow now 'n agin.

"No, sweet pea. You come by that all on your own."

Jessie chewed on that a while. "I just like to stand out, Mama. Is there somethin' wrong with standin' out?"

"Nothin' wrong a-tall, Jessie-girl," I tells her. "Means there's nobody else like you. But we already know'd that, didn't we?"

12

Jessie inspected her reflection in the tall, narrow mirror. Out of the five dresses she'd tried on since they'd closed Adornments for the day, this one had real potential for a sunset beach wedding.

"What are your thoughts on men's wear?" Amber called over the top of the curtained dressing room partition.

She froze for a moment and looked down at the navy blue dress she'd just slipped over her head. "Men's wear? I'm not really your Diane Keaton kind of girl. I don't think it's for me," she said, running two fingers over the intricate beading detail of the dress's Grecian neckline. "I really like this one though."

"Not for the wedding. For the store."

Jessie pulled back the lavender curtain and exited the dressing area.

"Oh, Jessie," Amber breathed. "That's perfect on you. And you won't need a necklace. The beading covers that for you."

She turned sideways and bent her leg to show off the hemline, above the knee in front and just below the knee in back. "What do you think of the length?"

"It's good. You should wear that one."

Jessie stepped back into the dressing area and examined her reflection again, head on.

"I took a call this morning—a referral from Francesca," Amber told her from the other side of the curtain. "The woman has a dozen suits and tuxedos in varying sizes that she's interested in placing for consignment. Tom Ford, Armani, Valentino. I was thinking we could open a little men's wear section on the other side of the handbags and shoes to give it a try."

"Men's wear," Jessie repeated. "I've never given any thought to that."

"But it couldn't hurt, right? Just a test section."

"I suppose. You really think so? We're only just establishing ourselves a niche market for women. Do you really think . . . *men's wear*? Really?"

"It's consignment." Amber stood behind her and shrugged at their reflection. "We give it a few months and see how it does."

"Okay." She shrugged. "Call her back and schedule a pick-up."

"Good." Amber nodded. "You should wear those silver platform sandals of yours with this."

She considered it. "Maybe. But I don't know if we're going to actually be on sand or not. Probably not. But I picked up these really cute flat sandals the other day with a simple clear rhinestone strap. I might wear those."

"Ooh, where'd you get them?"

"Promise not to laugh?"

"Of course."

Jessie peered around the corner to make sure they were still alone in the store before whispering, "Target."

"You shopped at Target?"

"Well, I needed a few things . . ."

"Hey, there's no judgment here," Amber said with a laugh. "I love Target."

"I know, right? I hadn't been in one of their stores in years, and it was actually pretty great."

"You know those rhinestone hoop earrings of mine that you love so much? I got those at Target."

"One of my roommates when I first moved to Los Angeles used to call it *Tar-jaay*."

Amber gasped. "You're going to wear a Bloomies dress with Target sandals." The two of them chuckled before she added, "You'll start a new trend."

"I don't even want to tell you about the panties I bought."

"You bought panties at Target?" Amber teased.

"Well, yeah. But . . . they had a three-pack for under twelve dollars. I didn't even remember you could *find* panties that cheap."

Riggs often made the joke that too much time away from the morning waves equated to that green fuzz around the edge of the shower. Left for too long without attention, and it was sure to get out of hand. That's how Danny felt this particular afternoon. Figurative green fuzz seemed to be growing under his feet at an alarming rate, and he longed for the cleansing waves of the Pacific Ocean—so elusive lately—to rescue him from the hours ahead of him planning and touring the Monarch Aristocrat Hotel with Rochelle Silverstein and her cronies. At the same time, eager anticipation rumbled in his gut as he led up to telling them that he had a lead about the loose lips intent on sinking their ship.

"The FiFis have been held here at the Monarch since year one," Rochelle told him as the five of them made their way in a cluster toward the banquet hall. "Because their largest venue only seats four hundred, it was perfect when we were just starting out. What it accomplished—and what we didn't expect as we gained more notoriety—is that holding the awards show in a venue of this size has led to a fervor for tickets while they're still available. We're sold out, and we have a waiting list of nearly three hundred. It seems we're *the place to be* at the start of the awards season."

"Unless we don't get this breach in hand," George Tercot chimed in from behind them, tugging at his bow tie. "If people think there's anything funny going on with our process, we won't be able to *give* the tickets away."

"That's why I'm here," Danny assured him.

Leslie McCann waddled ahead to keep stride with Rochelle and Danny. "How do you propose to solve our little mystery, Danny?"

"Right through here," Rochelle interjected, waving them all toward massive, ornate double doors.

Danny tugged open one of the doors and held it for the others to pass. Four massive crystal chandeliers hovered over the large room, their illumination helped along by small glittering sconces spaced evenly along walls papered in an elaborate silver pattern. Thick red carpet covered the floor all the way to the edge of a raised stage, empty except for a glossy-white baby grand piano.

Several uniformed workmen assembled round tables and framed them with chairs at one side of the ballroom while Rochelle led their party to one lone rectangular table at the back. While Rochelle unrolled the floor plan, Danny addressed them.

"Leslie, you asked me before how I plan to solve the mystery of your security breach. I'd like to answer that because I may have a pretty good lead."

Rochelle snapped to attention, dropping the plans and focusing on Danny. "Tell us, dear boy."

"I did a little research to find out where and when that first leak popped up, and I found myself looking at a reporter named Suzanne Lehmann at a thirty-minute local weekend show called *ScreenTime*."

"I love that show," Darlene declared.

"Did you call her?" Leslie asked Danny pointedly, her pudgy little nose curled up with curiosity.

"No. A reporter isn't going to tell me where she got her scoop. All my calling her would accomplish is giving her a heads up that we're looking into it."

Leslie deflated as if the air had been let out of her face. "What do we do now?"

"I have a couple degrees of separation from a reporter at the same local station. I've reached out to someone I know who can connect us, and I'll try to go in through the back door to see if I can find out anything solid. The interesting news is that two of the last three years of leaks have both originated in Lehmann's office."

"So you're on to something," Rochelle summarized. "That's wonderful, Danny."

"Meanwhile, I've pinpointed several areas I need information about. For instance, which security company have you used in recent years?"

"Weston Security," Rochelle replied.

"The agency is run by George's *nephew*," Leslie pointed out, and her expression might have made Danny laugh in different surroundings.

"Okay," he said, jotting down the name. "I'll need to get into the private areas and get the lay of the land. The green room, the dressing rooms, the bathrooms. And I need to see copies of the photos that were leaked so we can determine exactly where they were taken."

"I'll e-mail them over to you once I return home," Rochelle said. "But I can show you. Let's take a walk into the backstage area."

When they returned to the ballroom an hour later, Darlene, Leslie, and George went on their way, leaving Danny and Rochelle to gather the remnants of their mission.

"They serve a lovely cappuccino in the café here, Danny. Would you join me for a bite?"

He hadn't eaten anything all day, so Danny agreed. The two of them followed the glossy mahogany path through the pristine hotel and across the lobby to Features Café, and Rochelle told how fond she'd become of their simple cuisine and how she lunched there regularly. Once they settled at a clear acrylic table and opened their menus, Danny discovered how pricey "simple cuisine" could be.

Rochelle ordered half a Monte Cristo sandwich and a cup of minestrone with a large cappuccino. Danny struggled to find anything on the menu that appealed, but he settled on a grilled cheese with tomato and basil that came with a side of pasta salad arranged into a perfect mound and decorated with a sprig of something green. Dill perhaps.

"I was just delighted to hear from Francesca Dutton, by the way," she said before blowing on a spoonful of soup. "We had lunch yesterday, and I think we're on to something really exciting, Danny. I can't thank you enough for thinking of me when she told you what she wanted to do."

"Meant to be," he commented. "I just happened to overhear a conversation between Ms. Dutton and a friend of mine."

"Francesca told me that. I'm just so happy you made the connection. And so soon after our conversation. It's very timely for me, Danny. Ever since my husband had his heart attack—"

"I didn't know. I'm sorry."

"Oh, he's doing very well now, but the event caused John and me to become the typical cliché, I suppose. Living a life of excess, enjoying the fruits of our labor . . . and then in one instant, it's all hanging in the balance. We both started questioning whether we're making the most of what we've been given. John's done so much in the year since his bypass to contribute within his arena of films and television. This endeavor with Francesca is right up my alley, and I have you to thank. I was so impressed when you told me about all the charitable work you've done."

He wasn't quite sure how to respond without it coming off as blowing his own horn or—worse—making Rochelle feel as if she'd been living life with her head buried in her own sandy beach until he came along as a shining light or something.

"Thank you." Brevity seemed to be the way to go. "I appreciate you saying that."

"John and I would love to meet your friend Jessie."

Danny froze, the sandwich sort of hovering there in his hand. "I beg your pardon?"

"Kaye tells me she's lovely. She helped you solve Kaye's problem up at the cabin, I believe?"

He managed a nod in response.

"And Francesca says her little shop is just adorable. We share a love for cocoa, you know."

Danny narrowed his eyes and searched Rochelle's face for some hint or memory about the quirky love of hot chocolate. He didn't remember Jessie saying anything about—

"Coco Chanel," she clarified. "She evidently has a quote on the back wall of her establishment."

Ah. Okay. The word mural. He pictured it there behind the counter, but he couldn't remember the quote itself.

"'Dress shabbily, and they remember the dress,'" she quoted. "'Dress impeccably and they remember the woman.' One of my favorites."

He felt for a moment as if he'd been locked inside an absurd game of telephone where all of the outside elements of his life became inexplicably connected by one central theme: *Jessie.*

Not really so unexpected if he really thought about it. But he decided not to, at least not on this day. When his cell phone buzzed a moment later and he saw Piper's name on the screen, he chuckled. So much for that.

"Excuse me, will you?" he asked Rochelle. "This is my friend with the connection to the reporter."

"You go ahead. I'll just make a trip to the little girls' room."

He nodded and stood out of courtesy for her as he answered the call. "Piper. Thanks for getting back to me so quickly."

"Happy to help, Danny," she said. "I spoke to Cynthia Ross, and she's willing to meet with you in person if you're available late in the day."

"I can do that."

"Do you have a pen to write down her number?"

He quickly surveyed the room, noting no one within earshot. "I don't. Can you text it to me?"

"Sure."

"Thanks so much for this, Piper."

"Are you kidding?" she replied with a chuckle. "After everything you've done for Jessie? I'm just happy to help. I'll text you as soon as we hang up."

"Great."

"You two enjoy yourselves this weekend."

"Thanks. I'm pretty sure we will."

Things fell into place like a well-choreographed plan. Piper texted him the phone number and he called Cynthia Ross, who answered her phone on the first ring . . . she happened to have a break before filming her next segment . . . wasn't far from the Monarch . . . and she agreed to meet him there within the hour.

The waitress agreed to hold Danny's table while he walked Rochelle out to the valet. He carried an armful of her belongings for her, and they chatted amiably as they went. When he returned, the waitress had cleared the used plates and refilled his iced tea glass.

"We have a killer blackberry cobbler, if you're interested," she told him.

"Sounds good."

"Can I warm it for you?" she asked, and the tone of her voice drew his full and curious attention. She leaned a little closer than a waitress normally should as she added, "Maybe a little something . . . *extra*? Just for you."

Danny cocked one brow and stared at her. "Beg your pardon?"

"A scoop of vanilla to go with it?"

"Uh, sure."

She delivered the dessert to his table in a lightning flash of enthusiastic speed. "Coffee?"

"No. Thanks. The tea is fine."

The strawberry blonde shook her mop of curls and tapped the engraved nametag that labeled her *Lizzie*. A borderline creepy smile slithered across Lizzie's face as she slipped a folded napkin into his hand. "Let me know if you need anything else."

Danny watched her slink away before opening the napkin to find her name and phone number scrawled across it, punctuated by an odd-shaped lipstick kiss.

"Well," he muttered with the shake of his head. "*That* just happened."

Fortunately, the tasty cobbler occupied his time and filled the gap until a petite platinum blonde with sharp but pretty features slipped into the chair across from him. "Danny Callahan, I presume."

"How'd you know?" he asked with a grin, wiping his mouth.

"You're the only man sitting alone at a table." She offered her hand. "Cynthia Ross."

"Miss Ross, I appreciate you meeting me," he said as he shook her outstretched hand.

"If you don't call me Cynthia, I'm going to get up and walk out of here right now."

Danny laughed and gave her a nod. "Well, Cynthia, I can't have that. I need you too much."

"I like the sound of that." She grinned, but it melted from her face as she focused on something just over his shoulder. "But then I'm guessing there are a lot of us girls who would like a little sweet-talking from you."

He glanced back to find Waitress Lizzie standing nearby, seemingly hanging on their every word.

"Jealous girlfriend?" Cynthia teased.

"Attentive waitress."

"Ah. Well, I never begrudge a woman with good taste. How can I help you today, Danny? Piper said there's someone at my station causing some problems for you."

"For my client, possibly."

"You understand I can't go behind a coworker's back if it's something unseemly."

"I just need to patch up some holes that seem to have sprung a leak at the hand of a reporter named Suzanne Lehmann."

"Suzanne. Really."

"I don't want you to do anything that puts you in a bad position. In fact, I'm not entirely sure what I'm asking you to do. All I really need is a finger pointing out the general direction for me."

"Why don't you give me the details, and then I'll decide what does or doesn't put me in a bad position."

∞∞∞

"Danny wanted to speak with Cynthia Ross?" Jessie clarified. "Are you sure?"

"Positive," Piper replied. "In fact, I think they're meeting sometime today."

Jessie pushed her fork into the salad on the table in front of her and left it there. "I wonder why."

"Something to do with a case."

"He has a *fashion mystery* to solve?" Jessie giggled at her own joke.

"I guess so. Eat your salad."

She wondered why Danny hadn't talked to her about it. Cynthia Ross—a fashion reporter—couldn't possibly provide as much help in sorting out a mystery as she could. Hadn't she proven that to him several times over by now?

"Oh, wait," she realized. "It's probably related to the FiFis. He's working security for them. But I wonder what . . ."

Her words trailed off along with her thoughts. A moment after she returned her attention to the strawberry chicken salad in front of her again, she noticed Piper's pouty grimace.

"Sorry. Did you say something?"

"You're twisted up because he didn't bring you into his case, aren't you?"

She didn't even bother to deny it. "A little."

"Can I untangle your knot a little?"

"I don't know," Jessie volleyed back to her. "Can you?"

"You are in fashion retail. Danny, on the other hand, is an actual investigator." Piper raised both upturned palms as a symbol of weighing each side. "Fashion retail. Private investigator."

"All right, fine. I get your point."

"Do you?" Piper's nose wrinkled in amusement before she giggled. "You are nothing if not a renaissance girl. I'm thinking all those years of reading Hardy Boys and Nancy Drew mysteries might have been your downfall."

It was Jessie's turn to laugh. "You might be right."

"Can I get you ladies anything else?" the waiter asked them. "Save room for dessert?"

Piper shook her head, but Jessie jumped right in. "That depends. Do you have any pie? I have a taste for pie."

"Cream or fruit?" the young man asked.

"Fruit if it's got something crumbly on top. Otherwise, cream."

"Dutch apple?"

"Warm with a scoop of vanilla?"

"Certainly. And for you?" he asked Piper.

"Just coffee. But would you bring two spoons with hers? I like to save her from herself whenever I can. I'm a giver like that."

"Gee, thanks," Jessie said with a chuckle before turning to the waiter and adding, "I'd like coffee too, please."

"Sure thing," he answered before heading back toward the kitchen.

"So do you have any feelings about men's wear?" Jessie asked without missing a beat.

"Um. Well. I really like when Antonio wears it."

"I'm thinking of adding a men's wear section at the store."

Piper squinted as if trying to get a closer look at the idea in the air between them.

"It's just something we're going to try and see how it goes."

Jessie picked up her fork and speared a nugget of grilled chicken, a lettuce leaf, chunks of radish and cucumber, and a quartered strawberry. When she'd created the ideal last bite, she swirled it around in the raspberry dressing pooled at the bottom of the bowl and capped it all with a few candied pecans gathered at the side. She closed her eyes and slipped the concoction into her mouth. After a moment of sheer enjoyment, she opened her eyes and smiled at her friend.

"You do enjoy your food, don't you?" Piper teased.

"Don't you?"

"I thought I did. Until I met you."

"My Grampy says there's no use bothering to put something in your mouth if you're not getting something out of it. Nutrition, enjoyment, or both."

"He's a wise man," she remarked. "How's he doing anyway? You haven't mentioned him in a while."

"He seems to be good. Well, aside from the ongoing feud with Maizie Beauchamp."

"The next door neighbor? They're still arguing?"

"Going on three decades now. No sense in stopping now. Grampy says they'll still be fussing at each other while they wait their turns at the Pearly Gates."

My Jessie always liked a good mystery. From the time she could put one foot in front o' the other, she went lookin' fer somethin' to figger out. Usin' invisible ink from the variety store to pass notes to classmates 'bout her teachers. Peerin' over the fence at that irritatin' neighbor woman to see what notorious thing she mighta got up to.

"Grampy, when do you s'pose I'll be big enough for perfume?" she ask me one hot mornin' down by Pontchartrain nettin' crabs.

"Them crabs ain't enough stink fer ya?"

"Oh, don't be silly. I wanna smell like a real girl."

"Real girl, like who?"

"Like Nancy Drew."

Seemed Jessie'd been readin' The Secret of Red Gate Farm *agin and encountered some smelly clues by way of somethin' called Blue Jade perfume. Weren't enough she'd been thinkin' on Nancy Drew as a "real girl," but now she wanted to start wearin' perfume like 'er.*

My Jessie mighta been gearin' up to be a mystery-solvin' girly-girl if not for the louder call of mag'zines with stick-thin, fish-faced runway models on the covers of 'em.

13

Danny, thank goodness! We were starting to wonder if you'd changed your mind."

"*We* were not wondering that," Steph sang from around the corner. "My mother is the only one who wondered that."

He shared a grin with Jessie before leaning in to kiss Jean's cheek. "Good to see you. This is my friend Jessie."

"Hi, Jessie." In the same breath, she asked Danny, "Is that what you're wearing?"

He glanced down, grazing over his clothes with an eye of scrutiny. Tan linen trousers and an off-white, thin cotton shirt. "I asked Steph if I should wear a suit or something, and she told me not to."

"It's true, Mom. I threatened his life."

"No matter," Jean dismissed them both. "Marcus has plenty of suits. Let's look and see what we can find to fit you." She tugged at Danny's hand in an attempt to pull him along behind her. He'd forgotten how Jean could be.

"Hold on a minute," Steph called, and the soft swish of fabric preceded her. "Can I at least say hello to my Guy of Honor before you give him a makeover?"

Danny's heart fluttered slightly as Steph rounded the corner and headed toward him. Dressed in wide-legged white chiffon pants and a matching tailored blouse gathered at the waist with a thin rhinestone belt, she looked astonishingly ethereal. She'd swept her dark blonde hair back into an elegant twist, thin wisps escaping to frame her oval face. He felt happy—*and surprised*—to see that she had exchanged her usual government-issue shoes for three-inch spiked heels encrusted with rhinestones. Aside from flip-flops, he'd rarely seen grown-up Steph wear anything except the signature shoes of a Marine, and then a federal agent.

"I think you look perfect," Steph told him with a smile, and Danny took her into his arms and kissed the side of her head. "Don't you dare let my mother dress you up like a Ken doll." Over his shoulder, she chuckled. "Hi, Jessie."

"Hi, Steph. Happy wedding day. You look perfect."

She pulled out of Danny's embrace and took a step back. "You think so?"

"Exquisite," Danny said sincerely.

"Wait until you see Vince," she said with a wink. "He looks like the beach guy we always thought I'd marry."

"In the body of a fed."

"Right. And with a modified crew cut, of course."

Steph wrinkled her nose at Jessie and—for just a second there—Danny thought she seemed . . . giddy. Since Steph didn't exactly do *giddy*, he wasn't quite sure what to do with it.

"You look so pretty," she told Jessie. "Midnight blue is your color with that dark hair and those eyes."

"Thanks," she replied, and she fluffed the hemline that hung much longer in the back than the front. "I wasn't sure."

"Love the sandals."

Jessie chuckled as if guarding a tightly held secret. "Me too. Thank you."

"Yes, yes," Jean quipped. "Everyone looks lovely. Great wardrobe, wonderful shoes. But we have less than ten minutes before the ceremony begins, Danny. Come with me and we'll find you something more appropriate to wear."

Danny looked to Steph. After all, it was her wedding, not Jean's, and she'd approved the wardrobe choice.

"Mother. What was our agreement?"

Jean's sigh turned out like a groan, and she droned out what they had obviously discussed more than once. "Helping does not mean running the show."

"Exactly. And you got your big white tent, and your string quartet—"

Danny clucked out a laugh. *String quartet. She wanted a simple ceremony out on the beach.*

"—but you are not going to dress Danny like the guy on top of the wedding cake when Vince is trying so hard to dress *down* to a beach wedding."

"Can we at least add a nice jacket?"

"No." Steph held her ground, and Danny resisted the urge to crack the tension with a joke. "This is what I asked him to wear, and I think he looks handsome. Leave it alone."

"Fine." Jean clearly had no further retort, but Danny could see that she didn't like it. "But I hate to pin a jeweled rose to that thin shirt and have it tear."

"It won't tear. But if it does, I'm sure you'll MacGyver a repair. Now why don't you go ahead and get his boutonniere and my bouquet so we can get this show on the road."

When she left, Danny squeezed Steph's hand and whispered, "Steady, girl."

"She drives me nuts."

"She's your mother. That's her job. Listen, I brought you something."

He dug into the pocket of his trousers and produced the small shell he'd been holding onto for such a long time. When he placed it into her open palm, Steph's grayish eyes misted with emotion.

"You still have this?" she asked.

"What is it?" Jessie chimed in, leaning forward for a closer look.

"We were sixteen," Steph explained, clutching the shell to her chest with a smile. "The summer before senior year, and a big group of us went down to the Mexican Pipeline on a surfing vacation."

"The Mexican Pipeline?" Jessie asked them. "I've never heard of that."

"Puerto Escondido," Danny said. "On the Pacific coast of Mexico."

"Prime waves," Steph recalled, and she opened her hand and inspected the small shell. "I bought a choker of shells like this one, and it broke the first time I wore it. Danny rescued this one from the rubble and made a pendant out of it."

"Which also broke the first time she wore it," he remembered with a laugh.

"So he took it away from me and said I couldn't have it back."

Danny's heart flooded with a twelve-footer of good memories.

"It's funny you two were never a couple," Jessie told them, and they both burst with laughter, shaking their heads.

"We've known each other since we were kids," Steph told her. "He's been a brother to me for as long as I can remember. That would just be . . . unnatural."

"Against my every hope," Steph's mother stated as she came back into the master suite with floral boxes in her arms. "Danny was always my hope for Stephanie."

"Until you met Vince," Danny reminded her.

"Of course. Until Vince," she said with a grin as she pinned a lavender rosebud embellished with tiny crystals to Danny's shirt. "Any man who makes my Stephanie glow like that," she added, gingerly removing the bouquet from a square white box, "is the son-in-law of my dreams."

Jean placed the flowers into Steph's hands and kissed her daughter on the cheek.

"Oh, Steph," Jessie cooed. "It's perfect."

"Yes, she is," Danny added.

Steph's eyes darted to her mother, and Jean smiled and gave her a reassuring nod. "Beautiful. Are you ready, sweetheart? Your father's downstairs waiting for you."

Steph wrapped her arms around Jean's neck and squeezed. "I love you," she whispered. "Thank you for doing this."

"Doing what?" Jean joked as she stepped back, keeping the connection by placing her hands on Steph's shoulders. "You're doing all the work. You have to live with him. I'm just giving you a nice party to kick it off."

Jessie smiled at the elegant woman seated next to the empty chair on the aisle, and they exchanged pleasantries as she sat down beside her. She hadn't expected so many attendees, or the elaborate surroundings for the simple beach ceremony Danny had described.

The glass doors leading out to the Regniers' enormous back deck had been rolled wide open, creating one indoor/outdoor space. A dozen white chiffon panels gathered in the middle with thick purple ribbons and large sprays of lavender roses and green hydrangea matching the bridal bouquet cordoned off the reception tables and serving stations. Beyond the stone wall separating the deck from the sand, guests stepped out onto the wooden walkway leading to a large white tent placed just twenty yards or so from the surf. More lavender roses, green hydrangea, and sparkling ribbon accessorized the crystal chandeliers and flickering candles placed throughout the tent. Four short rows of ladderback chairs, opened by the aisle down the middle, had been adorned with thick ribbon woven between burnished silver slats.

"It's really beautiful, isn't it?" Jessie commented to the woman next to her.

"The bride's mother has an exquisite eye for detail," the woman replied. "Are you a friend of the bride or the groom?"

"The bride," she said. "Well. A friend of a friend of the bride, I guess. I came with the Guy of Honor."

The woman's expression softened with a knowing smile. "You must be Jessie."

She looked into the oddly familiar greenish-blue eyes of the striking woman. "Yes. Jessie Hart."

She clasped both hands around Jessie's and grinned. "Jessie, I was looking so forward to meeting you."

"You . . . were?"

"I'm Margaret Callahan. Danny's mother."

"Oh. I . . . Danny didn't say you'd be here. But of course you are. You live nearby, don't you? I'd forgotten that."

She pointed one finger over her left shoulder. "Just down the beach. Steph spent as much time at our house as she did her own."

"Their friendship is so lovely."

"Danny's father and I weren't blessed to give him siblings, so he filled the void with some spectacular friendships over the years." After a quick beat, she smiled. "Oh. I'd like you to meet my husband, Patrick." She leaned back slightly so that Jessie got her first glimpse of the dapper suntanned man seated on the other side of her. "Paddy, this is Danny's friend Jessie."

"Pleased to meet you, Jessie."

"You too," she managed.

Except for his smooth, clean-shaven skin and thick silver-white hair, the resemblance between father and son was unmistakable. When Patrick Callahan smiled at her, his dazzling blue eyes took perfect form inside distinguished lines and beneath dark groomed eyebrows that told the history of his now-silver hair.

A cellist at the front of the tent played the first notes of Pachelbel's *Canon in D*, and Jessie's stomach muscles tightened. A wave of nausea crashed as another beachside wedding skittered through her mind in quick musical flashes. The same piece of music had been played by a stringed quartet at her Malibu wedding to Jack.

Vince, his best man, and Danny took their places near a dark-suited reverend, and the cellist transitioned to an introduction of Mendelssohn's *Wedding March*. Jessie stood along with the other guests, and emotion choked her slightly as Steph—on the arm of her very handsome father—began the walk toward Vince. She admired Steph's sense of style. Her bold choice of chiffon palazzos and rhinestone-encrusted heels for bridal garments made Jessie take a new look at Danny's federal agent friend.

Once they passed, she turned her attention to the front of the tent where Vince watched his bride approach, his back to the spectacular pink and purple watercolor sunset and very blue Pacific Ocean. The groom's adoring expression choked her breath slightly, leaving it halted in her throat.

She caught Danny's eye, and he did a double-take when he spotted her companions. An entire conversation exchanged between them in that fleeting moment.

You're sitting next to my parents.

They're nice.

Be careful what you say.

Quit worrying. It's fine.

I kind of hate it when worlds collide like this.

Hush and look at your friend, the beautiful bride.

Her nose wrinkled and she suppressed a giggle as Danny broke the connection between them and nodded at Steph.

"Everyone, please be seated," the minister stated, and Danny's mother reached over and squeezed Jessie's hand as they complied.

"My son looks so handsome," she whispered.

"Yes, he does," Jessie replied with a grin. She decided not to add that she hadn't yet experienced a time when Danny didn't seem like the most attractive man in the room to her.

"Family and friends of the bride and groom," the minister said, "welcome to the celebration of marriage between Stephanie Ann Regnier and Vincent Robert Neff. This amazing setting serves to remind us that, like the ocean, our lives ebb and flow. To enter into the bonds of marriage does not also mean you're entering the proverbial endless summer where all your cares are washed away with the surf and healed under the warm rays of the sun—"

Well, that's for sure, Jessie thought, somewhat bitterly. *At least that's not what my marriage meant.*

"—but like the ocean, a solid commitment of this kind stands on the firm foundation that, as surely as the tide goes out, it will also return. Stephanie and Vincent share a deep and abiding faith in God, and they've asked Vincent's sister Rosalie to do a reading from Ecclesiastes."

A beautiful teenage girl wearing a bridal wrist corsage stood and accepted a wireless microphone. She grazed her brother with a nervous little smile before reading.

"From Ecclesiastes, chapter four," she said. "Verses nine through twelve. 'Two are better than one because they have a good return for their hard work. If either should fall, one can pick up the other. But how miserable are those who fall and don't have a companion to help them up! Also, if two lie down together, they can stay warm. But how can anyone stay warm alone? Also, one can be overpowered, but two together can put up resistance. A three-ply cord doesn't easily snap.'"

"Thank you, Rosalie," the minister said, and he turned to face Steph and Vince. "The third strand in the threefold cord of your relationship is the God in whom you have placed your faith. He is the foundation of your faith and the cornerstone of your marriage. If you start your lives with this in mind, you'll weather any obstacle or struggle you eventually face."

Emotion squeezed Jessie's heart, and she fought back a mist of tears. She couldn't help wondering . . . If she and Jack had started out their marriage as two cords braided together with a shared faith in God as a third, would they have endured?

No, she finally decided. Hindsight clearly revealed that she and Jack hadn't even been bound together—despite the whole cheesy *Now-We're-One* theme of their wedding—much less with a third cord of mutual Christian faith.

As Vince and Steph recited their vows, Jessie's mind drifted beyond them—past the minister and the wafting panels of chiffon, all the way out to where the waves lapped against the sand—and a scene replayed like an old-fashioned projector showing a movie against a white tent screen. It hadn't been so long ago when she and Danny had strolled along a similar beautiful beach and, while stopping to inspect the first tide pool Jessie had ever seen up close, their conversation had drifted to his own deep faith.

"I'm mesmerized by sea life myself," Danny told her that day. *"I often wonder how anyone can see all of this and not believe in the God who created it."*

"You really believe, don't you?" she'd asked him. *"With everything inside of you, you believe in God."*

"With everything," he answered with a nod.

Jessie's gaze floated to Danny now. As his mother had noted, he looked *so handsome* standing there behind Steph. Maybe even more attractive because of the solid belief that colored everything around him. She marveled at the fact that he'd been able to grab hold of such a faith after the vehicle he drove while intoxicated had drifted across the lane. A head-on collision had taken the life of his wife, Rebecca. And yet Danny had somehow managed to get out of bed after that . . . much less learn to love and worship the God in charge of things.

Jessie wondered if she would ever have the strength and where-withal for such a thing. Even though she'd been raised within the fringes of Christian faith, she'd never really embraced it for herself. She'd come close a time or two—like in high school when she and her friends sat whispering in the back of a church service, and one of the girls suddenly jumped to her feet and rushed to the altar to acknowledge Christ as her "personal Savior." She remembered seeing the angelic expression on Josie's face afterward and feeling overwhelmed with admiration—and even envy—for the courageous move that put it there.

"By the power vested in me by the State of California and our Lord Jesus Christ, I bestow on this couple every blessing and benefit our God has to offer. And I pronounce Stephanie and Vincent bound together as man and wife."

Such power given to a God they couldn't see or touch. But Jessie stood with the others, applauding for this God-ordained union. And the distant taste of that admiration and envy she'd felt for Josie Markoff's declaration of faith burned the back of her throat.

Made Jessie dress up nice each and ever' Sunday, and we'd walk the couple blocks to church. She didn't like it much, but I made her go anyways. The Good Book says you train up a child in the way they s'posedta go, and when they get older they'll remember it.

Still waitin' on the back end o' that promise. Still prayin' ever' night for those scales to come off her blue eyes so she kin see 'er Savior holdin' out his hand.

Ain't no promise in all the Scriptures that swirls the drain. If He promised it, He's gonna do it, and that's the fact. Sometimes it ain't easy for my Jessie to keep her head tilted up, but one day she'll look up at just the right time so's she and Jesus will meet face to face.

Take that as 'nother prayer for her, would ya, Lord?

14

It was a lovely ceremony," Jessie said as she embraced Steph. "I was really moved."

"As were Paddy and I," Margaret Callahan chimed in as she joined them.

"Marg," Steph exclaimed, and the women hugged like the old friends they were. "I'm so glad you made it."

Jessie repeated the name in her head. *Marg.* She didn't think she'd ever heard that variation on Margaret. Not in real life, anyway. With her short blonde haircut and long, elegant neck, Marg Callahan seemed like perfect casting for the role of Danny's mother.

"My three favorite women in one spot," Danny declared as he moved between Jessie and his mother and placed his arms around their shoulders. "Steph Neff, ladies and gentlemen."

Jessie giggled.

"I told you I'm keeping my name, loser."

"Ah, but I was hoping you'd change your mind. I can get a lot of mileage out of Steph Neff jokes."

"Behave yourself," Marg reprimanded him.

"Yes, listen to your mother," Steph teased. "Go do what you do best—"

"Class up the joint?"

"—and fetch your mother and your date a little sustenance."

Danny chuckled. Leaning toward Jessie, he asked, "Join me?"

"Love to."

"Mom?"

"No, your father is inside putting something together for us."

"Let's check it out." He took Jessie's hand, and the two of them crossed the threshold into the house.

The living room furniture had been removed and replaced with white leather couches and matching oversized chairs on one side of the massive stone fireplace; on the other side, several food tables with uniformed attendants. A beautiful white, three-tiered wedding cake topped with a crystal monogram and trimmed with sugar versions of the flowers of the day—lavender roses and green hydrangea—occupied a round table as the centerpiece of the room.

Danny took the open spot next to his father at the carving station. "Jessie, have you met the old man?"

They exchanged matching smiles, and Patrick Callahan's blue eyes sparkled. "Watch who you call *old*, son."

"We met outside, yes. The ceremony was beautiful, wasn't it, Mr. Callahan?"

"It was indeed." He nodded at the attendant and said, "Well done, please." Turning to Danny, he added, "You know your mother. If there's a speck of pink on her prime rib, she won't eat it."

"In recent years, my mother has become an epic fail of a vegan," Danny told her. "She loves animals of all kinds, and she really doesn't want to eat them. But prime rib is her downfall, so if the life is cooked out of it . . ."

"I get that," Jessie joked. With a grin to Danny's father, she added, "I suppose I'm a vegan at heart myself. My grandfather used to go crabbing with nets, and then he'd make a big crab dinner out of the little guys I'd already named and wanted to keep for pets. It became a sort of tradition—everyone else at the table had boiled crab, and I had a big plate of macaroni and cheese.

Unfortunately, over the years, I've become much less successful at living out my childhood esteem for anything with a face."

Danny laughed. "A recovering carnivore is what Mom calls it."

"Oh, I've given up on my recovery," she told them. "I'm a full-fledged, card-carrying meat eater now."

When they'd filled their plates to satisfaction, Jessie and Danny joined his parents at a table on the deck. One of the roaming waiters brought them each a glass of champagne, and Danny turned his in for a non-alcoholic version.

"Here's to Stephanie and Vincent," Patrick said, and he raised his glass.

"And to having a meal with our son and his lovely friend," Marg added. She grinned at Jessie and said, "It's been a long time since we've shared a table with Danny. Having you along makes it perfect."

Jessie devised a mental list of the few boys she'd dated before marrying. Not one of them—including Jack—had a mother so willing to include the object of her son's affections. In fact, she'd always experienced the polar opposite of Marg Callahan. Varying degrees of possessiveness, all of them with the one outlook in common: not one of them deemed Jessie Hart good enough for their son.

"Tell me about your store, Jessie," Marg broke into her recollections. "From what Danny has said, I think it was a stroke of genius on your part. Such a resilient spirit. Your family must be very proud of you."

Jessie propped her fork on the edge of her plate and wiped her mouth with the corner of her napkin.

"Both Jessie's parents are gone," Danny told her. "She was raised by her grandfather."

"Oh, I see. Is he still alive?"

Jessie nodded and smiled. "If I actually am resilient, I got that gene from my Grampy."

"Is he here in California?"

"Louisiana."

"I thought I noticed a slight bit of southern in you," Marg said with a happy grin. "What part of Louisiana?"

"Margaret," her husband interjected. "Let the girl enjoy her meal without being grilled like the shrimp."

"I'm sorry," she told Jessie softly. "I didn't mean to do that. Paddy's right. You should enjoy this wonderful cuisine."

"I don't mind answering your questions," she said with a grin. "It keeps me from embarrassing Danny and asking you all about *him*."

"Yes, tell them about Louisiana," Danny exclaimed. "And about the store. Don't leave anything out."

He and his father broke into a harmonious duet of laughter, and Jessie noticed again how similar the two men were.

"Slidell," Jessie stated. "I'm from Slidell, Louisiana. It's just across Lake Pontchartrain from New Orleans."

"New Orleans," Marg said, looking at her son. "Isn't that where you're headed next month?"

Jessie's neck snapped toward Danny. "You're headed for Louisiana?"

Home. From another life, granted. But still home.

"With Riggs," he said, nodding. "It's a mission trip, a few days to help get one of the schools up and running again."

"Why didn't you tell me?"

"I don't know," he replied with a shrug. "We've had a few dozen things occupying our time lately."

Music in the distance cut into their conversation.

"Oh, look. They set up a dance floor in the tent," Marg exclaimed. "You two should go have a dance. And Danny can tell you his plans for the trip, Jessie. Maybe you'll want to join up, and visit your grandfather while you're down there."

"Marg, really," Patrick commented, shaking his head.

"What? Jessie might like to do some good work alongside your son. In fact, you could stand to be a little more civic-minded your-self, Paddy Callahan."

Danny cracked the small blanket against the ocean breeze before spreading it out over a smooth patch of sand. He supported Jessie by the hand as she sat on the outside corner.

It seemed like an eternity before the wedding cake had been cut and served at last and most of the wedding guests had said their good-byes. A small group of stragglers brought their dessert and various beverages with them and gathered around a fire ring built on the Callahans' adjacent private beach.

Danny stoked the charcoal fire as Steph hiked up her wide-legged pants and plopped on the blanket beside her husband, across from Danny and Jessie. One of Vince's friends strummed a guitar and sang Bon Jovi's "Who Says You Can't Go Home?"

"I know it's my own cake," Steph told them between licks to the back of her fork, "and it might not be cool to say this, but . . . isn't this the best wedding cake you've ever tasted in your life?"

"It just might be," Vince replied, and he kissed the icing from the corner of his wife's mouth.

Danny chuckled at them, and he placed his arm loosely around Jessie's shoulder. He sighed as she leaned into the embrace and tucked her head beneath his chin.

"The Pacific Ocean is so beautiful at night," she said on an exhale. "I guess a full moon overhead doesn't hurt any."

He gazed off into the distant sky, a cloth of midnight blue set with a dazzling plate of silver light. Foamy surf capped leisurely waves as they sang to him a familiar, inviting song. He resolved then and there to set the alarm early enough the next morning to allow time for some wave therapy before church.

"Hey," he said as the thought occurred. "Do you want to go to church with me in the morning?"

Jessie stiffened against him before finally asking, "Really?"

"Yeah, really."

"I haven't been to church since I left Slidell."

Danny's heart felt tender to the touch of those words. "Time you paid a visit then, don't you think?" When she didn't answer, he kissed the top of her head. "They have donuts."

Jessie giggled. "With jelly in them?"

"Yep."

"Okay. Should I meet you there?"

Danny had almost forgotten the day Jessie had admitted to following him to see where he went on Wednesday nights. "That's right. You know where my church is, don't you?" Again, no response. Just a soft snicker. "I'll pick you up at nine."

Vince's buddy started a new tune, and Danny recognized it right away. One of his favorites. Funny that this complete stranger had chosen just that song, at just that moment. The Casting Crowns song "Voice of Truth" had been a pivotal part of the soundtrack of Danny's recovery after the accident that killed Rebecca. He'd had to learn how to forgive himself; and the more difficult feat—to move forward with integrity in the face of his vivid memories of such a massive lack of forgiveness.

Danny lowered his head until his stubbled cheek touched Jessie's soft one. "I'm excited to share this part of my life with you," he whispered. "It means a lot to me that you agreed to come tomorrow."

"I don't want you to be disappointed in me, but . . ." She paused and cleared her throat softly. "I can't really make any promises to you about believing like you do, Danny."

"There's no expectations, angel."

No expectations . . . *but plenty of hope.*

That hope carried Danny through a somewhat fitful night of near-sleep and into the morning when—at seven—he found himself sitting quietly atop Carmen in the sand, his head bowed, praying for the Holy Spirit to plow the road ahead of them that day.

"I can see your hand on Jessie's heart, Father," he silently prayed. "And you know better than anyone how the last year of her life has wounded her. For someone with a limited view of your love—like I had when Rebecca died—recovery hinges on meeting you face-to-face. Prepare her heart, Lord, so that when she does look into your face, she'll be open to reaching out." ·

"Get off your duff, Callahan," Riggs called out as he stomped past, his board balanced on top of his thick head as he headed straight into the water. "Surf's up."

Danny had wondered why Riggs's van wasn't parked out front the way it normally was on any given Sunday morning, but he glanced back now to find Frank stretched out in front of the run-down old thing, not a canine care in the world. He wished he felt as blithe as his dog—or as Riggs too, as a matter of fact. Nonetheless, Danny grabbed Carmen and headed out to find a wave with his name on it.

———

Jessie stuck close to Danny as they climbed the wide brick stairs and entered United Community Church along with a throng of other churchgoers. She could hardly believe she'd agreed to attend Sunday services when Danny invited her, but she couldn't think of a graceful way to back out of it—even though she'd spent the night tossing and turning over several considerations to do just that.

She glanced over at Danny—wearing blue jeans and a casual gray tee with sleeves just short enough to show off the circle of thorns tattooed around his bicep. A symbol of his faith, she recalled as they strolled up the center aisle and slipped into a carved wooden pew a few rows back from the altar.

When the music began, Jessie stood when everyone else did. Danny seemed to know the words to each of the songs, and she wondered what he thought of the fact that, even music as universal as "Amazing Grace," seemed obviously foreign to her. Although the original had been a staple at Grampy's church in Slidell, this version included something about chains being gone. She'd never heard that one before.

When the music concluded and a kind-faced pastor stepped up to the podium at the front of the church, she followed Danny's lead and settled into the pew again. A few moments later, something caught the corner of her eye, and she glanced across the aisle to find Allie waving at her, grinning. She subtly waved back before noticing *both of her parents* seated next to her. Charlotte grinned at Jessie, and she relaxed a little.

The pastor started out with a reading from the New Testament book of James, a passage that seemed comfortably familiar to her. He went on to explain that many people in today's world felt they could work their way to heaven on good works alone, but that the things people did for others was just a fruit of their faith. Jessie didn't fully understand the message, but she did feel oddly compelled to lean into it and soak up what she could. Toward the end of the sermon, she found herself thinking about the mission trip Riggs and Danny had planned to help rebuild one of the schools that had been damaged by Hurricane Katrina and never reopened in all that time. She supposed it was their faith in God that was the catalyst to do such unselfish things, and she wondered if she would be a less selfish person if she gave into the call to commit her life fully to the God who Danny and Aaron served.

At the altar call, she remembered her friend Josie again. She almost wished she still had it in her to make such a naïve, wide-eyed commitment to a God she couldn't see; to a God who had allowed Jack to deceive her for so long. No, she didn't have much wide-eyed teen left in her these days. That girl had been replaced by a woman beaten down by the hard knocks of reality. As the band played a moving song identified in the program as "I Need a Miracle," she watched a line of people file to the front of the church. Jessie inhaled sharply when she noticed that one of them . . . was *Charlotte*.

Jessie jerked her head toward Danny, only to find that his narrowed eyes had misted over with a pool of emotion. Something important had happened here to Aaron Riggs and his family. She didn't know what it was exactly—or how it would all shake out—but she could see that Danny had been profoundly moved by it.

After the service, Allie walked out with Jessie and Danny. Not one ray of light could be seen between Riggs and Charlotte as they left the church, locked together, Charlotte sobbing. Before she could figure out what had happened, Danny circled back to Riggs and whispered something to him. Riggs, in turn, kissed Charlotte's hand and spoke softly to her before he and Danny took off across the parking lot at a full run.

"Danny?" she called. "What is it?" When he didn't respond, she turned to Charlotte. "What happened?"

"They're chasing that guy," Allie exclaimed, and Jessie followed the invisible line between the girl's pointed finger and the rumble of male bodies on the ground across the lot.

"Allie, you stay right here," Charlotte demanded as she wiped the running streams of tears from her face with a wad of tissues. "I mean it."

Allie stomped her foot and clicked her tongue, but she didn't go anywhere.

Danny got to his feet and yanked someone from the ground while Riggs inspected what appeared to be a camera with a long lens attached. Jessie squinted to no avail in hopes of getting a better look at the young blond in Danny's grip. She stood frozen to the spot between Allie and her mother, watching, her mind racing with possible scenarios that could have sent the two of them flying across the church lot to tackle the boy.

"Do you know him?" Charlotte asked Allie.

"No!" she barked back. "Why do you automatically think this has to do with me?"

While the two of them bickered softly, Danny raised his arm and waved Jessie over to them. As she took her first step, Charlotte barked at Allie. "Not you. You're staying here."

The gap between them nearly bridged, Jessie stopped in her tracks with a gasp.

"Heath?" she cried out, and the young perfect-haired valet from Antonio's restaurant turned away from her.

———⦅∞⦆———

Just like her mama 'fore her, my Jessie always noticed the details. Ever'body else likely watchin' the main event, and she notices the guy in the corner with the blue hat and mismatched socks. Jessie always seemed to see the things the rest of the world walked right by and never saw. That's why it's been so hard on her times when she missed somethin' starin' her right in the face.

"Grampy, I can't believe I thought she was my friend."

"Grampy, how can you not remember what shoes I was wearin' Thursday night?"

That Jack Stanton she married was the worst of 'em.

"He fooled me, Grampy. How could I not have seen the truth? How could I have looked right into his eyes ever' mornin' and ever' night and didn't have one hot clue what he was upta?"

As unlikely as it seems, sometimes the truth is so unexpected, even the most observant ones of us looks right on through it.

15

Danny held Heath the Valet's camera by its lens, his pulse steadily increasing with each push of the arrow on the back of it. The large screen acted like a digital time machine, starting with Danny and Jessie on the stairs of United Community Church that morning . . . Jessie dancing with his father at Steph's wedding . . . sitting across a restaurant table from Piper . . . unlocking the door of her apartment . . . and the way-back machine ended—*or started?*—with the signage at Jessie's store.

"Oh, Danny," Jessie said on a sigh as she pressed in to look at the camera screen.

"You're how Stanton knew where to find us at the restaurant that first night," Danny stated. "How long have you been reporting back to him about Jessie?" When the kid didn't answer, Danny summoned every ounce of restraint within him. He leaned forward and glared directly into his eyes. "I'm trying not to throttle you, kid. It's your turn to talk. Was he paying you?"

Heath looked over at Jessie, and she seemed to hold his gaze captive for a long and frozen moment before he answered. "Yeah. He was paying me."

"Oh, Heath," she cried.

"Keep talking," Danny demanded. "When did it start?"

"I don't know. A while ago."

"Give me a frame of reference, kid."

"I don't know," he repeated with a little more volume to it. "A couple of weeks after the store opening, I guess."

Jessie gasped. "You've been—what?—following me around? And reporting back to Jack?" She moved closer and touched Heath on his free arm. "Why, Heath? Why would you do something like this to me?"

"I'm sorry," he whimpered. "I got to know Mr. Stanton when you used to come to the restaurant together. He was always nice to me. One night we got to talking about film school. You know. You were *there*. Well, the next day, he stopped by again while I was working and he gave me a fat check to help with tuition. I didn't ask him. He just did it, you know? He said he knew AFI isn't cheap, man."

"And that bought him the right to get you to stalk his wife?" Riggs chimed in. "Any one of us can say, 'Yeah, American Film Institute. That ain't cheap.' Are you kidding me, dude?" Brushing his forehead with the back of his hand, he almost looked like he might haul off and sucker-punch the kid. Instead, he groaned. "Stanton's nothing more than sewage. Don't you know that? But then he knew your price, didn't he?"

Danny pushed out a sigh. He knew Heath the Valet wasn't the one either of them wanted to deck.

The guy stole from his clients, ripped the rug out from under Jessie's life and left her with nothing, and then he turns Malibu Robin Hood to a random kid with tuition problems.

"I heard the talk, you know?" the too-pretty blond kid continued. "I figured he was long gone, and then he just showed up at my apartment first thing in the morning and says he needs my help and offers me a boatload of cash to make it happen. I guess I just . . ."

"Yeah. We know what you *just*," Danny said as he pulled his cell phone out of his pocket.

"I'm real sorry, Mrs. Stanton."

Jessie slapped her thigh with an open palm and sort of grunted in frustration. "I'm not *Mrs. Stanton*," she growled. Turning away, she added, "I never was."

Danny nearly called Steph before he remembered she and Vince were on their way to lounge on a beach in Waikiki 'right about then. Instead, he punched the numbers on his cell phone to call Rafe. He would know what to do from there.

"Now you're going to make it up to her by repeating your story to someone," he told Heath.

"What can they really do now?" Jessie asked him, and her voice broke. "Is there anything?"

He shrugged. "Maybe add to the charges against him. I don't know. There are new and tighter stalking laws in California."

"What's the law say?" Her voice cracked again as she asked the question.

"Well, stalking is defined as a pattern of willful and malicious behavior. I think the kid's camera proves it's a pattern on behalf of Stanton. And as far as creating a credible threat of harm, maybe a judge will see it our way since there's an order of protection against him." The instant Rafe answered on the other end, Danny nodded at Riggs. "Keep an eye out here."

Riggs wrapped one hand around Heath's arm and nodded him over to a line of large boulders at the edge of the parking lot. "Over here and sit down. Let's go."

Danny covered his free ear with the palm of his hand to hear Rafe over the grind of departure traffic from the adjacent lot. Jessie stayed tethered to his side with an invisible cable as he gave Rafe a quick overview of what had gone down.

Twenty minutes later, a squad car with Rafe and another officer pulled into the church parking lot.

"Where's Stanton staying while he's waiting for his hearing? Do you know?" Danny asked Rafe while the officer who came along led Heath into the back seat of the car. "I need to know where to find him."

"I have no idea where he is, and I wouldn't tell you if I did. It's not helping Jessie"—Rafe paused to nod a greeting to Jessie, and she tried to return it with a polite smile—"if you get yourself arrested for assault. Just let me take the kid, you hand over the camera, I'll alert the feds, and we'll see how it unfolds from there."

"Rafe, listen—"

"You listen, Callahan," he cut in, a soft understanding in his tone. "This is the way to go. Trust me. You go enjoy your Sunday afternoon, and I'll ring you later."

Danny groaned. "Yeah, all right."

Rafe placed his hand on Danny's shoulder and squeezed hard. "Good. Behave yourself."

As the squad car pulled away, he noticed Riggs as he jogged across the parking lot to where Charlotte and Allie still waited next to his van. He looked down at Jessie standing erect and still beside him. "Are you okay?"

She didn't reply. Or move. Or—that he could see—breathe.

"Jess."

When Danny leaned down closer and ran his fingers gently through the hair at the back of her neck, she closed her eyes and sighed. When she opened them again and looked up at him, one large round tear droplet dangled from a clump of lower lashes.

"It's better to know," he said softly. "Now we know."

She sighed again, and the teardrop let go, streaming down her cheek in a perfect straight line until it fell from her chin.

"I'm tired of knowing things. I think I'd like to go back to not knowing anything at all."

He smiled and dried her cheek with his thumb. "I know it feels that way, but you don't mean it."

Danny slipped his arm around her waist and led her into a little twirl until she faced him. With both arms around her waist, he drew her gently into him. It felt a little like embracing a porcelain doll; she just stood there, rigid and lifeless. He kissed the top of her head several times before she finally leaned into him a bit. Another few moments ticked past before her arms drifted around him limply. Finally, she angled her head slightly and rested it against his shoulder.

"I'm . . ." she murmured.

"You're—"

". . . hungry."

Danny laughed out loud at the unexpected shift of gears. "Let's go do something about that then."

He gingerly led her across the parking lot toward the Jeep, his arm firm around her shoulders. When they had almost reached it, she made an abrupt stop. She'd rolled her arm several times before he realized she had motioned to Riggs and his clan, still standing at the rear bumper of his van. Allie started toward them first, followed by Charlotte and Riggs.

"We're going to lunch," Jessie said. "Please come along?"

Charlotte looked to Danny for consideration. When he nodded, she grinned. "We'd love to."

"Ooh, Danny," Allie cried. "Let's go to that place where you took me for brunch on my birthday." Turning to her mother, she continued, "You can look out the window, and the ocean is right there. And they have lemon pancakes."

"Lemon?" Charlotte said, wrinkling her nose.

"Yeah, they're awesome."

"Lemon ricotta," Riggs corrected. "And they *are* pretty awesome."

Charlotte laughed, and Jessie looked at Danny with a question in her eyes.

"Coast," he answered it. "Over at the Shutters on the Beach hotel. Have you been there?"

"No. Let's go there then. I'm starving."

"And Danny, we can get Teenage Mimosas!"

Now Charlotte looked at him with the unspoken question.

"Orange juice," he said, and her entire face relaxed.

"Daddy likes the Bulls-Eye, don't you, Daddy?" she said, grabbing Charlotte's hand and then reaching for Jessie's. "It's a skillet, and it's real spicy. It has eggplant in it, which I didn't think I'd really like, but it wasn't so awfully bad. Do you like eggplant, Jessie?"

"Sometimes," she replied, casting Danny a lopsided grin. "It depends on how it's cooked."

"We can get a table near the window so we can see outside. At a booth, with blue striped pillows. And then you can tell Jessie and Danny our good news, Mom."

"Good news?" Danny questioned.

"Yeah, we're gonna be a family again."

His head practically jerked in Riggs's direction. "Are you now?"

Riggs shrugged one shoulder. "Yeah."

Danny felt a missile of relief shoot straight through his gut.

"I also want to hear your mother's other good news," he said.

"Is there more?" Allie asked curiously. "You have more good news, Mom?"

"I think he wants to know about when I went to the altar this morning."

"Oh, yeah," her daughter stated. "I have some questions about that, too."

<hr>

"Thank you, Mr. LaHayne," Jessie said with a sigh. "I appreciate anything you can do to keep me in the loop."

She disconnected the call and tucked her cell phone back into the outside pocket of her bag before glancing at Charlotte where she leaned against the lovely white picket fence that stood between her and the beach. The ocean breeze picked up the wide sleeve of Charlotte's pale blue blouse and rustled the long, dark ponytail gathered with a braided band and falling over the slope of one shoulder.

"That's your lawyer?" she asked as Jessie joined her there.

"Yes. He's been helping me navigate this whole mess with Jack."

"It's good that you have someone."

"I just don't know what Jack is trying to accomplish, you know?" she said, thinking out loud. "It makes no sense. He can't possibly think . . . I mean, we were never even legally married. What does he want out of me?"

Jessie's pulse thumped in her temples. She rubbed them with the tips of her fingers until Charlotte startled her by placing her hands on Jessie's shoulders.

"You are going to come out on the other side of this," she stated confidently, and Jessie smiled. She wanted so much to believe her.

"Promise?"

"Yes," Charlotte replied with a firm nod.

"Is this newfound faith after this morning's event at church?" Jessie asked. "Or are you always so optimistic?"

"Maybe a little of both."

Charlotte slipped her arm through Jessie's and stood there quietly, both of them gazing out at the water.

"Can I ask you something?" Jessie said.

"You want to know about me going to the altar."

She chuckled at her insight. "Is it too personal?"

"No," she replied. "Not at all. I've grown a little stagnant in my faith since Aaron and I split. But I've been feeling that tugging again recently, and I started to see God working in his life as well as ours . . . mine and Allie's."

"When did the two of you decide to get back together?"

"We've been talking for a while," she said. "It's been kind of gradual, but we sat Allie down last night and we discussed it as a family."

"Are you excited?"

Charlotte chuckled. "Having Aaron come home seemed like a big gamble at first, to be honest. But yes, I'm really excited to see where we're headed." A wide, sunny grin spread across her face as she added, "It's a whole new start for us as a family, and for me in my faith."

A stone dropped inside Jessie and bounced a couple of times before falling still. It had begun to feel lately like every new beginning she tried to forge fell as flat and heavy as that stone pressing down in the pit of her stomach.

"I'm really happy for you," she said with a smile that had to be forced upward. "I really am."

"I'm glad we're friends, Jessie."

Her cell phone rang as she replied, "So am I."

Amber.

"Excuse me for a minute?"

"Of course. I'll go find Allie."

"See you in a few minutes." Once Charlotte went back inside, Jessie answered the call. "Hi, Amber. What's up?"

"I'm just checking in to let you know Courtney called a few minutes ago. She wants to talk to you as soon as you have the time."

Another weight went right down into her stomach. "Did she give you any clues?"

"Nothing solid, but she did say she spoke to Perry Marconi. She said he told her there were some good options for Misha and Marianna."

"Okay. Well, that sounds almost promising."

"I said you would Skype her later in the day."

"Good, Amber. Thanks."

"Hey, Jessie?" she said carefully.

"Yep."

"Everything okay?"

"Yes, why?"

"You sound . . . I don't know. Not like yourself."

"It's been a very eventful Sunday for me, Amber." She grinned and shook her head. "I'll come over to the store as soon as we finish lunch and tell you all about it then."

Jessie disconnected the call and, before she had the chance to tuck away the phone, Danny touched her on the shoulder.

"Did you speak to LaHayne?"

"Yes. He's going to communicate with the agents and the prosecutor and fill them in on Heath."

"I hope you won't mind, but I called Piper while you were out here. She'll let Antonio know about the kid."

"Thank you," she said with a sigh. "I'm sure that was a noisy conversation."

Danny chuckled. "She had plenty to say."

"I can only imagine." Shifting gears, she asked, "Can you drop me at the store from here? I have to try and Skype with Courtney in London. Do you know what time it is there?"

"I'm pretty sure they're eight hours ahead of us," he said. After a quick mental calculation, he added, "So it's late evening. Almost eleven."

"Phooey. And she's got a small baby in the house."

"Still want to go to the store?"

"Yeah, I'd better try, at least," Jessie told him. "She told Amber she needs to talk to me."

"Good news? Or bad?"

"I think it's good. But I don't want to wait until tomorrow morning to know for sure."

"I'll drop you and then head home myself," he said. "I got a voice mail from Cynthia Ross earlier. I want to call her back and see what she has to say."

"The reporter?"

"Yeah, Piper hooked us up so I could get her help on—"

"A case. I know. She told me. Did she tell you to *stay stylish*?" she teased, but Danny's confusion spoke loud and clear through his expression. "That's how she ends her broadcasts." In her best Cynthia Ross voice, she sang, *"Stay stylish, Los Angeles."*

He laughed and shook his head. "Let's hit the road then."

"I'm ready when you are. But let's go back inside and say good-bye to our brunch companions first."

"I don't wanna talk about Jack, Grampy."

"Why's that?" I ask her.

"I don't want him muddying up any more of my water."

Good enough for me. Jessie and me have weekly phone calls where we talk about watchin' paint dry 'round Slidell, and who Maizie Beauchamp's old hound dog bit next. She tells me 'bout her store and the fish-faces who come 'n rent out her clothes like an overpriced hotel room for the weekend when they can hardly pay the rent on their crummy apartments. Don't understand the whole idea, but it seems to make Jessie happy talkin' 'bout it.

Subject o' that Stanton fella comes up an' I can feel my Jessie tense up straight across the miles.

"I really miss you, Grampy," she says to me.

"Get yerself on a airplane then. That'll solve it."

Her voice growed soft as a marshmallow center when she says, "I wish I could."

I don't tell her I'm hopin' she makes wishin' into doin' before the Good Lord pulls the plug on my time, or remind her she's been gone from 'er Luziann roots way too longa time. I don't tell her how much I need to see her neither. I just keep a-prayin' the Lord'll whisper in her ear when the lights go out and her head hits the pilla.

"Go see yer Grampy," I can hear Him say to her. "Get yer duff on a airplane soon, young Jessie."

Real soon, I'm hopin'.

16

Danny had spent a couple of hours catching up on paperwork, pressing Rafe about Heath the Valet, and chatting with Rochelle Silverstein about the upcoming awards event until Cynthia Ross finally called him back.

"It looks like I might have some information for you," she said in a somewhat cautious tone. "At least I think it might lead you in the right direction."

"I'll take what I can get here," he replied. "I appreciate you even talking to me about it."

"The awards committee has had a specific security firm under contract for the last couple of years," she began, and Danny already sensed where she was headed. His instincts had pointed him in that direction from the very first. "Weston Security has someone in their employ with ties to the governing committee. A gentleman with an affection for an actress by the name of Paula Peridot. He apparently set up a camera to take some pictures of her, purely for his own use—"

"Classy guy."

"—and he later discovered a lucrative market for pictures of that sort. From what I can tell, this is where it started, and the guy has been using his backstage connections to sell visuals and tidbits to the highest bidders ever since."

"Do you know his name?" Danny asked her.

"I'm sorry. This is a delicate issue since we're under the same umbrella."

"Could you confirm a name for me?"

The telephone connection hummed with silence before she replied. "Perhaps."

"Tercot?"

"I would pursue that avenue further if I were you, Danny," she said slyly.

"Cynthia, you've been more than helpful. Thank you very much."

"Happy to oblige. Give Piper my best."

"Will do."

Now to confirm that George Tercot's nephew did, in fact, run Weston Security. That should solve the mystery. Catching him in the act would be another matter.

Frank's low growl called Danny's attention to the open door, and by the time he reached it the dog had kicked into a full-on tirade of barks and snarls.

"Frank. Enough."

He stood outside the door, working to focus on the dark shape on the far side of the concrete patio out back. Someone appeared to be seated on the picnic table, doubled over with their feet propped on the bench below them.

Frank growled again, and Danny tugged at his collar. "Home." The dog obediently returned to the front door and sat in front of it while Danny made slow and steady work of closing the gap between himself and the stranger. As he moved closer, however, he realized it wasn't a stranger at all.

"Jess?"

Jessie jerked at the sound his voice and straightened.

"Angel, what are you doing sitting out here all by yourself? Are you all right?"

"Mm-hmm," she muttered, nodding.

"Something happen?"

She dropped her head and sniffled.

"Jessie."

He used the bench for a boost before dropping to the tabletop next to her. She responded to his arm around her shoulder by melting under it as if it were made of fire, immediately sinking into him. Before he even knew she'd started crying, Jessie pushed her head into his chest and wailed.

"Okay. It's fine. Just turn it loose."

The pain in her cries threatened to break Danny's heart straight in two, reminding him of an injured animal or a baby in crisis. He wanted to scoop her into his arms and carry her away to somewhere safe, but he had no idea where that place might be.

She began speaking to him—he felt the vibration of her words as they jammed against his chest—but he couldn't make out what she said. He crooked her chin beneath his finger and lifted her face, looking into those reddish blue eyes of hers.

"What are you trying to say?" he asked, using his thumb to wipe away the smears of mascara under her eyes.

"I . . . don't . . . have *tissues with me.*"

Danny couldn't help the laugh that popped out of him. "Let's go inside and I'll get you some."

He stretched his legs and stepped over the bench before offering his hand to Jessie. She wobbled slightly when she stood, and he wrapped his arm around her waist and lifted her safely to the ground. Frank, sleeping in front of the door, lifted his head and panted as they approached.

"Outta the way, boy," he said, and his nearly two hundred pounds of cow-dog complied with a groan. "Make yourself at home," he told Jessie, and she headed for the blue leather sectional while he went in search of a box of tissues.

When he returned with all he could find—a fresh roll of toilet paper—and handed it to her, Jessie looked up at him from the corner of the couch and tried to smile. "Thanks."

"You want coffee?"

"Uh-uh," she replied. "No."

Unrolling a wad of paper about five times as long as she'd need to blow that little nose of hers, she wadded it up and wiped her drenched face with it. She deposited the used clump of tissue on the sofa next to her leg before unrolling another handful and blowing her nose into it with a high-pitched trumpet blast.

"Water, maybe?"

"Huh?" she asked, her clear-blue eyes pinched and now a stormy shade of silver.

"Can I get you anything at all?"

"No," she said sweetly, her weepy eyes wide. "But thank you for asking."

He grinned—*Courteous to the end*, he thought—and he sat on the edge of the rustic farm table in front of her.

"Do you want to tell me what's going on?"

She blew her nose a second time, this time sounding off with a honk, as she shook her head. "No," she finally said.

"O-*kay*," he commented as he stood and went to one of the two tan club chairs on the other side of the coffee table and dropped into it. "But I'm pretty sure you didn't come over here just to borrow a roll of Charmin."

She giggled and wiped her nose.

"So I'll just sit here until you pull yourself together."

Frank circled the sectional and stood in front of Jessie—so tall that their faces almost met at the same height.

"Hi, Frank," she said without flinching. Casting a glance at Danny, she added, "He's already eaten, right?" The dog lowered his big head and sniffed Jessie's leg before giving her one comforting lick on the hand. "Oh. Well, thanks."

Danny sat watching her scratch the dog behind the ear and down the slope of his nose before he finally asked, "Do you want to tell *Frank* what happened?"

He achieved the intended result, and Jessie chortled with laughter.

"I think I might like to, yes." She leaned forward until their noses nearly touched. "Mean old Perry Marconi decided not to let me style his clients, Frank. And that's not just a blow to me, but a bigger blow to Courtney who took a chance on me and had to be the one to tell me Mr. Marconi doesn't think I'm a big enough deal in all-important Tinseltown to take a couple of outfits off the hanger and put them on his brass-plated actresses."

Frank snorted, like the good and understanding dog Danny knew he was.

"I know," Jessie continued. "Pretty lousy, right? I hope you never have a dog groomer who makes you feel like a complete and utter"—her composure crumpled—"*failure*."

Danny stood and stalked straight to the sofa. "Move, boy." Once Frank lumbered out of his way, he sat down next to Jessie and leaned forward with his elbows propped on his knees, his hands folded between them.

"Everything you've come through, and you're going to let a guy like this determine you're a failure?" he said softly. "That's not the Jessie I know."

"No?" she muttered.

"No. You're still standing." When she snickered, he clarified, "Figuratively. And your business is—against all odds—off the ground and running. Even expanding gradually. Didn't you tell me that?"

"I guess."

"And speaking of your expansion . . . do you have something in this new men's section that might fit me?"

Jessie cackled. "You want me to dress you," she stated suspiciously.

"I thought you might."

"For a specific event? Going to the opera? A museum opening?"

"Are you mocking?"

"Sorry," she said sincerely.

"An awards ceremony," he declared. "And until right now, I thought you might like to go with me, but now—"

"The FiFis?" she exclaimed. "Danny, you want me to go to the FiFis with you?"

"Please stop saying *FiFi*," he cracked.

"C'mon. You want me to go with you?"

"Well, I've scrapped that plan now. I would be happy to escort you to breakfast at Denny's, however. Or maybe we could grab a couple of dogs from the cart outside of Costco?"

"Are you finished?" she said on a laugh. Then she sighed, leaned back into the soft leather couch, and rubbed her tear-stained face. "I'm so tired." As if it came as a sudden revelation, she added, "And hungry. Got anything good to eat in there?"

One chuckle clucked out of him. "Probably not. Riggs was here earlier."

"Mind if I look?"

Danny lifted one shoulder in a shrug before leaning back and stretching one arm along the back of the couch. "Knock yourself out."

Jessie dragged herself forward and stood. After a full-body stretch, she kicked off her shoes and padded into the kitchen. Frank yawned and looked at Danny as if to question this action as she opened the refrigerator and stared into it.

"I warned you," Danny said, but Jessie waved her arm at him without turning around.

"Hold your horses, smarty pants. I see something that might have promise. Do you have any bread?"

"In the box on the counter."

She pulled several items out of the refrigerator and used her foot to kick the door shut behind her. With the little room she had left in her hands, she grabbed the open bag of potato chips on the counter. Danny got up and walked into the kitchen area, shifted his weight to one side and folded his arms across his chest.

Chips. A package of bologna. A couple slices of American cheese wrapped in plastic. Yellow mustard. Butter. Every bit of it—except for the bread—came into the house with Riggs.

I really need to go to the grocery.

"Jessie. What are you searching for?"

"A skillet."

He walked around her, opened the cabinet next to the stove, and handed her the skillet.

"And a spatula."

"Second drawer."

He watched as she turned on the burner under the skillet and dropped four thick slices of bologna into it, cutting slits into the edges with the tip of the spatula.

"What on earth are you doing?"

"Oh, the cuts help keep the bologna flat so it—"

"No," he interrupted. "I mean, what are you *making*?"

She tore off two paper towels from the roll and set them on the counter, then she placed four slices of bread over them. "A very special entrée I learned to make during my time at Chez Grampy," she replied without looking up from her work.

After turning the bologna in the pan, she squirted mustard on all four slices of bread and topped two of them with shiny cheese she freed from plastic covering. Danny winced as she added the bologna to the sandwiches, crunched up a few potato chips and added them, then spread butter on the outside of each before placing them carefully in the pan again.

"Grilled cheese . . . with potato chips and bologna?" he exclaimed. "Are you serious?"

"Fried bologna sandwiches," she said, pressing them down with the spatula. "Don't judge."

"I'm not judging." He shook his head at her. "I'm trying to imagine the woman I met in the Malibu house at the beach frying up bologna and potato chip sandwiches for Jack Stanton's dinner."

"Yeah," she commented with a giggle. "That didn't happen."

"No," he said dryly. "Really?"

"But every time I visit Grampy in Slidell, it's the first thing I make."

"On purpose?"

She crinkled her nose and glared at him, the spatula hovering—looking about as adorable as he'd ever seen her. "Ha. Ha. Ha. Just reserve judgment until you try it, comedian."

He peered down into the skillet and snickered. "Oh, I'm not eating that."

"Please?"

Danny glared at her. "Really? You're going to use the please card on me?"

"Did it work?"

"Whatever. I'll try it. But I'm not eating the whole thing."

"Thank you," she sang, cracking a smile. Returning her attention to the contents of the skillet, she muttered, "And we'll see about that."

⁂

Jessie took a huge bite out of the fried bologna sandwich. Crushed potato chips fell from the other end of the bread, but she didn't care. Salty . . . garlicky . . . kinda greasy . . . the over-processed gastric delight of her childhood. After the day she'd had, this was the only sustenance that would do.

When she glanced across the table and caught the comically contorted expression on Danny's face after his first bite of her creation, she nearly sprayed him with half-chewed bologna.

"Oh, come on," she said, placing her sandwich on the paper towel in front of her. "You can't tell me it's not delicious."

"I can't, huh?"

"Danny, come on."

"Jessie, this is disgusting. You want me to lie?"

"Kinda. I mean . . . are you highly opposed to lying?"

"Little bit, yeah."

"Oh, fine. But you're crazy. This is fantastic southern cuisine in front of us right now. And besides, it makes me feel better. It's Cajun comfort food."

"Jessie, you are not Cajun."

She opened her mouth to object . . . or explain . . . but she couldn't manage it. "Yeah, all right. I'm not."

"And on behalf of all Cajuns everywhere, I don't really think you should inflict this concoction on their culture and expect to be allowed to cross the Louisiana border, even for a visit."

"Speaking of which . . ."

He pushed his sandwich toward her. "Speaking of what?"

"Returning to Louisiana for a visit," she replied. "When are you and Riggs headed down there on your mission trip?"

"On the tenth."

"For how long?"

"Five days, four nights," he answered. "Why? Interested in strapping on your tool belt and doing some construction in ninety-degree heat and six hundred percent humidity?"

She chuckled. "Uh, no. I'm not exactly your tool belt kind of girl, or hadn't you noticed?"

"Oh, I noticed."

Jessie's heart fluttered. "I thought I might go visit Grampy at the same time, and . . . maybe . . . you might like to come to Slidell for a couple of days afterward."

He seemed to freeze for a moment before he asked, "Are you serious?"

"Uh, unless you think we're not . . ." *there yet? No.* ". . . or if you don't think . . ." *you want to meet my Grampy. No.*

Jessie struggled for the words to complete her stammering thoughts, and silently thanked him when Danny interrupted.

"Oh, I'm there," he said, and he brushed her hand with his fingers. "I am so there. I'll e-mail you the itinerary, and you can book yourself on the same flight so we can fly in to New Orleans together. Let me know your return flight, and I can try to rebook on that one."

Jessie's pulse rate doubled, and she could feel the beat of it in both ears. The last time she took a man back to Slidell . . . it was Jack. And that flew like a two-ton solid gold balloon.

My Jessie-girl was born with a pretty face shaped like a heart. "My little Valentine," I usta call 'er. Dark hair, eyes blue as a crystal stream, and a perfect little face shinin' the Lord's light.

Done a lotta prayin' for her over the years. Started prayin' for the right man to come into her life 'fore her mama even left the earth and she came to live with me full-time. When she brought that Stanton fella home to say they was engaged to be married, ain't gonna lie, rocked my faith a little. From the minute he walks in my door, he was lookin' around, evaluatin', turnin' his nose up at the whole town o' Slidell. Couldn't find nothin' to like about the fella 'sides the happy smile on my Jessie's heart-shaped face.

I know'd I hurt her feelin's when I didn't make the trip to LaLa Land for the weddin', but I couldn't stomach such a thing. Walkin' my Jessie up that aisle t'wards him, handin' her off to him like I was all fer such a union. I know'd right off he was gonna hurt her, and I know'd I'd eventually work up a real hate fer 'im if I didn't watch out. What I didn't know was how mad I could even get, or how awful that boy would turn out to be.

Here in Luziann, we gotta sayin'. "You mess with my kin, and I don't retreat. I just reload."

When Jessie filled me in on what he done, I was madder'n a mule with a mouth fulla bumblebees. Same time though . . . felt like a fat trout floatin' downstream in a river o' relief. Ain't nothin' more soothin' than a loved one bein' set free.

17

I can't believe you get to go to the FiFis," Amber said. "I'm green. All the freedom fighters will be there."

Jessie sat cross-legged on her bed, bits and pieces of her makeup kit scattered around her. "What's a freedom fighter?" she asked as she carefully applied blush to the apples of her cheeks.

"You know. The more . . . *conservative* professionals. The ones who stand up for family values in the Hollywood community."

She grinned at Amber through the reflection in the mirror. "Isn't that an oxymoron? Family values and the Hollywood community."

Amber popped out a laugh. "That's funny," she said in relative surprise.

"What did Danny end up choosing? The Armani or the Valentino?"

Amber chuckled. "Valentino. But he didn't like it."

Jessie's entire face curled. "Who doesn't like Valentino?"

"Oh, he liked the way it looked. He just didn't want to wear it," she said. "It tickled me the way he kept tugging on the tie, and buttoning and unbuttoning the jacket."

"But he took the suit, yes?"

"Yes. And do you know what *you're* going to wear?"

Amber flopped onto the bed and Jessie squealed, yanking the liner brush away from her eye. "Hey!"

"Sorry."

She twisted shut the eyeliner and dropped the tube into her makeup case. Before curling her lashes, she warned Amber, "Don't jiggle the bed. I don't want to have to wear fake eyelashes to cover for the ones you make me yank out."

"Okay. So just *who are you wearing, dahling?*"

"Wait until you see the dress I found at Maxim's on Melrose."

Amber gingerly pushed upright. "Where is it?"

"Hanging on the back of the door in the closet. Why don't you bring it in for me."

As she applied mascara to her freshly curled lashes, a smile widened. She could hardly wait to hear what—

"Oh no you didn't!" Amber screeched.

Yep. Just the reaction she'd hoped for.

When Amber returned to the bedroom, she stood in the doorway—the hanger around her neck and Jessie's beautiful sleeveless dress dangling in front of her like a one-dimensional masterpiece covering a paper doll.

Jessie sighed. Flesh-colored illusion fabric trimmed with pink rhinestones topped the perfect sweetheart neckline of the black velvet bodice. The stunning tea-length skirt—pink satin peeking out from beneath a three-quarter overlay of black tulle—was set off by a stiff black satin ribbon tied in a generous bow at the waist.

"It's even more beautiful than I remembered," she observed.

"You are so going to rock this dress, Jessie. And I know just the shoes. You have to wear your Manolos."

"Which ones? Because I was thinking—"

"The silver metallic ones with the Swarovski crystal studs. I'll go get them."

"Well, grab the pink ones too," she called after her. "They're on the second shelf."

"The peep toe satin with rhinestone heels?" she shouted back to her.

"Yes. I was thinking—"

Amber reappeared with only the pink ones before she could complete the thought. "Yeah, you're right," she said, holding one of the shoes up to the dress. "They're perfect with this *gorgeous dress*. Which bag?"

"I'm not sure."

"Oh good! I know which one."

And with that, Amber dropped the shoes and galloped around the corner to the second-bedroom-turned-walk-in-closet, the dress flying off to the side as she went. An instant later, she appeared yet again, this time without the dress necklace and holding a soft cloth drawstring bag with both hands. She sank to her knees and carefully set the dust cover on the edge of the bed. As if opening a sacred scroll, she peeled back the drawstring with two fingers to remove one of Jessie's treasures: *Lily*. The black Marchesa box clutch with black crystals and beads, finished with a clear quartz clasp.

Perfection, Jessie thought.

"It's perfect," Amber breathed in unison.

⬦

Even after having the Jeep detailed, Danny knew it was still no ride for some Joe in a Valentino suit with a woman like Jessie on his arm. With barely enough time to spare following his initial walk-through of the dressing rooms and backstage areas at the Monarch, he took a ride over to his folks' place in Newport Beach to borrow his mom's Infiniti and get back to Santa Monica. He tried for fifteen minutes to make the tie look the way it had when Amber had just about choked him with it, then finally gave up and stuffed it into the pocket of the single-breasted slim-fit jacket.

"I never noticed how tall you are," she had told him. "I guess we're lucky Eddie Whatever-his-name who preowned these suits was a tall drink of water like you, Danny."

He just nodded without admitting to Amber that this wasn't his first rodeo with a designer label. In fact, he preferred the Ralph

Lauren in his closet to this Valentino getup, if she'd really have wanted to know—but that jacket turned out to be too tight when he tried it on, and the trousers didn't drape the way they once did.

After he knocked on Jessie's door, Piper opened it. She grinned and tucked her short strawberry-blonde hair behind one ear, her green eyes glistening as she greeted him.

"Well, look at you," she exclaimed. "Did you forget your tie?"

Danny plucked it out of his pocket and let it dangle from one finger.

"No bow tie?" she teased, taking it from him.

"The Armani had a bow tie, but it didn't feel right around my neck."

Piper stood on her tiptoes to slip the tie into place. She arched one perfect brow and looked him in the eye as she tied the thing. "You look very dapper, Danny."

"I guess that makes me *Dapper Dan*?" he said, and she giggled.

The instant she finished his tie and tapped his shoulders with her hands, Danny caught sight of Jessie standing in the doorway to the hall, a vision in black and pink. His breath caught in his throat as she smiled at him and fidgeted with the large satin bow off to one side of her small waist. He'd heard about moments like this one—mostly in movies, now that he thought about it—when one look exchanged between two people signaled the end of life as they knew it. Corny as it was, Danny felt pretty sure nothing would ever be the same again.

"Jess, you look so pretty," Piper declared.

Danny managed a nod of agreement.

"Thank you. I just need to grab my lipstick and wallet, and I'll be ready."

He nodded again like some kind of mute idiot.

The heels of her pink satin shoes were encrusted with clear rhinestones that glistened at him as she walked away. When she turned around again, tucking a couple of things into a small beaded purse, her smile just about burned his eyes.

"Danny, you look really handsome."

I should have cut my hair.

"You," he said, and it trailed away from him, lost in a cloud of uncharacteristic speechlessness. *What is wrong with me?*

"She looks beautiful," Piper prodded.

"Yes," he finally managed. "You do. Unbelievably beautiful."

"Thank you," Jessie replied, and she tucked the little purse under her arm and touched his hand. "Ready?"

Danny covered her hand with his and held it there. "Ready."

"Before you two leave," Piper said, and they paused at the front door. "Two things. First . . ."

She lifted her iPhone and snapped a picture.

"You look too good to let you leave without a pic. And second, I just wanted to let you know that Antonio fired Heath. We both just want you to know how sorry we are about him."

"I told her they didn't have anything to do with the havoc Jack causes everywhere he goes," Jessie said. "He's a plague of destruction, and he took Heath down with him."

Danny chuckled. "No apologies necessary from you, of all people, Piper. You're Jessie's biggest fan. She knows that, and so do I."

"Well, thank you. I just felt it needed to be said."

The three of them left the apartment, and Danny took Jessie's keys and went to work on securing the door.

"Whose car is that in the driveway?" Jessie exclaimed.

"I thought the Jeep was inappropriate for two people who look like they belong on the cover of a magazine," he said dryly. Nodding back at Piper, he added, "I mean, the paparazzi has already started snapping our picture."

"Where did you get it?"

"I stole it on my way over. It was between this one and a red Porsche, but that clashed with my eyes."

"Nice."

Piper squeezed Jessie's wrist and chuckled. "You two were made for each other." Waving to Danny, she called back to them on her way down the driveway. "Have a good time."

Danny opened the door to his mother's hybrid and waited for Jessie to slip into the soft leather passenger seat before closing it behind her. He willed his heartbeat back into submission on his way around to the driver's side.

"Seriously," Jessie said as they reached the corner of the street. "Where'd you get the car?"

Danny dropped his head back and laughed out loud.

Merging into traffic was a challenge, but the ride was pretty smooth all the way out to the Monarch. Unfortunately, things jammed up six blocks back, and he started to worry about how late they might be. Instead of parking in the garage as planned, he pulled right into the valet circle and surrendered the car to one of several dozen uniformed attendants.

Rochelle spotted Danny and Jessie immediately, and he actually heard her very high silver heels clicking on the marble floor as she rushed out of the open doors toward them. The long tank dress she wore—one hundred percent covered in silver sequins that nearly blinded him when it reflected the insistent flash of cameras on the sidelines of the bright red carpet—boasted a thigh-high slit up one side.

"I hardly recognized you," she said. "Who knew you cleaned up like this? And who's your beautiful friend?"

"Jessie Hart, meet Rochelle Silverstein."

"It's a pleasure," Jessie said as they shook hands in that timid way females sometimes did.

"Same here. Danny, Leslie is waiting with your security credentials at the door to the green room. Miss Hart, why don't I show you to the table where you and Danny will be seated. You'll have a bird's-eye view of everything."

"Sounds good. I'll see you later then?" Jessie asked him.

"I shouldn't be too long. I'll meet you in the ballroom."

Jessie leaned closer and muttered, "I was pretty sure I'd never hear you say those words."

Danny chuckled. He took her hand and lightly kissed her knuckles before they parted.

Leslie McCann's shiny green dress flagged his attention even before her flapping arms. "Danny. Over here. *Daaaan-ny*." Holding the door open with her sizeable derrière, she greeted him with an odd little smile. "Don't you look . . . *unexpected*," she said as she pressed the red badge to his lapel. "Handsome," she clarified. "Very handsome, Danny."

"Thank you. And you look stunning."

Her high-pitched cackle caught Danny by surprise. "Rochelle said I should show you to the backstage area," she announced. "Why don't we go and have a look around."

Leslie led the way through the large green room—which, in spite of its name, was a deep *blue*. A couple dozen formally dressed people mingled and draped on rigid couches and wide chairs. He recognized a few famous faces, but they mostly just ran together with their sequins and beads and bow ties. When it looked as if Leslie intended to join him through the hallway that led to the dressing rooms and backstage area, he stopped her.

"I've got it from here, Leslie. Thanks."

"Oh. All righty then."

He waited for her to turn away before crossing the room again with one goal in mind. "Evening, Mr. Tercot."

George looked up from the appetizers on his small china plate. "Danny. Everything in form?"

"So far, so good," he said with a confident smile. "I was wondering if you might point out your nephew to me."

"My nephew?"

"He's the man to know at Weston Security, I believe?"

George gave a strange twitch before nodding. "Indeedy. He's been here for hours, and I think he has everything on track . . . but I suppose you two could meet. Come with me."

Danny followed the little man down the hallway, past the dressing rooms, and out into the large open styling area backstage. Every one of the tall leather chairs in front of mirrors and tables was occupied, makeup and hairstylists fussing over their subjects. George led the way toward a lanky young guy wearing a red security badge on the lapel of his oversized tuxedo jacket.

"Frasier Tercot, my nephew," George said. "Meet Danny Callahan, your security liaison."

Frasier gripped Danny's hand as if he had something to prove, and he shook it awkwardly. "Nothing to worry about here, Callahan. We have it all under control."

"I said as much," George announced. "I'll be needed out front in a few minutes. You boys play nice."

Once his uncle had moved out of earshot, Danny turned to Frasier with the intent of casually buddying up. "I'm not really up on the Hollywood community. Anybody of note here?"

Frasier's expression instantly told Danny he'd accomplished his goal. "It's part of our job to know who these people are, Callahan. How else can we protect the security of the FiFis if we don't know who's in attendance?"

"Yeah," he said with a nod, "I guess you've been doing this a lot longer than I have. I figured you were the guy to know here tonight."

As he straightened his bow tie and sniffed, the resemblance between Frasier and his uncle became abundantly apparent. "In my mind, there are a few major players here that need our extra attention."

"Yeah? Who are they?"

"Over there in the makeup chair," he nodded. "In the blue dress. That's Saundra Elliott."

"Actress?"

"Reality star. We brought her in through the back so she could avoid the red carpet. The paparazzi are circling for her like sharks because she's supposedly pregnant and everybody's aiming for her baby bump. I'm going to stay on her like jelly on bread all night."

"Good thinking," Danny remarked. Then he made a mental note to keep his eye on Tercot while he kept an eye on Saundra Elliott.

"Down at the end, that's Michael Dellacourt. He's walked the carpet already without his married girlfriend. Victoria Morningside? Well, she's in dressing room number three. The press will risk homicide to get a shot of them together, so I've got a couple of guys ready to escort them out separately just before the show wraps."

Danny nodded. "I admire your forethought. You've really got this thing going like a well-oiled machine, Tercot."

"Well, I should hope so, Callahan. I've been at this a while now."

And betting on being the only one to get those lucrative pictures no one else can get, no doubt.

"Jessie Hart?"

Jessie looked up at the plump woman in the very shiny green dress. "Yes?"

"I'm Leslie McCann. I'm on the governing board."

"Oh. It's a pleasure to meet you."

"Jessie, Danny doesn't think he's going to get out here to be seated before things get underway. He wanted me to ask if you'd like to sit out here without him, or if you'd like to join him backstage."

"Oh." She picked up her clutch and stood. "If no one minds, I'd love to go wherever Danny is."

"I'll take you right to him. Just walk this way."

Walk this way. Jessie pressed back the laughter as Leslie McCann waddled in front of her.

"There he is," the woman pointed out, and Jessie nodded at Danny where he stood to the side of the styling area where a young woman with several sewing kits knelt at the feet of that year's *Most Beautiful Woman*—according to Buzz Magazine— stitching the hem of her stunning gown.

"I'm sorry," he said as she reached him. "I need to stick around back here."

"Something exciting going on?"

"See that guy over there?"

She followed his line of sight—past a woman at the mirrors having her hair styled by one person and the low back of her dress supported by a frame of two-sided tape by another—until she landed on a guy who looked a little like Barney Fife. "In the tuxedo three sizes too big?" she teased.

"That's the guy. As much as I'd like to make use of this monkey suit I'm wearing and enjoy the evening with my beautiful date, I need to stick close to him. But if you're hungry, there are snacks and drinks on a table at the end of the hallway."

"Is there a ladies' room back here?"

"The doors all the way down this hallway are dressing rooms. They should be empty by now, and two of them have private bathrooms. Number one, and number six."

"Excellent. I'll make a quick stop, and I'll go grab some munchies for us and be right back."

"Jess," he said, taking her hand. "Thank you for being so chill about this."

"Are you kidding? I'm backstage at the FiFis with the cutest guy here. I'm great."

She gave his hand a quick rub before heading toward the hallway. The first door on the right had an ornate number 6 on it, and she turned the knob and poked her head inside.

"Hello?"

When no one answered, she stepped in and closed the door behind her. The dressing room walls, painted a steely lavender-gray, held a long row of silver frames around stunning black-and-white still photographs from classic movies. She gave each of them a closer look as she slowly passed.

She supposed the small door at the other end of the charcoal sofa to be the restroom, and she turned the knob.

"Who's there?" a woman's voice called out.

Jessie jumped back. "Oh, I'm sorry. I didn't think anyone was here."

"Are you alone? Can you help me?"

"Um, yes," she said, a frozen grip on the knob. "Is something wrong?"

"Please come in."

Jessie pushed the door open and looked up into instantly recognizable—and striking—violet eyes gazing back at her through the reflection of the mirror over the sink.

Carolyn Coleman!

"My dress," Carolyn said, and she turned to show Jessie that the side seam of her delicate lace gown had completely unraveled. "Can you help?"

"Wait right here, Miss Coleman," she exclaimed. "I saw someone with a sewing kit just a few minutes ago. I'll get it and come right back."

"Thank you, child."

Jessie's heart thudded in her ears as she hurried out of the dressing room and closed the door behind her. After taking three strides at a full run, she slowed herself down and tapped her heart with the palm of her hand.

Carolyn Coleman. Carolyn Coleman. Carolyn Coleman.

Rushing straight past Danny, she hurried to the now-empty chair and rummaged through the makeup utensils, hair products, and random papers on the table. She spotted a fairly substantial sewing kit in a small plastic box hiding under a program from the awards show. She snatched it up as Danny reached her.

"Taking souvenirs?"

She chuckled and showed him the kit on the open palm of her hand. "Carolyn Coleman's seam let loose. I'm going to help her. I'm like a fashion Red Cross."

Jessie hurried away, and his resonant laughter floated down the hall after her. When she reached the door with the number 6 on it, she tapped twice and let herself in.

"Miss Coleman?"

Carolyn Coleman cracked open the bathroom door and peered through it. "Did you find something?"

"I did," she said gleefully, showing her the kit. "Do you want to slip out of your dress? We can sit out here on the sofa where the light is better and I can sew it for you."

Thirty seconds later, the very beautiful Carolyn Coleman handed Jessie her dress and stood there in the doorway in just a bra and half slip. She made a valiant effort not to stare, but Jessie couldn't help noticing how striking this woman in her mid-fifties still looked. Once the dress repairs were underway, she looked up and smiled.

"We've never met or anything, but there is a connection between us, Miss Coleman."

"Oh?" she replied as she sat at the other end of the couch.

"Well, your stylist Perry Marconi works with an associate of mine, Courtney Alexis."

"Oh, yes. I love Courtney."

"She's in London and just took custody of her newly adopted daughter," Jessie said as she carefully stitched the seam.

"Did she?"

"Katie. She's just as pretty as her mother," she editorialized with a grin. "Anyway, while she's over there, Perry came into my shop to see about pulling some dresses for your Lifetime Achievement Award ceremony next month."

"You have a shop?"

"Adornments. In Santa Monica."

"I hope you found something wonderful for me," she said.

"Well, I thought I had, but Perry wanted to go with someone more established than me, so . . ." Jessie shrugged. "He'll come up with something perfect for you."

"I certainly hope so," she replied. "And let's hope it stays together all evening, unlike this one."

Jessie giggled. "I'm sure it will."

After a few moments of silence ticked by, she asked, "What's your name, dear?"

"Oh. I'm sorry. I'm Jessie Hart."

"It's a pleasure to meet you, Miss Hart."

"Call me Jessie," she insisted.

"And you shall call me Carolyn." Jessie thought it sounded very much like a royal order from the queen. Her heart thumped. She wasn't sure she could call this iconic Hollywood actress so casually by her first name.

The moment passed quickly when they were interrupted by a commotion outside the door. When Jessie recognized Danny's voice, she handed Carolyn her dress. "I think that's my date out there, and I don't like the sound of things. I'm pretty sure the seam will hold now. Go ahead and get dressed again, and I'll come back to check on you and let you know if the coast is clear."

Carolyn nodded and hurried into the bathroom with her gown draped over her arm. The instant Jessie stepped into the hall, she locked eyes with Danny standing with Rochelle Silverstein and two men in front of an adjacent dressing room door that stood gaping open. All three of them sported the same red badge as Danny's.

"What's going—"

She couldn't get the entire question out of her mouth before the younger of the two men—the one Danny said he was watching—tried to push past him to leave.

"I don't have to take this from you, Callahan. Not from any of you. I'm out of here."

"You feel free to do that," Danny said. "But I'm sure you won't mind emptying your pockets before you do."

"For what?" he spat. "I'll do no such thing."

"I need to make sure you haven't picked up any additional devices before this one."

Jessie spotted a small contraption in Danny's hand, only about a third of the size of the palm that held it.

The guy turned his pants pockets inside out with two yanks. "Happy?"

"I'll see that he's escorted out," Rochelle said. "George? You'll accompany me?"

The older gentleman huffed, and the three of them stalked down the hallway toward the green room. As Jessie approached him, Danny turned to the final lingering guy and shook his head.

"Do you have any special allegiance to Tercot that I need to know about?"

"No, sir," the smooth-faced guy replied.

"Good. In addition to Saundra Elliott," he said, holding up the small device, "he was also very interested in someone named Victoria Morningside. She was in number three. Why don't you go check that one, and I'll spot check the rooms on the opposite side of the hall."

"You got it."

Danny's eyes thinned to suspicious lines as he watched after the guy.

"What in the world is going on?" Jessie asked. He lifted the device between two fingers and held it out for her to inspect. "What is it?"

"Do you remember Cassie Clinton?"

"The medical student. Someone was taking pictures of her in her bedroom through her cell phone." Jessie remembered Cassie very well. And she particularly remembered that she'd been the one to crack the case when she'd innocently tagged along with Danny.

"Same thing here," Danny said, gazing down at the small circular device. "He's been planting them in the dressing rooms so he can get compromising photographs of celebrities that the rags will pay top dollar for."

"Like a devious nanny cam." Jessie moved closer and stared at the thing. "That's horrible."

"I need to check out the other dressing rooms and try to track down any more cameras."

A sudden thought hit Jessie like a brick in the forehead and she gasped. "Danny, can you come to room six first? Carolyn

Coleman is still in there, and until just a minute ago she was walking around in just her intimates."

He nodded toward the dressing room. "Let's go."

When they reached the door, Jessie rapped lightly. "Miss Coleman? Are you decent?"

"Come right in, Jessie."

She opened the door and leaned inside before seeing Carolyn seated on the sofa, fully clothed again. She pushed through the opening and waved at Danny to follow.

"Carolyn, this is my friend Danny Callahan. He's a private investigator, and he's been handling security for the event."

"I hope everything is all right out there, Danny."

"Just fine, Miss Coleman."

"Carolyn," she told him with a smile.

"I just need to have a look around the dressing room, if you don't mind."

Carolyn cocked a brow and inhaled sharply. "Oh?"

"It won't take but a minute."

"Do whatever you need to do, my boy."

While Danny walked the perimeter of the room, running his hand around the framed artwork on the wall and along the bottom of the bookshelf, Carolyn stood and turned to the side.

"It looks as good as new, my dress," she told Jessie. "You did a very nice job."

She inspected it more closely and nodded. "It does look pretty good."

"But I'm certain I've missed all the fun out there, haven't I?"

"It's not quite over yet. Why don't you go on out?"

"Oh, I'm afraid I'm all *funned out* for this night. I think I'll go home."

Jessie noticed Danny as he discovered another small camera like the one he'd shown her.

"Another one?" Jessie exclaimed as she moved in for a closer look. "They're so small."

"Technology is pretty amazing these days," Danny told her as he turned it over in his hand. "Ten years ago, no one could have imagined—"

"A camera?" Carolyn interrupted. "In the dressing room?"

"Nothing to worry about," Jessie reassured her. "Danny figured it out before anyone could get their hands on them."

"Are you certain?" she asked. "I don't want to stop at Albertson's for a quart of milk and spot myself on one of those papers at the checkout wearing nothing but my bra and underwear."

"Not to worry," he told her. "Jessie, why don't you wait here while I finish a walk-through of the other rooms. And Miss Coleman, it was a pleasure meeting you."

"You as well, young man. Thank you for protecting what little virtue I may have left at this age."

He chuckled. "My pleasure."

As soon as he closed the dressing room door behind him, Carolyn smiled at Jessie. "Well, he's quite delicious, isn't he? Well done, my dear."

Jessie giggled and lifted one shoulder in an awkward shrug.

"You say your shop is in Santa Monica?" Carolyn asked.

She nodded. "It's nothing much. Very small."

"Adornments. Didn't I see a piece about you and your store on the weekend fashion report a while ago?"

She smiled. "They've featured the store twice."

Carolyn leaned forward and cocked one brow. "How about I pay you a visit at your store later this week, Jessie?"

She swallowed around the lump in her throat before croaking, "Really?"

"Well, I'm looking at you right now and admiring your very elegant style, and I can see from your charming dress—not to mention your handsome date—that your taste is impeccable. I'd like to see if your fashion sense can translate to an old bag like me. How's Wednesday morning for you?"

———⟨∞⟩———

"I was thinking about that whole experience thing, Grampy."

Four simple syllables never sounded so filled with meaning. *Experience.*

"And how's that?" I ask 'er, wonderin' how she planned to get around the need fer it when searchin' out her first job there in LaLa Land.

"Well, you always say I'm a pretty personable girl, right?"

"Yeh."

"So I think once I get in the door to meet with them, I'll be able to sell myself as the right person for the job. Don't you think so?"

"I think there's a need for exper'ence and a personable girl when it comes to hirin'."

"But how else am I gonna get experienced if nobody gives me a chance? A secretarial job is just what I need to keep on payin' the rent. I don't want to spend all my money before I get my first modeling job."

My Jessie's winnin' personality didn't get her that secretary job she wanted so bad. But it did get her a spot behind a perfume counter at a highfalutin department store a while later. And that department store got her a no-account husband who left her high 'n dry.

18

So I just wanted to tell you straight out what happened, Court."

Jessie sat on the floor between the sofa and coffee table. She took a sip from her cup of tea and folded one leg underneath her. "I hope you know I'd never go behind your back, or even Perry Marconi's. It was just a completely accidental connection, and I couldn't go to bed for the night until I spoke to you."

Jessie watched the computer screen carefully, scrutinizing every detail of Courtney's reaction. She looked away just long enough to set down the cup, and Jessie flinched when her friend sighed.

"I believe you, of course. I have no doubts about your integrity, Jessie. But at the same time, I've been working with Perry for years. And so has Carolyn Coleman."

"Do you think I should cancel the appointment with her?" she asked, all the while silently chanting *Please say no. Please say no.*

"What I think is the right thing to do is for me to Skype with Perry and just tell him straight out what happened. He may say he wants to be there, which, of course, he'll have to clear with Carolyn on his own. But I feel like full disclosure is going to go a long way in this circumstance."

"Okay. You'll let me know how that goes?"

"Of course. I'll try to reach him before Katie wakes up and needs some breakfast. Hey, are you in your jammies?"

Jessie giggled. "Yeah."

"Is it one piece?"

"Nah." She tilted the laptop screen downward to show her. "A short tee and capri pants that tie at the waist, basically."

"I like the print. You look very *groovy flower child*."

Jessie looked down at the pattern of large daisy-like flowers drawn in bright colors on the pale yellow background. "They're really comfy."

She decided not to confess that she'd bought them at Target.

Courtney looked pretty with barely a speck of makeup and her dark hair swept upward into a ponytail at the top of her head. When she smiled directly into the camera, it reached all the way from London and straight into Jessie's heart.

"I don't want you to worry about this, Jessie. I'm glad you told me, and I'm sure we'll work it all out."

"I hope you're right. She's very sweet and down-to-earth. I'd love to work with her if it comes to that."

"Something to keep in mind if you do . . . She likes the classics. Chanel, Alexander McQueen, Valentino," Courtney told her. "And she loves experimenting with color. She's very Helen Mirren like that."

"I'll send you JPEGs of what I pull for her."

"Good. And avoid orange. She hates orange. It's only a myth that it's the new black."

Jessie chuckled. "We got a fantastic crepe Balenciaga into the store just yesterday that would be stunning on her. But it's black."

"Throw it into the mix and see what she thinks. Oh! And if you have another couple of minutes, I'd like to talk to you about writing a blog for me on the FiFis. Are you interested?"

"Of course."

Jessie left her closed laptop on the coffee table after they finished their Skype chat and padded off to bed with the last of her tea in hand and memories of her evening with Danny rolling around in her mind. The acidic knot in the pit of her stomach had dissolved since talking to Courtney, replaced with a rush of adrenaline about the events of the evening. She'd gone to the FiFis excited to see the celebrities accept their awards, but she hadn't witnessed even sixty seconds of the event . . . and had left without feeling the least bit deprived.

She pulled back the sheets and slipped in between them, resting the teacup on her blanket-covered knee. Leaning into the pillows propped behind her, Jessie supported the cup with her hand and closed her eyes. Grinning, she replayed the Goodnight Finale with Danny just a little while before; from the easy conversation between them on the drive back to her apartment to the goodnight kiss in the middle of her living room. His lips had been warm and tender, and he'd done that thing he sometimes did— raking his hand through the hair at the nape of her neck.

Jessie swooned slightly at just the memory.

"He's quite delicious, isn't he?" Carolyn Coleman had said after meeting Danny. *"Well done, my dear."*

She giggled just thinking about it, and a shot of joy pelted through her. In response, she quickly set down the cup, replacing it with the phone.

"Piper? I'm sorry if I woke you. I couldn't wait until morning to tell you all about tonight."

———

The precinct was pretty active for nine in the morning. Danny nursed the coffee he brought along with him for more than thirty minutes while he waited for Rafe. One of the detectives, his dented metal desk angled into the corner across the small room, grew frustrated with trying to open his bottom drawer and kicked the thing with the full force of his boot. Danny chuckled.

"Easy there, MacKenzie," Rafe joked as he stalked past him. "I'm sure you can get a confession out of that desk without beating it out."

MacKenzie grumbled after him, and Rafe smacked Danny's shoulder before folding into his chair. Danny made a quick save of the coffee in his hand and set the cup on the desk.

"Sorry, Callahan. It's a madhouse in here today."

"No problem."

"Where were we?" Before Danny responded, Rafe belted out, "Oh. Right! You said his name is Frasier. What's the last name again?"

"Tercot," he replied, and spelled it out for him as Rafe typed it into the computer screen before him. "The security company is Weston."

"I've heard of them," he remarked without looking up from his two-fingered typing for several minutes. When he did, he picked up one of the three small devices Danny had deposited to the desktop and held it close for better inspection. "Who'd think something this small could do so much damage, huh? You found three?"

"Plus the receiver."

"And that's the digital photo frame," he said, picking up the contraption and turning it around several times.

"The cameras are motion-sensitive, and they take one frame every fifteen seconds as long as they detect movement."

"And he's been doing this for several years at the awards show?"

"Then selling whatever compromising photos he's been able to get to various gossip outlets, starting with a local television reporter here in town." Danny tapped Rafe's notepad with his index finger. "I wrote down all of her information while you delivered him to the holding cell."

"Can you tell me exactly where you found each one?" Rafe asked, and he dropped the camera to the desk again and positioned his fingers over the computer keys.

"Two of them on some decorative shelves in the dressing rooms, and one attached to some questionable wall art in the green room."

"Good."

He continued laboring over the keyboard until Danny asked him, "What's next for Tercot?"

Rafe leaned into the chair back and angled his head slightly. "California prohibits filming or photographing people anywhere that's considered a private place, which means a locale where people feel reasonably safe from unauthorized surveillance. Like a locker room or changing rooms in a clothes store, that kind of thing."

"Or a backstage dressing room."

"Or a backstage dressing room," Rafe repeated. "The penalties may have changed, but there's the expectation of a couple grand in fines, as well as possible jail time. Since this sleaze has been doing it for a couple of years, and if we can back that up with proof, he could spend a couple years looking at the inside of a cell."

"My clients are going to be very happy to hear that," he said. On second thought, he added, "Well. All but one of them."

"The uncle," Rafe stated.

"Yeah. I'm guessing he'll have some very mixed emotions over all of this."

"So where are you headed? Will you be around at lunchtime?"

"Sorry. I've got a couple of things to take care of today," Danny replied, and a satisfied smile slipped upward.

"Let me guess. Lunch with Jessie?"

"Dinner and a movie."

"Ah. Well, go on. I'll take care of the rest of this. You go make yourself pretty."

"Hey," Danny objected. "I am always pretty."

"Are you kidding? With that mug?"

"Jealous much?"

The two old friends simultaneously raised their hands and clasped them together in a quick shake.

"Later," Danny said as he slapped the desk and headed for the door.

The precinct neighborhood, with its cracked sidewalk, was littered with paper cups and wadded cellophane. The morning sun washed the unattractive surroundings in bright yellow warmth. The brown-blue skies looked almost clear despite the smog Danny had noticed hovering already early that morning. He snickered at his own sugary frame of mind.

Next thing, I'll be humming "Walking on Sunshine."

As he drove, Danny tried to recall whether he'd ever felt this way about a woman before Jessie. Even with Rebecca, he didn't remember that *the-world-is-a-wonderland* way of thinking. He couldn't put his finger on exactly what it was, but something about Jessie just . . . energized him. Even though he was due to pick her up in just six hours for a quick dinner before the movie, he found he had to work hard to resist the urge to make an excuse to drive over to see her in the interim.

Danny had read about the reopening of the vintage Marquee Theater in Santa Monica in the paper a few weeks back, but he hadn't given it much thought until he stopped for coffee that morning on his way to meet Rafe and saw a flyer. Classic movies from the 1930s, '40s, and '50s would grace the large new screen all month, and the third movie showing that very night at 10 p.m.: *The Treasure of Sierra Madre.*

His conversation with Jessie about the origination of the term *bogarting* had cascaded like a waterfall. She'd never seen it, and that was a tragedy he simply had to rectify.

"Did I wake you?" he asked when he couldn't help dialing her number despite the early hour.

"Yes," she admitted, and her sleepy voice confirmed it. "But it's okay. Is anything wrong?"

"Yes. But I can fix it." Never having seen an Oscar-nominated film starring Humphrey Bogart and directed by John Huston— well, that was just *so* wrong.

"Oh no."

"I'm being a smart aleck. If you're not busy tonight, I'm calling to ask you out on a date."

He heard the rustle of the covers as she tossed them back, and the creak of her bed springs—"You are?" She groaned, and Danny imagined her stretching. "Where are we going?"

"You'll see tonight. But you're going to love it."

Dinner at Misfit . . . with a takeout order of a few of those chocolate chip cookies with sea salt to munch in the movie . . . walk off dinner with a stroll toward the pier . . . followed by a late showing of *Sierra Madre*.

Danny stopped, jarred by the memory of Rebecca looking him straight in the eye.

"You should never start something with the expectation of it being amazing," she'd said. "It's a sure way to be disappointed."

"That might be the saddest thing I've ever heard," he'd replied, and he followed the declaration with a very convincing argument that she should look forward with eager excitement to their trip north for his three days of R & R. It would be a new start for them. A kick start. "An amazing time," he'd promised her. "Trust me."

And so she did.

The long weekend had started just like he'd vowed it would. A barbecue on the beach behind his folks' place. Surfing with his old Newport buddies. A few carefree days of liberation from the restrictions and regulation of the United States Navy.

But then they decided to attend a party up in Northridge and Danny had so much to drink that Rebecca finally called a girl-friend to drive her back to Newport. Danny woke up under a tree in some stranger's front yard at six in the morning. He some-how managed to drive himself back out to the beach—chugging beer the whole way—and picked up his gear and his wife in time to make the two-hour drive back to the base. Just as Rebecca had predicted, their "amazing" weekend together had ended in disappointment.

And when her half-drunk husband lost control of the car he insisted on driving—crossing the median, sailing over an embankment, and plowing into oncoming traffic—embers of disappointment were stoked into horror and regret as the young and beautiful Rebecca Callahan—who had trusted her husband against her better judgment yet again—slammed into the windshield.

Nothing had been the same for Danny since that moment when some anonymous doctor in blue scrubs called out, "DOA." A heartbeat later, a cop snapped handcuffs on Danny and hauled him away from her body. In some ways—as strange and unfair as it seemed—the drastic changes resulting from that tragedy had been a blessing. In other ways . . . not so much.

At the light on Broadway, Danny checked his phone for the bookmarked page he hadn't visited in ages. After scanning the different possibilities, he landed on an early afternoon meeting in the basement of the Lutheran church over on Ocean Park. Since the coffee at those meetings was notoriously disgusting, he stopped and picked up a cup to go before heading over.

Danny took a seat in the back as the leader of the group moved up to the front.

"Hi, everyone. I'm Bob, and I'm an alcoholic. Welcome. Is there anyone new here who wants to introduce themselves?"

He hesitated, hoping someone else would beat him to it before standing. "My name is Danny."

"Hi, Danny," some of those in attendance greeted him.

"I'm nine years sober," he said, emotion climbing up his throat as he added, "after killing my wife in a car accident while driving drunk, going to jail for it, and being discharged from the Navy."

"That's rough, Danny," Bob said from the podium at the front. "What brings you here today?"

"I've met someone," he stated, staring at the floor. "I mean, I've dated a few women over the years, but never let myself . . . you know . . . complete the connection we might have made, if that makes sense. I just felt like I could never take a chance on hurting somebody like that again. But this one—Jessie. She's a game changer."

Danny Callahan. An Irishman. Been wonderin' a while now if this ain't the man I been praying for all these years.

Phone chats with my Jessie been filled up with "Danny this" and "Danny that," and that's a way a grampy purdy much always knows it's a foreshadowin' of things to come.

"He believes like you do, Grampy. He's got a strong faith."

"Danny says this is the best way to go, Grampy. I think he knows about these things better'n I do."

"Danny had the pasta 'n I had a berry salad with . . ."

"I never thought I'd be on a surfboard, Grampy, but I stood right up on it and used a paddle. Went glidin' across the water, 'n Danny said I done pretty good."

Yeah, my Jessie-girl's been doin' a lotta Dannyin' in her calls to me since that varmint husband o' hers went packin'. Hope I getta meet 'im face to face. Kin tell a lot about a man when you look 'im in the eye.

19

I'm not a fan of goat cheese," Jessie remarked as she lingered over the menu at Misfit. "I don't like the aftertaste."

"Yeah, I could easily live in a world that didn't have any," Danny said with a chuckle. "The cheese, not the goats. How about going old school. The burgers are great."

"I wouldn't be opposed to tasting *yours* . . . but I think I want to try the mac and cheese."

"They have mac and cheese?"

"Right here," she said, leaning across the table to share a look at the menu. "Baked with cheese and green chilies, and made with brown rice pasta."

"Hmm."

Jessie grinned. She loved the way—when Danny became very serious—his dimples deepened next to the corners of his mouth.

He lifted his eyes to glance at her, then did a double take. "What?"

And there it was. The smile that completely did her in, and the dimples that went from a shadowy impression beneath the haze of stubble to two full craters of charm and heart-stopping appeal.

Jessie snickered and darted her attention back to the menu. "Why don't you order the burger and I'll get the mac and cheese, and we'll share," she suggested.

When the waiter appeared and they put in their order for a Misfit Burger and an order of mac and cheese, Danny also asked for four chocolate chip cookies in a takeout bag. "For the movie," he told her.

"Assuming they make it that far."

The cookies were still confined to the inside of the bag as Jessie and Danny walked back toward the deck where they'd parked the Jeep. Instead of heading for the car, however, they instinctively locked arms and strolled to the railing. In the distance, a midnight gray sky hosted a half-moon, and Jessie noted that the throng of people enjoying the Ferris wheel, carousel, and shops along the boardwalk probably missed it completely.

When she turned toward Danny to give voice to her thoughts, he'd moved his face so near to hers that she nearly jumped. As he dug his hand into the hair at the nape of her neck and drew her close, Jessie felt her knees weaken, and she wondered if she might lose her balance. He pressed his warm lips to hers. They tasted tangy, like the green chilies they'd had at dinner.

I love you. Danny, I love you.

Why wouldn't the words come out? The timing was just right to remind him that he'd changed her life. That nothing would ever be the same for her again, now that she'd met him.

"Danny, I . . ." she began.

But just as she opened her mouth again to complete the thought, someone shouted. Someone standing nearby. "Daniel Callahan!"

Danny spun toward the woman, his hand still resting at the base of Jessie's head.

"Jackie," he said, and the woman smacked his arm—hard!— with the full force of her handbag.

Danny nudged Jessie behind him and planted himself between her and the woman he'd called Jackie. The middle-aged man with her hooked her arm like a horseshoe around a post.

"Danny?" Jessie muttered.

"Jackie," he repeated without answering her. "Brent."

"Is this your next victim?" the woman snapped, and Jessie heard Danny softly groan as he lowered his head for a moment. "Does she know?" The woman repositioned herself to peer around Danny and glare at Jessie. "Do you really know this man you're kissing in the moonlight, young lady? Are you aware that he is a murderer?"

Jessie touched Danny's back with the palm of her hand. "Danny, who is this?"

"Rebecca's parents."

His late wife.

"Jackie and Brent, this is Jessie Hart."

The woman turned to her husband, and his face contorted slightly with pain . . . or possibly embarrassment. Maybe a little of both.

"So Danny Callahan is roaming around free," she told her husband, "kissing pretty young women and enjoying the moonlight . . . while our little girl is cold in the ground."

"Jackie," he managed, and Jessie could hear the pain in his tone. "I'm sorry."

"You're . . . *sorry?*"

"All right, that's enough," Brent said softly, tugging on Jackie's arm. "Let's go."

"Jackie," Danny said, and he took a step toward her. "There's hardly a day that goes by when I don't think about what my carelessness took from you. From all of us. There aren't adequate words to express to you how sorry I am."

The woman turned away as if she smelled something foul.

"Danny hasn't had one drop of alcohol since that night," Jessie spoke up, and all three of them turned toward her, varying degrees of surprise in their expressions. "He served his jail time, and he's changed his life as a result of that horrible thing that happened—"

"It didn't just happen to us—" Jackie exclaimed. "What was your name again?"

"Jessie Hart."

"Jessie. Can I give you a slice of advice, Jessie?" She didn't wait for a reply. "Run away from Danny Callahan as fast as your legs will carry you before he's the something that *just happens* to your life too."

Jessie weighed the various responses that jumped to mind, propelled by defensiveness on behalf of this wonderful man she'd come to know. And love.

"Let's go," Danny said softly, and he wrapped his hand around hers.

As they turned away, he nodded at Brent and the two of them exchanged a glance that Jessie interpreted as one of simple coexistence.

Jessie looked back at them for a moment. "I'm very sorry for your loss."

As she and Danny walked away, Jackie called after her. "And I'll be very sorry for yours because, believe me, this one destroys everything good that gets close to him."

Her lips parted with a sharp reply, but Danny squeezed her hand and urged her along. She heaved a deep, burdened sigh and followed in silence.

Once they'd buckled up inside the Jeep, he turned the ignition and allowed the car to idle for a while before he finally spoke.

"Jessie. Would you mind if we skip the movie?"

Nosh, the little French café at the other end of the strip mall from Adornments, had become a regular hangout for Jessie. She'd ordered two skinny vanilla lattes and took a seat at one of the white wrought iron bistro tables near the chiffon-draped window to wait for Piper's arrival.

"Oh, the poor thing!" Piper exclaimed once Jessie had unfolded the details of the previous night's interaction with Danny's former in-laws. "He must have been devastated."

"He was," Jessie replied, and she folded her arms on the edge of the table and dropped her chin to the top of her clasped hands. "It was just *painful*."

"Well, I'm proud of you for speaking up to the old bat."

"Piper."

"I know," she repented. "I'm sorry."

"The woman lost her daughter," Jessie said. "It's nine or ten years later, and she's still grieving. I get it. But she's just so wrong about Danny, and she couldn't even hear anything about how much he'd changed, or how sorry he was—*still is!*—for what happened."

"I know you're supposed to turn the other cheek and all that," Piper said. "But I'm not sure I'd have that in me for someone responsible for Antonio's death, you know? And I can't begin to imagine losing *a child*."

"I know," she said with a pensive nod.

"Hey . . . changing gears . . . you mentioned going down to Louisiana. Do you think you'll still do that?"

"Oh, I don't think so. Now that I've got this meeting with Carolyn Coleman and several blog posts due to Courtney . . ."

"You know," Piper interrupted. "I think now might be a good time to remind you that your granddad won't be around forever. How long has it been since you've been back to see him?"

Jessie sighed. "A while."

"And let's not forget the whole Jack ordeal. It might be a really good time to just escape for a bit, don't you think?"

She shook her head and groaned. "Oh, I don't know."

"I think you should go."

"Well, speaking of going, I have to get over to the store. Danny should be here within the hour to return the suit he borrowed for the FiFis."

"Oh," Piper exclaimed, and she immediately started to root through her large Chanel boy bag. "I can't believe I forgot all about this."

"About what?"

With a smirk, she yanked a folded publication out of her bag and slapped it to the tabletop. Jessie stared down at the cover of *Hollywood Daily*, her heart pounding out a Samba beat at the sight before her.

"Is that . . . ?"

"Yep," Piper answered. "It's your boy."

Beneath the screaming headline—"Mystery Man Turns Heads on Red Carpet"—a large photograph extending to both sides of the fold. In full and living color . . . Danny, donning his Valentino suit, his gorgeous dimples in full neon, kissing the hand of a woman who disappeared just below her elbow.

"Is that your hand he's kissing?" Piper inquired slyly.

"I hope so."

"It is. Look. Your bracelet."

Jessie leaned down and took a closer look. "Yep. That's my hand." She scanned the headline again. "Yep. He did turn some heads that night."

"He was rocking that Valentino. I wonder what he'll say when he sees it."

"Oh, he'll go insane," Jessie said with a chuckle. "Can I keep this? I can't wait to show him."

Piper laughed. "Sure. I picked up several."

Jessie folded the paper and tucked it under her arm. "Ready to go?"

The two friends ambled out the door and down the sidewalk. Jessie spotted Piper's Jaguar parked in front of the store and walked with her toward it. She spotted Amber standing outside the front door to Adornments, both hands on her hips, glaring straight ahead.

"Hey, Amber," Piper called, and her car chirped as she unlocked the door.

"Amber? What's wrong?" Jessie asked.

When Amber remained motionless, seemingly frozen to the spot, and Piper appeared at Jessie's side with a dramatic frown of concern.

"Jess," Amber said, nodding toward the lot where three dark blue nondescript vans sat parked.

Jessie spun around to look at the object of Amber's laser focus. It took a moment to process the activity going on inside the store, but Amber clarified as she muttered, "They told me I had to leave."

"Who did?" Jessie demanded.

"It's the FBI. They're raiding the store."

"They can't raid my store," she objected, looking from Amber on her left to Piper on her right. "Can they?"

"They're the FBI," Amber said. "I think they can do pretty much anything they want to do."

Two men in FBI Windbreakers—dark blue with large block letters, labeling them like generic cans of peas or stewed tomatoes—emerged from the store just then and headed purposefully toward one of the vans.

"Excuse me," Jessie cried, following after them. "Excuse me. I'm Jessie Hart. Adornments is my store."

"*Was* your store," another guy in a three-letter jacket remarked as he came up behind her.

"Who's in charge here?" she asked him as he passed. "Who do I talk to about this?"

He nodded toward the door and sort of grunted. Jessie rushed the next person to exit the store, a lanky woman with frizzy hair she'd attempted to tame into a twist.

"Please," she said, her hand on the woman's arm. "Please don't rush past me. I need some answers."

"What are the questions?" she asked dryly.

"I'm Jessie Hart," she stated, pausing for a sharp intake of oxygen. "Adornments is my store, and I'd like to know what you're doing."

Producing a tri-folded bulge of paperwork that she handed to Jessie, the agent told her, "There's a halt to any further business dealings on the premises until further notice."

"No. That can't be right." Jessie ruffled the papers, her heart pounding, her hands twitching. "Please just tell me what's going on." Realization hit, and she gasped. "It has to do with Jack, doesn't it? What's he done now? He doesn't have anything to do with my business. We are . . . *Not. Even. Married!*"

"Everything I can tell you is right there in the injunction," the woman told her. "Beyond that, I'd suggest you contact your attorney."

Jessie grabbed her arm, this time with more force. "Please. I have personal items inside. What do I do about—"

The agent twisted her arm free as she called out to one of the other agents. "Douglas, escort Mrs. Stanton inside, will you? And—"

"Hart!" she shouted, then clenched her teeth and spoke through them. "My name is not Mrs. Stanton. It never was. My name is Jessie Hart."

"And," the woman repeated for effect, "make sure it's personal items only. No files, financials, drives, inventory, or computers."

Jessie handed off the paperwork to Piper as she passed her, following Agent Douglas through the doors of her own store. In that one instant of eye contact, she and her friend succinctly exchanged all the confusion, panic, and anxiety both of them felt.

"There were so many restrictions on what I couldn't take," Jessie told Piper and Amber when she emerged from the store just a few minutes later with a makeup bag and the raincoat she'd left hanging on the back of her door a few days prior. "I just stood there trying to figure out what to grab. I don't know what to do. Piper, what do I do?"

"Take a few deep breaths, first of all. From what I can see," she said, rattling the open papers in her hand, "the store was bought with funds from your ring. And your ring was bought with the ill-gotten gains of Jack's crimes. So until they sort it all out, it seems you're caught in the meat grinder we lovingly call Jack Stanton."

"It's like that game," Amber remarked as Jessie tried not to hyperventilate. "The Three Degrees of Kevin Bacon."

"Six degrees," Jessie countered, her fists clutching her pounding chest. "It's the *six degrees* of Kevin Bacon. Shouldn't I get three more degrees?"

❊

"Jessie. You have to calm down. Take a few deep breaths, will you?"

"I . . ." She tapped her throat, and her usually serene blue eyes looked to Danny as if they might bulge right out of their sockets. ". . . can't."

He placed her hand between both of his and stroked it. "Yes, you can. Jessie, look at me." She closed her eyes and snorted in a breath, reminding Danny of the first time Steph had taken a direct hit by a fifteen-footer. He'd dragged her out of the water and, although she was conscious, she flailed in a sort of panic. He'd only been able to calm her by creating a connection between them, regulating her breathing by regulating his own. "Jess. Look at me."

Jessie opened her eyes, but her gaze fluttered back and forth.

"Right here, angel. Look at me."

When she finally plugged in, her glazed blue eyes meeting his and locking there, he smiled. "Let's do this together. Breathe in slowly through your nose. Like this." They inhaled in harmony. "Now out through your mouth, like this."

After several rounds of breathing exercises, one corner of Jessie's mouth twitched in an attempt at a grateful smile.

"Good. In through your nose, and out through your mouth."

Just as it seemed as if she might make some real headway in the breathing department, the receptionist stood and smiled at them. "Mr. LaHayne has asked me to show you into the conference room. Right this way."

As they followed her down the hallway, Jessie continued to cling to Danny's hand until it ached. Strange, guttural noises bubbled out of her throat until the receptionist turned and asked, "Are you going to be all right?"

"Maybe we could just get her some water," Danny suggested.

"Of course. Have a seat . . . the second door on the right. I'll bring in some cold water."

Danny led Jessie into the conference room and to one of the leather chairs on the far side of the polished mahogany table. "Sit here and just keep trying to breathe."

"D-Danny, what am I . . . going . . . to . . . do?"

"You're going to stop talking and start breathing. There's no shot at sorting this out if you're passed out under the table when your attorney comes in."

"O-kay. Y-you're ri-ight."

The noseful of oxygen she sucked in sputtered out immediately, as if she'd sprung an untimely leak.

"You're going to be fine, angel." He spoke in soft, even tones. "We're going to work this all out and you're going to be fine."

"H-how?" she clucked. "I mean . . . *how?*"

"That's what we're here to find out."

He wished he had a better answer for her. The best thing he could do for now was to keep his own temper in check and just provide a calming influence while they sorted things out. As he stroked Jessie's hand, Danny focused on taking a few of those deep cleansing breaths himself.

"Jessie," LaHayne greeted her as he walked in and closed the door behind him. "Danny. Good to see you both. Now tell me what's occurred."

Jessie's lips parted, but nothing coherent came out. Just a low sort of grunt as she threw the paperwork across the table at him.

"They showed up at the store this morning and ran through it like a tribe of banshees," Danny explained on her behalf. "She was allowed to go in with an escort and remove a couple of personal items, but they loaded up a couple of vans with business records and computers."

Jessie whimpered and, as Danny turned toward her, she simply folded like the paperwork in LaHayne's hands. Her head thumped softly against the tabletop. The attorney didn't even glance up at her; he simply continued skimming the paperwork, page by page.

"Well," he finally said as he dropped it and smiled warmly at Jessie. "This is quite an ordeal, isn't it?"

She straightened and nodded frantically, wide-eyed and wordless.

"I know it seems like your life has crumpled with this, but it's fairly routine, Jessie. The authorities are dissecting Jack's business dealings, organism by organism. They're tracking every cent. When he spent embezzled funds on a three-carat diamond ring, that opened the door for investigating the trail of those funds. That's all they're doing right now. They're fact-finding."

"Yes, but . . ." She sniffed back a cascade of emotions and clutched her stomach with both arms. "Am I going to lose everything?"

"I don't think so," he said as he stood and crossed the conference room. He picked up a box of tissues from the credenza on the short wall and slid it across the table toward Jessie as he sat again. "We have to let them perform their due diligence, and cooperate with them wherever we can until this plays out. If we have to go to court to fight the injunction, we'll know that soon enough."

"What should I do?" she asked around a shuddered breath. "In the meanwhile."

"I'll make a few calls this afternoon and gather as much information as I can. This won't be fast or easy, but I do think it's going to shake out on your side." He glanced at Danny, a slight twitch to one brow as he did. "Is there somewhere you can go, Jessie? Somewhere to relax and step out of the caldron for a few days?"

"Leave?" she exclaimed. "I can't leave when I don't know what's happening."

"That's my point. This may be a bit of a marathon. You aren't equipped to handle it at this stress level straight out of the gate."

"She had plans to head down to Louisiana," Danny chimed in. "To visit her grandfather."

"No!" she cried. "Danny, I can't go now!"

"I think you should go forward with those plans. Get some perspective and try to relax for a few days or a week. Meanwhile, I'll get to the bottom of things and see what we're in for."

"I . . . can't . . ."

In through the nose, out through the mouth. Danny could almost hear the words echo through Jessie's head as she closed her eyes and followed the blueprint for better breathing. When he touched her arm, Jessie spun toward him, her eyes dancing with flames of fear.

"There's nothing we can do until your lawyer gets all the facts," he reassured her.

"But if he needs me to do anything, if he needs anything from me, I have to be here." As a new wave of hysteria rolled in, she straightened and gasped. "I paid for my apartment with the money from my ring too. Are they going to take that, Mr. LaHayne? Will I go home and find the FBI there too?"

"They will not land you on the streets," he replied confidently.

"And most of your furniture," Danny pointed out, "and your car, that all came from Antonio and Piper."

"Good," the lawyer said. "I don't see that being an issue. Just give me time to sort things out with the FBI. I'll speak to Jack's attorneys, and we'll talk again as soon as you get back. But be sure to leave your contact information with my secretary."

LaHayne stood, rounding the table to stand face-to-face with Jessie as soon as she made it to her feet. He shook her hand and smiled down at her.

"I'm going to get to the bottom of this, Jessie."

She nodded and croaked out an attempted, "Thank you."

He left the conference room, and Jessie just stood there like a statue in a garden. Danny placed his hands on her shoulders and tried to nudge her into taking a step or two toward the door.

Instead, she folded in half and lowered to the chair again. He surrendered and occupied his own chair as well.

After several minutes of tense silence, except for the hum of her deep breathing, Jessie swiveled the chair and faced Danny, her eyes brimming with conversation that showed no signs of initiating.

"Let's go," he said. "Are you ready to go?"

She shook her head.

"Okay, angel. Just sit here for a minute and get your bearings."

"No," she chirped.

"No?"

"You."

"Me?" he tried to clarify. "Do you need me to do something?"

Jessie nodded. "Pray with me. Can you do that? Will you pray with me?"

He smiled and lifted her hand, kissing the trembling knuckles.

"I can do that," he whispered.

⸻

Phone didn't ring in a week's time when I didn't expect my Jessie on the other end.

"Grampy, I'm needed at the store. Please don't be dis'pointed."

"You can't believe how busy I am, Grampy. I'm sorry, but I just can't come to see you this time."

"I been thinkin' Christmas might be a better time to get away from the store, Grampy."

Could throw a dart'n land on any one of the dozen reasons I 'spected she might use. When a girl gets 'er life goin' in a place like LaLa Land, haulin' back to Luziann to see her gramps ain't got the kinda competin' edge it once did.

Couldn't help sayin' a prayer anyhow. Needin' a visit with my Jessie-girl purdy soon, Lord.

228

20

Jessie's entourage of two—namely, Danny and Riggs—accompanied her to the Hertz counter to rent a car before she dropped them at an airport motel where they'd meet up with the others on the mission trip in the morning. She and Danny lingered in the car for several minutes while Riggs checked into their shared room.

"Danny, no," she'd said when he placed the Visa gift card he'd purchased back in Santa Monica before they left into her hand.

"Jessie. Yes," he stated. "LaHayne said he didn't think they'd freeze your personal account, but he couldn't guarantee it. Maybe you won't even need it, but it's there if you do."

Her stomach flopped over on its side and moaned. By some miracle, she had managed not to think about the Jack Stanton cyclone that had consumed her life since somewhere over Austin at thirty thousand feet.

Danny initiated one last kiss before climbing out of her rented Toyota Corolla, and Jessie leaned into it. It would have to carry her for a few days.

She hadn't been looking forward to the drive on her own; however, minutes after finding her way to I-10 East in Metairie, she tuned the radio and turned the volume down so that the music played softly behind her thoughts. Jessie realized she hadn't been alone with them—her thoughts, that is—for quite a long time.

The replay of Jack's return and the subsequent maelstrom he'd brought with him was somehow cauterized by thoughts of Danny and wonderings about how he might interact with her grandfather. After all, Grampy was a very unique person, not like anyone she'd ever met before—particularly in Los Angeles. Danny's converse family life would surely cause him to view hers as unsophisticated at the very least; hayseed at worst. And yet Jessie's adoration of the grandfather who'd raised her trumped those concerns. For the first time in she didn't know how long, Jessie yearned for the strong arms of home . . . and everything that came with it.

About ten miles into the twenty-four-mile trip across the Lake Pontchartrain bridge, Jessie glanced at the speedometer and noted she was traveling at almost 75 m.p.h., further proof of her eagerness to arrive in Slidell. Jessie grinned as she eased her foot off the accelerator. She didn't know how long she'd been speeding but, when she finally made the turn off Markham onto Eton Street, she realized she'd made the drive from the airport in New Orleans to Slidell—a drive that should have taken just under an hour—in less than forty minutes.

The sharp, straight edges of sidewalks formed a perfect frame around a neighborhood she thought she might still be able to navigate with her eyes tightly shut. Short, stout ranch homes, each with a distinct personality of its own and yet symmetrical in their similarity, lined the street on both sides. Jessie pulled into the familiar concrete driveway leading to the small red brick house with the miniscule white porch and gracious black shutters, and the same old red pick-up in the carport. She turned off the ignition, leaned against the headrest, and sighed at the sight before her.

Home.

She climbed out of the Toyota and stretched.

"Jessie Hart," Maizie Beauchamp called out from just inside her gaping front door, and Jessie chuckled. Finally, someone got her name right. And she only had to travel sixteen hundred miles to hear it. "Ain't you a sight fer sore eyes?"

It figures. That old bitty has her nose in everything that moves on Eton Street.

"Hey, Miss Maizie," she returned with a friendly wave Jessie wasn't feeling. "How are you doing?"

"Got a leak in the roof and a hole in the pipe under the kitchen sink," she bellowed. "But thankin' the good Lord it's the house and not this old body fallin' apart around me."

Jessie removed her sunglasses and squinted to get a better look at the old woman through her screen door. Aside from a full head of silver hair rather than the salt-and-pepper version she remembered—albeit still smoothed into the exact same bun—and, of course, far deeper trenches of wrinkles across and around her scowling face, Maizie Beauchamp looked exactly the same. In fact, Jessie felt pretty sure she remembered that flowered dress.

"Good to see you again, Miss Maizie."

As Jessie turned her attention back to the house, her heart stopped for an instant, along with time itself.

"Jessie-girl," Grampy half-whispered, and his act of resting his hands on his hips looked as if he'd planted himself there at the edge of the carport.

Tears erupted out of nowhere and squirted from her eyes propelled by the full force of the emotion churning in her heart.

"Grampy," she called, taking off at a full run toward him.

She'd been craving one of his hugs for so long, and she buried herself inside his strong arms and tucked her head under his fleshy chin as she breathed in the jubilant and wonderful Old Spice scent of him that she'd nearly forgotten.

"I've missed you so much," she cried, the words partially blocked by his solid shoulder.

When they eventually parted, she looked up to find a surprising pond of tears standing in his warm and familiar eyes. Those wonderful eyes, not a cloud in their clear-blue sky. Despite his thinning fawn-gray hair and the brownish age spots on his forehead and beside one eye, the rosy apples of her grandfather's cheeks and the clarity in his crystal gaze transported her back a hundred years. To jubilant days and secure nights tucked into a contented lower middle-class existence, wrapped tightly in the love of the one person in the world who meant more to her than anything—or anyone—else ever could.

"I've missed you so much," she repeated, and her tears spilled down her face in hot, steady streams.

"C'mon." He nodded toward her rental as he wiped his moist eyes with the back of his hand. "Let's get you and your bags settled in. What, ya bring a dozen suitcases? Maybe two dozen?"

She playfully smacked his arm. "I brought one bag and a cosmetics case."

"This I gotta see." Jessie popped the trunk, and her grandfather peered down into it. "Well, I'll be."

He groaned as he yanked the larger of the two cases from inside. She reached around him and tugged the handle upright to make it easier to wheel her Louis Vuitton to the house. She hung the long chain of her handbag over one shoulder and slipped her hand through the wristlet of the smaller round white leather case. Grampy faltered a bit as he pulled the case through the front door, and Jessie resisted the considerable urge to take it away from him.

"You remember the way?" he asked.

"It's burned in my memory."

His hearty laugh tickled her emotions with a sugary sweetness.

The carved wood frame around the dark green sofa had lost some of its luster, but Jessie couldn't pinpoint a single thing out of place in the front room. From the sheer white panels under the thick tan draperies to the wrinkled covers fitted over the arms of both brown leather chairs, the living room looked as if it had been preserved in time over the five years or so since she'd last visited, that time with Piper in tow. Beyond the formal dining room and across the open counter, the kitchen still wore the dull oak cabinets and cracked linoleum floor like a favorite old cotton housecoat. Jessie peered through the glass to the oversized sun porch along the length of the house, and she smiled at her old friend—the loveseat glider angled into the corner like always, waiting quietly for her arrival.

The wooden door to her old bedroom creaked as Grampy pushed it open, a lyrical song from days gone by, and the walls—papered with large pink roses settled against a pale green background—welcomed her home as she passed through to the tall canopy bed draped in faded pink and white Swiss dotted ruffles.

"Guess the room needs a makeover, huh?" he quipped.

"To bring it out of the sixties?" she teased in return.

"You wasn't even born in the sixties. Whatcha know 'bout the sixties?"

"Still. Couldn't hurt."

She set her cosmetics case on the round lime green beanbag chair hiding in the corner beside the imposing wardrobe, and she hung her purse on the frame of the ornate mirror hanging over the dresser.

"It feels so good to come home, Grampy."

"Might think you'd do it more often then," he remarked as he headed toward the door. "Red beans 'n rice for supper. Five 'clock like always."

"Can I help?"

"You get settled while she cooks. Nothin' to do now but let 'er."

Grampy closed the door as he left, the soft click of the latch igniting another spark of memories at the back of Jessie's mind. The last good-nights of the day, shrouded in storybooks and hushed nighttime chatter and final drinks of water, always punctuated by the gentle click of the door closing behind him.

As she looked around, Jessie's gaze landed on the crisscrossed ribbons on her precious memento bulletin board above the tall bureau. Among the ticket stubs and photo booth strips and opened envelopes sat one gaping, empty hole where something used to be. The weekend she and Piper had paid a visit—the last time she'd been to Slidell—Jessie had slipped a wallet-sized version of her favorite wedding photo into that spot.

"Mixing old with new," she'd remarked. "For good luck."

A bitter chuckle popped out of her as she remembered. So much for good luck.

She spent a little time unpacking—hanging things in the closet, folding a few more on the wardrobe shelf and lining her shoes along the bottom—before stowing the Louis Vuitton in the closet and placing the unopened cosmetics bag on the seat of her mother's old rocker in the corner. With a huff, she did a backward free fall into the beanbag chair and draped her arms over both sides. She'd spent a lot of hours in that beanbag, crying and dreaming and making her big plans.

From that perspective, she almost felt sixteen again.

Danny had met two of the mission group members—Bill and Susan Wentworth—when they went to Honduras two years back, but the rest of the dozen folks at the table were strangers. Riggs seemed to be making it his own personal mission to spend a few minutes getting to know each and every one of them as he made his way around the couple of tables the hostess had pushed together in order to accommodate the size of their gathering.

"So this is our group," their leader, Benny Oates, told them as he stood at the head of the tables. "Get to know each other and enjoy your meals, then get a hot shower and a good night's sleep over at the Super 8. For the next few nights, you'll be sleeping in tents set up on a dirt parking lot and waiting in line to share the portable toilets."

Cathie Oates touched her husband's arm and smiled. "There are two up sides," she told the rest. "The food should be good because we've got a local restaurant providing two meals a day onsite. And there are three hundred displaced kids and teachers who have been jammed into trailers since Katrina hit. Construction was started and abandoned—twice—but when we're through, they'll have their school back."

"So let's get acquainted and then go across the street to the motel. Tomorrow's going to be a long, hard day."

When the waitress stopped next to Danny's chair, he changed his intended order—a mushroom Swiss burger—to mirror what he'd heard Abigail, the woman in her mid-fifties seated next to him, request.

"Sounds good," he said. "I'll have a club sandwich as well. With fries and iced tea."

"Sweet tea?" she asked with a deep Southern drawl.

"No. Just . . . regular."

Abigail and Brad, her thirtyish son, made for pleasant dinner companions. Later, Danny made the walk across the street to the Super 8 alongside them. When they'd nearly made it across the parking lot, his cell phone rang.

"I need to grab this," he told them. "Great to meet you. I'll see you both in the morning."

"Continental breakfast in the lobby at eight," Abigail reminded him.

"See you there."

He pressed the Talk button on his phone. "Are you home, or still lounging around in Hawaii?"

Steph's familiar chuckle was like a song he'd been eager to hear again. "We got back this morning. Are you home? I thought I'd—"

"I'm in New Orleans," he interrupted. "With Riggs."

"No good can come from the sound of that."

He belted out a laugh. "We came down for a mission trip."

"Oh. Okay. That's better."

"So what's up?" he asked her. He'd never known Steph to call to arrange a drop-in without a solid reason.

"I called in for an update on Jessie," she replied. "I heard about the activity at her store. Is she all right?"

"Define *all right*."

"You think I should give her a call?"

"You can, but she's not back there either."

"She go with you?"

"She's got family here, about an hour out. She's visiting her grandfather while I'm on this trip, then we'll meet up in Slidell after."

Steph's silence ticked by, but Danny clearly heard the grind of the wheels as they turned. "Meeting the fam," she finally said. "Interesting."

"Is that it?" he teased as he pushed the key into the lock on Room 142. "Or do you have anything constructive to say?"

"Just that I think this stuff with Jessie is a blip. She'll have her store back soon."

"How soon? Any hot tips on that?"

"They're just doing things by the book, Danny. They can't take any chances."

"Well, while they're doing things by the book," he said, closing the hotel room door behind him and flipping on the light, "Jessie's world is turned upside down and frozen there."

"I know. But it won't be for long."

"Can I quote you?"

"Better not."

"Yeah. As I suspected." He dropped to the bed by the window and kicked off his shoes. "But I hope you're right. I don't think she can take much more, Steph."

"I know. I really felt for her when I heard the story. On the flip side, I heard you interviewed very well."

"I'm charming like that."

"And not full of yourself *at all*."

The door opened with a crash. Danny's head jerked in time to see that Riggs paid no attention to the fact that he was mid-conversation on his phone. "Man, it's hot out there. I mean, it's not so much the temp as it is the humidity. You forget about that when you live in SoCal, don't you?"

"Steph, I've got an explosion in my room. I gotta go."

"Is that Steph?" Riggs exclaimed. "How were the waves?"

"Tell him they were rockin'," Steph said. "Swell conditions ideal out near Diamond Head. It was so beautiful, Danny."

"And the honeymoon?" Riggs interjected without waiting for him to repeat her answer. "Fulfilling, no doubt?"

"Class act," he muttered.

"Hey, does she know about me and Char?"

"Charlotte has lost her mind and reunited with her ex-husband," Danny told her.

"If I knew her better, I'd call and set her straight," Steph teased. "Listen, give me a shout when you get back, will you?"

"Sure thing."

When Danny disconnected the call, Riggs sat on the bed across from him. Resting both arms on his knees, he asked, "Where'd they ride?"

"She mentioned Diamond Head."

"Sweet. Talk to Jessie?"

"No," he admitted. "I don't want to be a reminder of things at home. I'd rather she just enjoy her time with her grandfather."

"Yeah," Riggs said with a solemn nod. "Because I'm sure she's not thinking about things at home without you reminding her to."

Danny shook his head and laughed. "I'll go for a walk outside and give her a call."

"Don't bother. I'm gonna grab a shower. Call the girl."

Danny punched the pillows behind him and crossed his feet at the ankles, waiting for the sound of water falling into the chipped tub. Once he heard it, he called Jessie. She answered on the first ring.

"Danny?"

"How's it going?"

"Okay. How about there?"

"It's a good group," he told her. "We set out first thing in the morning, and I wanted to touch base with you before we did. I'll bet your grandfather is happy to see you."

"It's mutual," she remarked somewhat offhandedly. "We had red beans and rice for supper. I haven't had that in forever. But you'll never guess who came over with a pecan pie for dessert."

"Pecan pie. Man, that sounds good right now. Who?"

"Miss Maizie from next door," she told him, and he could tell she'd cupped her hand around the phone. "She's the woman I told you about that my Grampy can't stand, Danny. He could *never stand her*. And now she's bringing pie and making coffee in his kitchen like she's lived her whole life here. I think she might be"—she whispered—"his *girlfriend*."

Danny chuckled. "Maybe he's tired of being alone."

"Oh," she whined. "Don't say that. I feel terrible for staying away for so long."

"I didn't mean anything by it, angel. I just think it might be nice for him to have some companionship. Don't you?"

"I . . . guess. But *Miss Maizie*? It's just not . . . the match I would have imagined for Grampy."

"Doesn't make it wrong," he reminded her. "Not every couple looks like a no-brainer on paper, huh?"

She giggled. "What are you trying to say to me, Danny?"

"That your grandfather deserves someone to share his life with, just like anyone else."

"Yeah," she said, stretching the word out longer than it needed to be. "But Miss Maizie. That's just *strange*."

He hesitated before he broached the subject of home. Finally, he opened with, "Steph called a while ago."

"Oh, are they back?"

"Yeah. Just landed this morning."

"Was it wonderful?" she sang.

"Sounds like. They surfed Diamond Head."

"Oh, I've been there," she said. Her words froze to a sudden stop for several beats before she added, "It's beautiful."

Danny realized she must have been there with Stanton. "Good surfing there," he remarked.

"I have a hard time picturing Vince on a surfboard," she said with a chuckle. "I don't know why."

"She probably wouldn't have married him if not." He swallowed around the trepidation stuck in his throat, then figured he may as well scale the wall. "Listen, she checked in with her colleagues at the bureau, and she felt really bad when she heard what happened with the store." When she didn't respond, he continued. "She said she got the impression it's just a temporary glitch and you'll be back to business in no time at all."

"Really?" The softness of her voice cut Danny to the core.

"Yeah. No guarantees, of course. But that's the way she sees it."

"I hope she's right."

The water shut off in the other room, and he sighed. "Listen, I'm going to let you go."

"Oh." She sounded disappointed. "All right."

"The Oateses, the group leaders, are heading to see relatives in Bay St. Louis when we're through here, so you won't have to come back this way to get me. They'll drop me."

"That's great. I can't wait to see you."

"You just saw me."

"You're nice to have around," she cracked. "What can I tell you?"

"Your grandfather's okay with me staying there at the house?"

"He's so thrilled you're not Jack, I think he'd put together a parade for you if he had the time."

Danny chuckled. "Save me a slice of pie."

"I can't promise anything. Miss Maizie makes a mighty fine pie, and I might not be able to resist."

"Try."

She giggled. "Okay."

⸻⸺⸻

Got my Jessie back fer a spell. All seems right in the world.

At least fer a minute or two.

Got a chance to fatten her up a little with some starchy stuff, remind her what's what. Fact, make sure she even knows what's what. Gonna get a chance to size up the new boy too. Hopin' and prayin' he ain't a carbon copy o' the last un she brung home.

21

"You better come clean, you old coot."

"Hush up, woman."

Jessie giggled as she padded into the kitchen to find Grampy and Miss Maizie going at it. "Are you two still cat-fighting?" she teased. "You were saying the same things to each other when I left Slidell."

"Yer old gramps is a fool," Maizie said, drying a large pot in front of the sink. "Don't know why I give 'im the time o' day."

"Wish you wouldn't," he snapped back. "Be a lot more peaceful 'round these parts if you'd just stay on yer own side o' the fence."

"Grampy," Jessie said with a laugh, and she took the big pot from Maizie and tucked it into the cabinet. "The fence between our houses came down years ago."

"Only temporary. Gonna replace the thing."

He'd been vowing to replace the fence for ten years.

"You want me on the other side of the fence?" Maizie snapped. "Gonna get yer wish, ya old coot."

The old woman tottered out of the kitchen, her exit punctuated a moment later with the slam of the front door.

"Good riddance to 'er," her grandfather mumbled.

Jessie circled his chair and leaned down from behind, wrapping her arms around his shoulders. "Do you want some more coffee, Grampy?"

"Nah. Got 'nuff trouble sleepin' on that lumpy old mattress. Don't need to give this old body more reasons to stay 'wake."

"It's decaf, Grampy."

"Still."

"Okay. Then let's go sit on the sun porch and chat," she suggested. "Like we used to."

He squeezed her arms, still wrapped around him, and nodded. "Meetcha out there."

Jessie kissed his cheek before doctoring her own fresh cup and heading out to the porch. She folded her legs beneath her and settled back into the faded blue paisley pillows. As she tilted her head and gazed through the glass ceiling of the sun porch, a few stars welcomed her home by winking at her from the navy blue sky. "Where've you been?" they seemed to ask her. "It's been a long time." And it had. She'd missed those Louisiana stars, even more than she'd realized.

Los Angeles stars tended to be restricted to red carpets and the Walk of Fame down Hollywood Boulevard. The kind that dwelled in the overhead sky remained pretty much hidden behind the brownish gray haze left over from smoggy days. Jessie smiled. From the corner of that glider, she'd always imagined Hollywood as a shimmering and magical place tucked beyond a sandy shore and foamy ocean waves, with sunny, blue daytime skies and glittering nighttime ones. In truth, Hollywood's streets were lined with discarded trash and broken dreams, and the Hollywood sign on the nearby hilltop often appeared as merely an outline from behind a smoggy haze. And that beach she'd imagined somewhere close behind the towering gates of glamorous movie studios—well, it could take an hour to reach it by car if traffic on Sunset was typically jammed.

Grampy sat beside her on the glider, and he tapped her knee with the palm of his hand. "Dreamin' again, Jessie-girl? Whatcha dreamin' 'bout now?"

She angled toward him and smiled. "Not dreaming, really," she said. "Just thinking."

"Good to have you doin' yer thinkin' here at home," he replied with a sigh. "Tell me 'bout that boy who's comin' to call. He what you're thinkin' 'bout?"

"Danny?" Jessie's heart squeezed a little at the mention of his name. "He's been so good to me, Grampy. Especially with all the mess Jack left."

"He still messin'?"

"Like only he can," she replied. "But Danny's been a rock for me to lean on. He's a good man, Grampy. I think you're really going to like him."

"Do ya now? I remember 'nother so-called man I was really gonna like. But now he's leavin' messes fer you and yer Danny to clean up."

She lifted one shoulder in half a shrug. "Sure enough. But Danny's nothing like Jack. You'll see when you meet him. He's really kind . . . and strong. And he has such a solid faith."

"Faith in what, that's the 'portant question," he remarked.

"Faith in the things that are important."

"And what's that, Jessie-girl? What's he think's important?"

"God."

"Whose God?"

A mist of tears glazed her eyes as she turned and looked squarely at him. "Yours, Grampy." After a moment, she swallowed around the lump of emotion and added, "Yours and mine."

<hr>

Danny's white tee shirt, drenched with a T-shaped river of sweat down the front and immersed completely on his back, clung to him like additional skin. The relatively mild low eighties temperature in this stretch of Louisiana simmered because of the sky-rocketing humidity levels. He removed the band from his hair and raked his hands through it before securing the wet ponytail again.

"Hey, buddy." Riggs said, and he handed off a bottle of cold water before giving his dripping curls a good shake and showering Danny in the process.

"You look like Frank when he comes out of the surf," Danny told him with a laugh as the two of them joined Benny Oates and Bill Wentworth, parked on some wooden crates for a short break.

"We're making some good progress," Benny declared as he wiped sweat from his forehead and retied the bandana like a headband to keep it from streaming into his eyes. "We might get this drywall completely up by the end of the day."

"When's the group from the school scheduled to arrive?" Riggs inquired.

"Not until our last day. They'll put things in place and do the painting once we finish the framing and drywall. Tomorrow we'll start laying the floors and tiling the roof."

"I expected a much larger school," Bill commented. "You say it's a private school with three hundred students?"

"Three hundred, including teaching and office staff."

"Why has it gone so long since Katrina without repairs?" Danny asked, and he wiped his face with the hem of his tee shirt.

"Katrina changed things for everyone down here," Benny said. "There were so many wounds in this region, and just not enough supplies to heal them all. While they were still trying to figure it all out, there was the BP oil spill and the devastation that caused to an already suffering local economy. The focus had to be on rebuilding homes and getting people back into the workforce. This particular school was just one of many sitting pretty low on the list of priorities."

"I talked to one of the teachers when he stopped by the site this morning," Bill added. "He said they made do with the trailers for so long, just grateful to have a place to meet. They're over the moon about us coming down to help usher them back to a sense of normalcy that they'd almost forgotten."

"I think if anything impacted me from going to Honduras," Danny said, "it was how easily you can represent the hands of

Christ to someone who has lost so much. A little bit goes a pretty long way."

Riggs nodded in agreement as he downed the last of the water. "Bill, your wife mentioned the possibility of distributing some food at a mission down near the French Quarter if we head back that way in time."

"Yeah, we're ahead of schedule, so it looks like we might be able to dedicate our final day to that. We'll see how it goes."

Danny leaned backward onto both elbows and stretched. He was in his thirties and in pretty good physical shape. He could only imagine the difficulty some of the others were having with so much physical work. Many of the volunteers had a decade or two on him, not to mention an additional fifty pounds or more. As Abigail and her son passed them by, balancing heavy buckets, Danny noticed Abigail wince under the weight before the wide grin she'd worn reappeared.

"I'm back at it," he said, excusing himself from the break, and he jogged toward her and relieved her of two of the three buckets she carried. "Where to?" he asked her.

"Oh, thank you, Danny," she replied. "We're helping lay the restroom floors. If you can spare some time to give us a hand, we might finish them today."

"I'm all yours."

"Careful," Brad joked. "She'll take full benefit from a statement like that."

Jessie tried to fit into a pair of the old jeans hanging in her closet, but she couldn't manage it. Relegated to wearing the far newer ones she'd brought along in her suitcase, she pulled an old pair of sneakers and the Garth Brooks tee—the one from his *Fresh Horses* tour in the nineties—out of the wardrobe to top off her "I'm home" outfit. The sentiment worked too because, as she stood at the back corner of Grampy's red Chevy pick-up truck and watched him load the bed with a couple of folding chairs, fishing poles, and that same old tackle box, a wave of childhood nostalgia consumed her. It didn't hurt that Grampy confirmed it . . .

"Ya look fifteen agin standin' there," he said. "All's missin's the pigtails."

"I haven't worn pigtails in months," she teased. "Hey. That tackle box of yours is probably as old as your truck, Grampy."

"Nineteen hundred and fifty-two," he said. "Clementine has held up purdy good, huh, little girl?"

"Like a champ," she said, adding the cooler she'd packed with egg salad sandwiches, potato chips, and glossy red apples. Their traditional lunch for a day of fish-and-chat.

"Red apples to match your red truck," she used to tell him. But old Clementine's red didn't look quite so glossy any more.

"Can I drive?" she asked, expecting the same reply she'd always gotten each of the twelve hundred times she'd asked that question. *Sure kin. When I'm too old to see the road and too stove-up to climb behind the wheel.*

"Sure," he answered instead, and he tossed her the keys.

When they landed in her cupped hands, Jessie just stood there, mouth gaping, hardly breathing. "Are you serious?"

"You still got a license?" he asked.

"Of course."

"Then let's see if you 'member the way out to Picayune."

Jessie grabbed the steering wheel to pull herself up into the cab. With great jubilation, she turned the key and revved the engine.

"*Aht.*" That was the noise Grampy always made when he wanted to stop somebody—namely Jessie—in her tracks. "Clementine's not young's she usta be. Gotta treat her with a little kindness, Jessie-girl."

"Clementine wasn't young when *I was*," she retorted.

"She's an old girl. Likes to be treated with respect."

He made the "*Aht*" noise again when she nearly missed the turn in Pearl River County, but for the most part it was an amiably quiet drive. Jessie rolled her window all the way down and rested her left arm on the top of the door, just like Grampy had always done. She let the wind whip her hair into a frenzy and found herself wishing she had one of Danny's ponytail bands.

"Funny," she said, pulling off to one of their favorite spots, "it used to seem like such a long drive out here. It only took us twenty minutes."

"And looky there. Our fav'rite squat spot's open," Grampy announced.

When he yanked open the passenger door, it groaned loudly. But not as loudly as he did when he hauled himself out of the truck. Jessie grabbed the folding chairs and the lunch and headed down the embankment. Just a few minutes later, they were all set up—Jessie in one chair with the book she'd brought along, and her grandfather in the other holding on to one end of the line he'd just cast into the water.

"Whatcha readin'?" he asked her. "One of your mysteries?"

"Yeah. I picked it up at the airport, but it's not really very good."

"Nah? Why not?"

"I think maybe I have too much intrigue going on in real life. I'm a little overloaded with it."

He tossed his head back and laughed, hearty and rich. Just the sound of it brought joy to Jessie's soul. She closed the book and let it slip to the ground next to her chair and swatted away a buzzing mosquito. She scanned the area until she found the orange top to the can of insect repellent and retrieved it to give the bare skin of her arms a quick coat. She remembered then that she and her friends used to joke that the real *repellent* was the odor of the spray, but anywhere near the bayou . . . it was the "perfume of choice."

Jessie's gaze wandered over the scenery, pausing to watch the muddy water as it lapped lazily against the river bank. After spending so many years formulating her plans to escape Louisiana for a more glamorous life, she hardly knew what to do with the disarming realization that she'd never really left any of it behind.

It had traveled with her, and despite all those years working so hard to be Mrs. Jack Stanton, the truth was . . . the muddy waters of that river bank still coursed through her Southern veins.

After several minutes of silence, she finally turned to him and sighed.

"How did I get so far away, Grampy?"

"Packed up 'n drove as I recall. Lookin' for a new start."

She chuckled bitterly. "Well, I sure found that, didn't I?"

"S'pose ya did." After several beats of silence, he asked, "Whatcha got on your mind, Jessie-girl?"

"I don't know," she replied. "I'm just thinking about my life and all the ways it's crumpled lately. I can't help wondering if maybe God's trying to tell me something. Did you ever feel like that, Grampy? Like God's talking, but you're not listening, so he has to talk a little louder? And before you know it, he has to shout at you?"

He gazed at her with an odd expression that scraped the edges of her heart.

"What?" she asked.

"Ain't never heard you give such a nod in God's direction, that's all. I'm guessin' he did have to talk a little louder'n he ever has. Nice that yer listenin' though. That boy with the strong faith in Jesus have somethin' to do with that?"

Jessie sighed. "I think so."

"Tell me."

"He told me about something that happened to him. He was a pretty wild guy, I guess, married and in the Navy, drinking a lot. Well, one night he was driving home and had too much to drink, and he was involved in a pretty bad accident. His wife died in the crash that night."

Her grandfather clicked his tongue and shook his head. "That'll do a fella in."

"That's the weird thing. His wife died and he spent some time in jail. But instead of caving into it, Danny completely changed his life. He hasn't had a drink of alcohol since that night, and he goes on mission trips and he's involved in his church. Grampy, he has stronger faith than anyone else I've met out there in California. And he's surrounded by friends who believe too."

"Sounds like God did some shoutin' at that boy too."

"That's what I mean. I can't help wondering if maybe God's been shouting at me."

"Whatcha s'pose he's sayin'?"

She reached over and rubbed the arm of his short-sleeved, plaid cotton shirt. "I just wish I knew."

His fishing line pulled suddenly, and Jessie jumped.

"You've got something," she exclaimed.

"Think it's a big'un," he said as he yanked back on the rod and reeled in the line. "Looks like a speck."

Jessie grabbed the net, then gasped when she saw the size of the fish at the end of her grandfather's line.

"Oh, Grampy, he's enormous."

"Yeh," he answered, working to reel him in.

"You know, Grampy . . ." Her heart pounding, she nibbled the corner of her lip. "We'd never be able to eat a fish that big."

"Yer boy don't eat?"

Emotion choked her a little as she suggested, "Grampy, let him go."

He froze for a second, then turned and looked her in the eye. "Let 'im go, huh?"

She pushed a smile upward. "Please?"

The old man got to his feet and netted the fish himself. Jessie looked away as he pulled the hook out of its mouth, and she didn't look back again until she heard the splash.

"Comin' out to fish usually means you go home with supper," he said.

"I guess I hadn't thought about you actually catching something," she admitted. "I just always liked the talking we'd do out here. Tell you what, Grampy. I'll treat you to a pizza for supper. To reward you for throwing him back."

"Pepp'roni?" he clarified.

"Sure."

He stopped to think it over. "Might as well go on home then."

"No, we have to eat the lunch I packed!" He glared at her until she laughed. "It's our tradition."

She produced hand sanitizer from her bag, and her cell phone rang as she extended the bottle to him. The screen identified the caller as Charles LaHayne.

"Grampy, I have to take this. You clean up, and I'll get the lunch out as soon as I'm finished."

"Yeh."

Jessie's insides gave one violent lurch as she answered. "This is Jessie, Mr. LaHayne. How are you?"

"Jessie, good," he said. "You're still in Louisiana, I presume."

"Yes. In fact, I'm sitting here on a river bank with my grandfather."

He paused, then joked, "I haven't been on a river bank since I had hair."

She chuckled. "Has something happened?"

"It wasn't easy, but I've convinced a judge to hear us about detaching your holdings from Jack's. She's given us a morning court date next week on Tuesday."

"Oh. Mr. LaHayne, that is wonderful."

"You'll be back by that time?"

"Yes. Danny's on a mission trip in New Orleans, and he'll join me here in Slidell for a couple of days. Our flights back are booked for Monday morning."

"Excellent. I'll need you at the courthouse by nine on Tuesday."

"I'll be there. Thank you so much."

"I can't tell you everything is going to be okay. We have a lot to prove, Jessie. But I'll work on that while you're out of town. Keep your chin up."

"That will be a lot easier after hearing this."

"See you soon."

Spent a coupla days with my Jessie-girl. Done a lotta eatin'. Red beans 'n rice. Black-eyed peas casserole. Eggs 'n grits, biscuits 'n milk gravy. Almost had a trout supper 'cept it was the one that got put back.

Done a lotta talkin' too. We's overdue on our talkin'. Seems Jessie been facin' some hard times, all 'cause of that husband o' hers. Not even her husband neither. She didn't wanna tell me, but she finally come clean about the feds takin' holda her store. But a coupla helpin' hands got her back. Her ole grampy done some extra prayin' fer 'em too.

Heard once that keepin' a secret acts like water in a dam. Both of 'em wanna get out, the secret and the water. Jessie's secret finally come out. But not mine.

Been keepin' a secret from my Jessie. Keep findin' myself fightin' against the dam, tryin' to figger out if it's gonna make any difference whether it stays in or goes out. One thing I know. Once the dam lets the water go, ain't nothin' or nobody gonna coax it back.

22

"Grampy, what aren't you telling me?" Jessie maintained the scowl as she stared her grandfather down across two plates of eggs and grits. "It's not normal. Do you think I don't know not normal when I see it?"

"Whatcha yappin' 'bout, girl? Eat yer breakfast."

She groaned and fell back against the vinyl chair with a thump. Just as she parted her lips to voice her further objection to his underestimating her, the front door chimed and Jessie's stomach did a little flop. "Danny."

"Well, don't just sit on your duff. Let the boy in so I can get a look at 'im."

She stood, then balanced against both hands on the edge of the table. "Don't think we're not going to talk about this later."

"Heaven forbid. Go get the door."

Jessie reeled, hurrying through the living room. An involuntary smile lifted both sides of her mouth—and her entire face, for that matter—as she pulled open the door and looked into Danny's gray-blue eyes. He looked so handsome standing there with the open screen door resting on the duffle bag protruding from his shoulder, his sunglasses propped on his head and holding back his beautiful blond hair.

"You made it," she cried, and she leapt forward and wrapped her arms around his neck. The duffle strap slipped, and the bag thumped to the concrete. "I'm so happy to see you."

He touched her lips with a warm, tingly kiss before asking, "Can I come in?"

"Oh, of course. Sorry. Yes, come in and meet Grampy."

He grabbed the bag and stepped inside. As he took a look around, leaving Jessie wondering about his first impressions of her humble beginnings. Did he imagine it this way, or had he more likely pictured a two-story plantation home with a wrap-around porch and big white columns? Had he wondered when he pulled up whether there would be mint juleps awaiting him?

"We were just finishing breakfast," she said as she led the way toward the kitchen. "Have you eaten?"

"I haven't."

Jessie stopped him, whispering, "Grampy made grits. Have you ever eaten grits before?"

"No," he replied. "What do they taste like?"

"Wallpaper paste. But if you add a lot of butter, they're not bad. It's an acquired taste."

He snickered and shook his head, passing her by and leaving her standing there in the center of the arched doorway.

"You must be Jessie's grandfather," he said, extending a warm handshake across the table.

"And you must be her rock. Good to meetcha, Danny Callahan. Take a load off."

Jessie swallowed air instead of spit. "I'll get you some coffee."

"Jessie tells me you been doin' yer part in the wake Katrina left."

"Yes, sir," he said, nodding thanks to Jessie as she set down his coffee and refilled her grandfather's cup. "It's appalling how long it's taken this area to recover, but our group managed to put together the bones of a school in just a few days."

Jessie sat in the chair adjacent to Danny on her left and Grampy on her right. She stared down into her own coffee cup for a few moments.

"Went with a group from my church up to Baton Rouge last year," he told Danny, pausing to slurp from his coffee cup. Jessie cringed at the loud sound of it, feeling a little embarrassed by it. "Worked with one of them habitat char'ties. Rebuilt sixteen houses and three storefronts."

Jessie's attention jumped to her grandfather. "Grampy, you did? Why didn't you ever tell me that?"

"Don't gotta go 'round advertisin'," he told her. "Just gotta go 'round doin'."

Danny smiled broadly. "Yes, sir."

"Now, Danny. Let's get this outta the way right quick. How are you different from that Stanton varmint?"

Danny let loose a hearty laugh, but Jessie's heart stopped. "Grampy!"

"It's okay, Jessie," Danny said, touching her hand. "It's a fair question."

"No . . . it's not . . ."

"Let the boy talk, girl."

She leaned back into the chair and lowered her head. Was this really happening?

"I'm different from Jack Stanton in every way that means any-thing, sir," he said, straightforward. "He took your granddaughter in every way he could; my heart's desire is to meet her needs if I can. He's a liar and a cheat; I'm not saying I haven't lied in my life, but I've never stolen from anyone, and I haven't lied to Jessie."

"You love 'er?"

Jessie crumpled and growled softly.

"I do, sir."

She opened her eyes wide and peered at Danny over the top of her astonishment. Straight out like that, no hesitation, no dis-comfort. Just, *"I do, sir."*

"You Southern?" Grampy asked him, and Jessie felt like she might die from the relief at the change in subject.

"Does southern California count?"

"Not hardly."

"Then, no. I'm not Southern. I was born and raised in Orange County, California."

"You ate grits any, son?"

"I haven't, sir. But I hear if you load them up with butter, they hardly resemble wallpaper paste at all."

Her grandfather's laughter was resonant and clear, and Danny's sounded like music when he joined in. Her favorite song, Jessie determined. The shared laughter of the two men she adored most in the world.

"Don't just sit there, Jessie-girl," Grampy snapped. "Dish 'im up a plate and let's put 'im to the test."

Jessie used the door of the cabinet over the counter to hold the torn paper so she could read it as she went.

"Add enough oil to drippings in the Dutch oven to measure half a cup," she read aloud. "Then add flour, and cook over medium heat. Stir constantly for twenty to twenty-five minutes until the roux color looks like chocolate."

She poured a bit of liquid Crisco into the pot and stirred in the flour before turning the burner on beneath it.

"Now . . ." she began, but the smack of the back door caught her attention.

She turned to find Miss Maizie had let herself in. The woman ambled over to the kitchen table behind her and plunked into one of the chairs. Miss Maizie sure did wander in and make herself at home these days.

"What's cookin'?" she snapped, more like a declaration than an actual inquiry.

"I found my mama's recipe for chicken and sausage gumbo. I haven't had it in years, and I thought I'd try my hand."

"You ain't much of a cook, as I recall."

"No," Jessie said with a chuckle, turning her back on the woman and skimming the recipe again. "I'm really not."

"Your grampa don't take ta too much spice nowadays. Go easy on the Creole seasonin'."

"Yes, ma'am." Jessie considered several dozen ways of asking her to leave, but not one of them struck her as civil.

"That andouille gonna give it enough punch fer him."

"Yes, ma'am."

"Quit *ma'amin'* me, child. That your new beau left in the truck with him?"

My new beau.

"Danny. He's helped me with some issues I've had since my marriage ended."

"Not much of a marriage, you ask me. Heard it weren't even legal."

Jessie tapped the spoon several times on the edge of the pot and set it into the spoon rest before turning around. She placed both hands on the back of the chair in front of her and sighed as she looked across the table at Maizie Beauchamp.

"Don't get yer dander up," she said before Jessie could speak. "Your grampa told me all about it."

That's hard for me to imagine. Why would he do that?

"Says you met a real nice boy in that Danny."

Her so-called *dander* rose higher with every statement this woman made.

"You want some help with that?" she asked Jessie, nodding toward the stove. "Made a messa gumbo in my day."

Before she could think of a way to decline the offer, Miss Maizie stood and lumbered around the table, using the backs of the chairs for balance as she went. She lifted the glasses attached to a chain around her neck and pushed them up her nose.

"Let's have a look at dis." Jessie didn't budge from in front of the pot as Maizie skimmed the recipe, her lips moving as she read to the bottom of the page. "Half a teaspoon o' dried thyme, says here. Look up in the cabinet next to the Frigidaire. Brought over some seasons outta my garden a while ago. I think there's some thyme there."

Jessie cocked a brow before heading to the cabinet and opening it. At the front of the first shelf, a line of identical glass bottles stood like little toy soldiers, each of them labeled with perfect round letters.

Oregano.

Basil.

Parsley.

Thyme.

"Got some *filé* up there too. Pull that out, why dontcha?"

"I saw the recipe called for that, but I don't know what that is," Jessie said as she returned to the stove with the requested items.

Maizie took the filé jar from her and held it up. "Spicy herb," she said. "Get it from a sassafras tree."

"I thought you said I shouldn't make it too spicy for Grampy," Jessie said with a smirk.

"I said go easy on the Creole seasonin'. Ain't gonna be gumbo without the filé and the Creole season. Old coot don't know when to quit eatin' neither, so don't let 'im dish it up fer his self. You do it fer 'im."

Jessie suppressed a grin. "Would you like to join us for supper, Miss Maizie?"

The woman chuckled and tapped Jessie's arm. "Got me some French bread raisin' over yonder. That oughta go good with some gumbo, ya think so? Now you do the choppin' and I'll get to bonin' that chicken."

Danny heaved the bag of bark mulch off the push-cart and over the gate of the truck. It landed to the bed with a thud. Jessie's grandfather climbed into the cab and slipped behind the wheel with inspiring ease for his age.

"I'll just stow the cart." Danny wheeled it to the coral before hopping into the passenger seat. As they backed out of the parking spot, he looked over at his driver. "You didn't really need me to help you buy mulch, did you, sir?"

"Whatcha mean?"

"Well, you get around pretty good. And the improvement store has people to help you load things. So I'm guessing you have something to say to me that you wanted to say without an audience of one."

The old man laughed. "Pretty smart cookie."

"Do you want to tell me what it is?"

His expression hardened slightly and he sighed. Without taking his eyes off the road in front of them, he said, "Been prayin' a while for you to git here, ya know."

Danny grinned. "I appreciate that."

"Been waitin' fer a righteous man to light my Jessie up like ya do."

"It's a mutual light, sir."

"Kin see that. Thing is . . . been keepin' a secret from 'er, and I don't know what Jessie might do with it. Don't know if it needs to come out right quick, or if we can let it set a spell."

"And you want to share it with me?"

"Want you to keep it fer me. Just 'til the timing's right. You think you can do that, son?"

"Honestly, I don't like the idea of keeping anything from Jessie without a really good reason. But you've known her a lot longer than I have, sir. You know better than anyone what she can handle and what she can't, especially in light of everything she's been through lately. If you think it's the best thing, I'll try to honor your wishes."

"Yer a good man, like she said. I 'preciate yer love for my girl." As he stopped at the red light ahead, he turned toward Danny and gave him a tired smile. "Thing is . . . looks like I'm gonna be a-dyin'."

Danny's heartbeat double-timed it, and emotion crowded his throat.

"Ain't nobody but the good Lord knows how long I got," Grampy continued. "But the doc wants me to start chemother'py. Know anythin' about that, son?"

"Not too much, no."

"Pump a body fulla chemicals 'til it can't stand it no more. I got no designs on dyin' slow by chemicals when I can die faster without 'em."

"You don't think you should talk that over with Jessie?"

"Nah. Cancer ain't a friend to nobody, least of all Jessie. Got her mama—my daughter April—too 'n we watched her suffer through the 'fects o' chemo."

"I'm so sorry," Danny offered, and it seemed hollow. He wished he had something more substantial to offer. Advice. Experience. Wisdom. But at that moment, as the light turned green and the red truck lurched them forward, he felt he had absolutely nothing.

About a mile from the house, Danny wiped both palms on the knees of his jeans, then rested on them. "You know, sir, I can't see how it's going to help my relationship with Jessie to hold back the information you've shared with me today. She's going to want to know that her time with you is limited."

"Yeh. Reckon you're right."

"And she'll never forgive me if she knows I helped you keep it from her."

The old guy's expression didn't even twitch. He just stared straight ahead as he drove them closer to home. Danny's gut lurched as the weight of this new secret pressed down on him.

"You have to tell her," he said as they pulled into the driveway of the modest ranch house Jessie had known as home.

"Guess you're right." He navigated the large truck into the carport and turned off the engine. "But not today."

Danny prayed all the way into the house behind Jessie's beloved grandfather.

"I'm so glad you're both back," she exclaimed when they walked through the door. "I made Mama's gumbo."

"Gumbo," Grampy said. "What kinda gumbo?"

"Remember she used to make it all the time. It has chicken and sausage—"

"Yeh. I 'member. Ain't quite hungry yet though. You ever had gumbo, boy?"

Before Danny could reply, his cell signaled an incoming text. He shrugged at Jessie as he produced the phone from his pocket. "I've had it with shrimp, I think," he said.

Danny felt as if the one sharp intake of breath at the sight on the screen might be his last, and his heart pounded as his throat constricted. "What the—" Poking the phone in front of Jessie's face so she could see the image attached to Riggs's text, he barked, "Uh, did you know about this?"

Jessie's eyes grew wider and wider until they formed two perfect Os. She stared at the screen without blinking. Or possibly breathing.

"Jessie? Did you know they used my picture on the cover of an L.A. entertainment rag back home?"

She snickered before recovering. "I . . . meant to . . . Well. About that."

<hr>

Jessie sat next to her Grampy, facing Danny across the table, Miss Maizie seated beside Danny. Aside from Grampy and Maizie's random pops of chatter, a couple of spoons clanging against bowls, a slurp here and there, dinner was pretty quiet. Maybe the quietest meal she'd ever eaten at a table with three other people.

Danny's reaction to his photo on the cover of *Hollywood Daily* still lingered like a haze of smoke after a fire.

"I don't know why you're angry with me," she'd said to him once she recovered from the look on his face. "I didn't have anything to do with it. I just forgot to tell you about it."

"So you've seen it," he clarified.

"Yes, but only about thirty seconds before the FBI showed up at the store."

Danny had immediately gone out to the sun porch and sat down on the glider, and Jessie had left him alone there until it came time to serve dinner.

"Do you like it?" she asked him now, softly.

He lifted his eyes, and they were narrowed. Troubled. "It's really good."

She sighed and smiled at him.

"I'm sorry about before," he said, then he glanced at the others around the table as well, his gaze coming back to land on Jessie. "That was . . . quite a shock."

"Ya looked like one of those pretty boys they put on covers," Maizie stated. "Seems reasonable to put you on one."

Jessie giggled. "You did look really handsome that night, Danny."

He simply peered up at her over his bowl of gumbo.

"You with him at the shindig?" Grampy asked, and she immediately recognized why he asked.

"Yes, Grampy. That was my hand he was kissing."

"Wonder why you didn't make the cover," Maizie cut in.

Jessie had to admit she'd wondered that herself in those few seconds she'd had between seeing the cover and watching the rest of her life swirl around the Jack Stanton drain. "Mystery Man Turns Heads On Red Carpet," the headline had read. But then she supposed it was only fitting. A label-less vintage dress didn't stand a chance against the forceful, undeniable power of Valentino.

"How 'bout the bread?" Maizie asked them, just a decibel too loud. "You like the bread?"

"You make it?" Grampy asked.

"Why? That make a difference in whether you like it or not?" After making a funny little sound that sounded like a cat hissing, she muttered, "Old coot."

"It's good bread," he said. "It's fine. You want a sky-writer or somethin'?"

Maizie nodded at Jessie. "Don't you tell 'im which of us made the apple roll for dessert. The confusion'll have 'im wonderin' all night long whether he liked it or not."

"Fool woman. You think I can't figger out you made the apple roll? You been makin' the same thing for twenty years."

"Go on. Choke a little on it," she said, and Maizie pushed out of the chair and headed for the back door. "You kids enjoy your evenin'."

And like a sudden clap of thunder, the slam of the door punctuated the dark cloud hanging over their supper table.

⸗∞⸗

Yeh. He's the boy. The one I prayed t'ward my Jessie.

Now if the good Lord'll just give 'em both a shove. I ain't gettin' any younger here.

'Sides, I got a bushel o' things to talk to her about where's she might need a good strong somebody on the other side of 'er. My Jessie's heard enough bad reports over the years. Hate havin' to dump another one on 'er now.

Got no choice.

23

Danny hadn't meant to spend so long out there on the sun porch, but the night sky on the other side of that glass ceiling had captivated him. A midnight-blue velvet sky, silver glitter stars, and a bright crescent moon lounging in the midst of it all provided a great accompaniment for maybe the best cup of coffee he'd ever had and a third slice of something called apple roll.

"It's hard to break away from it, right?" Jessie teased softly as she appeared and sat next to him on the glider. When he looked at her, she clarified, "The night sky here. It kind of gets under your skin."

"It really does."

"Can I get you more coffee?"

He snickered and grinned, shaking his head. "Only if you want me awake until next week."

"I don't think it has as much caffeine as regular coffee," she commented.

"I didn't mean to have another cup, but it's pretty tasty. I usually take mine black, but even with the creamer, it's like no coffee I've ever tasted."

"Grampy loves this blend," Jessie said with a grin. "It's made from chicory, and you can apparently *only drink it* with a splash of warm cream added."

Realization set in. Of course. An old Louisiana tradition.

"He can tell you about it better than I can," Jessie said as she noticed her grandfather heading out to the porch.

"Whassat?" he said as he made his way to an easy chair on the other side of the small porch.

"Grampy, tell Danny what's so special about your coffee."

He grunted as he shifted in the chair. "Coffee shortage during the Civil War," he said, and it took him a few beats to get comfortable enough to expound. "Union blockades cut off the ports, 'n Nawlins folk heard tell 'bout a root you could roast up'n add to extend the life o' their coffee drinkin'. Evolved a bit o'er the years, but chicory coffee become a Nawlins tradition."

"Well, I'm not from New Orleans or anywhere close, but I'm feeling this coffee," Danny proclaimed.

"Maybe got a little Southern in ya after all, heh?"

"Must have."

Jessie beamed at them both, a sort of relief at the base of it. Danny imagined she must have wondered if the two of them would connect in a meaningful way, hoped it wouldn't be as awkward as it had been when her grandfather met the upscale, full-of-himself man she married. No, he and Stanton couldn't possibly have been more polar opposites. The only similarity or common ground they ever could have found rested in the saucy little brunette with the crystalline eyes sitting next to him. And when *he* finally married her, it would be for real.

His own thoughts stopped Danny in his mental tracks. Had he really just speculated so casually about marrying Jessie?

"This sounds serious, Grampy. What's going on?"

The trepidation in Jessie's tone of voice transported Danny back to the moment. What had he missed?

"Well, it is, Jessie-girl. Rather not have the talk a-tall, but your boyfriend there feels like I need ta be up front with ya, else he will."

Jessie turned toward Danny, embers of confusion and fear dancing at him in the dim light. "What's going on?"

"I'll leave you two with some privacy," Danny said, and he started to stand.

"Nah, you stay here now," the old man stated with a raised palm. "You might be needed here'n a minute."

He relaxed into the spot again, and Jessie reached over and grabbed his hand tightly without taking her eyes off her grandfather. "You're scaring me."

"Nothin' to be scared of. Not in the long run anyhow."

Danny formed a pocket around her rigid hand with both of his. His heart rate kicked it up several notches, and breathing fell shallow as a sense of dread shrouded them both; she for the news to come, and he for the pain he wasn't able to shield her from.

"Looks like I got cancer, baby girl."

"What?" she whimpered. Slipping her hand from Danny's, she rushed to her grandfather's chair, knelt in front of him, and took his hand inside both of hers just the way Danny had done. "Are you sure?"

"Yeh. It's fer sure."

"How bad is it?" she asked him.

"Purdy bad. By the time I figgered out somethin' weren't right, the catfish was nearly cooked in the skillet."

Jessie turned and gazed at Danny over the slope of her shoulder. "How long have you known?"

"I just found out too."

"Don't give him yer guff, girl," the old man said. "Just wanted to give him a chance to catch ya when I told you the news."

Jessie clasped his hand and laid her head to rest on it. "I can't lose you," she whispered. "You're all I have."

"Nah. You got a whole world built 'round ya now. I weren't goin' nowhere 'til that happened."

"Grampy," she said, gazing up into his weary eyes. "You're my only connection to Mama. To this place. To Louisiana."

He clucked out a laugh and shook his head. "You got Luziann in yer blood, Jessie-girl. And me an' yer mama right there in yer heart. None of us are goin' nowhere."

"Are you on medication?" she asked hopefully. "In treatment? What are they going to do for you? Are you in any pain?" She gasped. "Is that what Miss Maizie meant? I overheard her telling you to come clean about something. Does Miss Maizie know?"

Danny stood and placed his hand on Jessie's shoulder, sharing a knowing exchange with her grandfather. "I'm going to leave you two alone now." Grampy gave him a nod and the flicker of a smile. "I'll be in the kitchen finishing up those dishes if you need me."

He had the odd feeling as he left them that the air had been sucked out of his lungs, and his throat burned with acidic torment. The kitchen felt slanted, as if the floorboards had given way beneath every step. Instead of stumbling straight to the sink, he crumpled into the nearest chair and tilted his full weight toward the table. His mind went blank. Completely gray. He couldn't even think. His eyes ached, and he had to work at it to blink. He groaned, yet no sound escaped his seared throat.

After—he didn't know how long—he finally managed to bow his head.

I have no words, Lord. I just . . . have no words.

The house was so still. Jessie didn't think she'd ever known such a solemn silence. She sat upright in her bed, the indistinct muffled sound of her blankets cutting through the quiet with a sharp steel blade. She stared at the murky darkness of the bedroom she'd once known with such intimacy, but it looked like a stranger now. Some distant, cloudy memory of a place.

She thought she heard something in another part of the house, so she perked her ears and froze. There it was again, the creak of the floor. Probably in the living room. She climbed from bed and straightened the long tee that fell to mid-thigh. In case it was Danny wandering the house—one that would have seemed even more foreign to him than it had to her just a few moments prior—she tugged on a pair of jeans before opening the door.

Jessie felt relieved to find Danny seated in the easy chair on the sun porch, mostly because it meant Grampy might actually be asleep. He needed his rest. Danny glanced up at her with a tired smile as she approached.

"I'm sorry. Did I make too much noise?" he asked.

"No. I couldn't sleep."

"Me neither."

Jessie didn't give a second thought to slipping into the fold of Danny's outstretched arm and lowering herself into it, propped on the arm of his chair and folding down to his shoulder so that her head nested beneath his chin. He kissed the back of her head, and she sighed.

"What a terrible day," she muttered. "I don't know what I'll ever do without him."

"I . . . know."

"Talk to me about where he'll be, Danny. After, I mean."

"You mean, heaven?"

"Yes. Tell me. I want to hear about it."

And so he did. For over an hour, the two of them spoke in soft whispers about the eternity Danny believed awaited her grandfather.

Morning came more quickly than it should have for Jessie, and her midnight conversation with Danny out on the sun porch replayed on a loop in her mind before she ever opened her eyes. She'd finally kissed him goodnight sometime after two, slipped beneath the covers, and remained awake for quite a long while before sleep finally found her. And now it cruelly eluded her again.

She tossed back the blanket and used her toe to open the window curtain, craning her neck upright to peer out at the gloomy day before her. It seemed like Slidell had gotten the same news she had received about Grampy, and the sun just couldn't manage to shine on such a dark and terrible day. Apparently, the gray skies of Louisiana knew full well what a dreary world it would be without Grampy in it to brighten things up.

Just about the time she gave any real consideration to getting out of bed and making breakfast, Grampy's recognizable soft rap preceded the click and creak of the bedroom door.

"Haul yourself up," he said through the slight opening. "We're goin' out for mornin' grub."

Jessie grinned. "I just need fifteen minutes."

"Make it five. I'll turn the crank'n get the truck revved up."

She plucked a maxi dress with cap sleeves from the closet and slipped into bejeweled sandals before she even hit the bathroom to brush her teeth and straighten out her messy mop of bedhead. She added some powder and lip gloss, grabbed her purse from the bedroom doorknob where her Grampy had hung it like he used to, and hurried out the front door.

He had already backed the big red truck out of the carport, and Danny stood next to it with the passenger door gaping open. Shaking his head, he pulled what looked to be a five-dollar bill from his wallet and handed it to Grampy.

"What was that?" she asked, and she pulled herself up into the truck and slid across the seat to leave room for Danny.

"I told your grandfather there was no possible way you'd make it out here within ten minutes, and he bet me five bucks you would."

"Ye of little faith," she said on a giggle as he climbed in next to her.

"Brekkers on me," Grampy announced. "I'm feelin' all kinda flush right quick."

The ride toward Tilley's became increasingly familiar to Jessie as they headed up Pontchartrain Drive. Grampy had always loved having breakfast at Tilley's, and she recalled having a particular fondness for their cinnamon French toast with whipped cream and chocolate shavings. Before the days of trying for enlightened sensibility. Before the breakfasts of green smoothies and egg-white omelets (and heart-wrenching deprivation).

Several members of a new wave of regulars greeted Grampy as they filed in, and the waitress in her mid-fifties handed Danny a stack of menus and waved them on toward a table by the window. Jessie didn't actually *see their family name* engraved on it, but from all indications it may as well have been there.

Although her beloved French toast no longer graced the plastic encased menu, a similar treatment of pancakes caught her immediate attention. She gulped back her disappointment and moved on to more sensible offerings, landing on a veggie scramble with wheat toast and a pot of hot tea.

"For you, sugar?" the waitress asked Danny.

"I'll have the number four combination with ham and a biscuit."

"How would you like your eggs?"

"Over easy."

"Home fries, hash browns, or grits?"

Danny cocked a brow and smiled at Grampy. "I'll try grits."

"Coffee?"

"Please."

She smiled at Grampy. "The usual for you then?"

"Yeh."

"Okay. A veggie scramble with wheat toast and tea for you, young lady," she recapped. "Then two number fours with ham, biscuits, grits, and two coffees."

Jessie and Danny exchanged strange smiles before she looked to her grandfather. "Nice sales job, Grampy."

"Whatcha mean?"

"You must have told him the right breakfast to order, right?"

"Nah."

Danny chuckled. "He never even mentioned what he orders. Only that this is his favorite place to eat a few mornings a week."

Jessie's scrambled thoughts gave an amusing tap inside her head. Danny and Grampy were far more alike than she'd ever realized. *Or imagined.*

"Seriously?" she asked him.

Danny chuckled as he raised his fingers in a Boy Scout pledge. "On my honor."

"The boy and me got good sense, Jessie-girl," Grampy said as the waitress reappeared with a small pot of hot water for her tea and two steaming cups of black coffee. "Don't know what's such a mystery with that."

Jessie giggled, then she swallowed back the trepidation that came with her next thought. "Grampy," she broached. "I'd like to speak with your doctor."

He lifted his narrowed eyes, his coffee cup suspended between the table and his lips. "What fer?"

"I want to know what we can expect, what the plans are for your treatment, whether he thinks you need a second opinion."

"You don't think I ask 'im those things?"

Jessie sighed. "Did you?"

"Course."

"Then what are the answers?"

"To which 'uns?"

She resisted the pressure to spin out completely. Inhaling sharply, she asked, "What's your treatment plan?"

"Doc went over a coupla options, thought pumpin' me fulla chemicals was the best bet. And I ain't int'rested in that 'un."

"Grampy, chemotherapy is—"

"Save yer breath. Ain't goin' that route."

"At least let me contact another doctor for a second opinion on—"

"Don't need none."

Jessie glanced over at Danny who seemed inexplicably fascinated with the inside of his cup.

"He says antiques like me make the same decision all the time," Grampy continued. "It's a rough road considerin' the odds it'll work."

"Grampy, please."

"Please'n thank ya very much, Jessie," he snapped. "Now that's the end of it."

Jessie felt as if the lining of her stomach had separated from the rest of her body and had begun to swirl and churn, unanchored. After a somewhat long and uncomfortable silence, she let Danny and her grandfather carry the burden of talking around the elephant on the table, and their conversation felt nonsensical to her in the glaring light of everything not being said.

It irritated her, in a way, to hear Danny laughing and conversing with her stubborn old goat of a grandfather about topics like crabbing, woodworking—which she didn't even know Grampy still practiced—and Civil War history. Since when had Danny developed his knowledge about the differences between thingamajigs like "7-shot Spencers" and "16-shot Henry rifles"? Had the whole world turned upside down?

When her cell phone went off and she checked the screen to see Piper's name, she almost could have kissed her friend for the means of escape. She'd texted her a simple, three-word message before she finally fell asleep the night before: *911. Call me?*

"I need to take this," she commented, sliding out of the vinyl booth and heading for the front door of the restaurant. "Hi. It's Jessie," she answered, waiting until the glass door closed behind her to sit on the wooden bench out front. "You are a lifesaver, Piper. Thank you for calling right now."

"What's up?"

"Where do I start?" She took a quick look behind her. Grampy and Danny sat there chatting like old friends, and it galled her. "Grampy has cancer—"

"What?!"

"—and he's refusing chemo. Danny's remaining maddeningly quiet and supportive of this ridiculous decision—"

"Well, Jessie, you can't really blame him for—"

"Oh, and get this. On top of everything else that's gone completely crazy down here, I think Grampy is involved with Miss Maizie."

"That awful woman next door?"

"Yes, can you believe that?"

"Sweetie. Like you needed all this. What's the prognosis?"

"On Grampy's cancer, or his fling with Miss Maizie?"

Piper giggled, forcing a smile out of Jessie. "The cancer?"

"Who knows," she replied, exasperated. "He won't let me talk to his doctor, he won't get a second opinion . . ."

"What can I do?" Piper said.

"I have no idea."

"Oh, by the way, if you don't mind, I'd like to give Amber a part-time job until things get back on track."

"Oh. Really?"

"She's struggling financially, and I knew you couldn't afford to lose her to another job, so I'm thinking of having her help coordinate a charity event."

"Piper, are you serious?"

Jessie's heart flooded with emotions, from gratitude to relief to an overpowering sense of wonder—yet again—at Piper's many kindnesses.

"Well, I guess one of your benefactors at the store started up a nonprofit kind of like Dress for Success."

"Yes, Francesca Dutton and Rochelle Silverstein."

"Right. Well, Amber called me to see if I could advise them on launching, so we all had lunch together."

"You did?"

"Yes, it was lovely. But these two women need some serious cat-herding to get it off the ground. Amber is just the kind of shepherd that can take them on and give the charity a fighting chance at success."

Jessie chuckled. "Yes, she's good at that."

"So it's okay with you?"

"Of course."

"With your granddad sick, are you going to stay longer than expected?"

"I don't really know yet. Give me time to sort things out here, and I'll call and let you know."

"Good. Anything I can do from this end, just say the word."

Jessie placed a hand over her heart and sighed. "I love you."

"Love you back."

No sense in tellin' Jessie 'bout the first round o' chemicals they pumped into this old skeleton. How I lost what little hair I did have, didn't know if it'd grow back a-tall, but it did. Neither to tell 'er 'bout how sick a fossil gets while all that's happenin' inside his tired old body. And I don't guess she needs to know 'bout all the volts o' radiation they shot at me thinkin' it might kill somethin' that just won't die.

Nah, all Jessie needs to know is her old gramps stuck with her while she needed 'im. Looks like she's good now. I can rest easy knowin' she's standin' on her own two feet.

And Danny's two rock-solid feet too. That don't hurt none.

24

The morning sun hadn't yet climbed to its rightful place, but the Louisiana sky overhead waited in jubilant and colorful expectation. The rounded glass ceiling of the sun porch reflected the sun's efforts with golden-orange prisms of light that reached through the doorway to the rest of the house.

Jessie sipped from the cup of coffee Danny had brought her, and her vision grew blurry until she blinked back the mist of tears standing in her eyes.

"Danny, I just don't know how I can leave him right now."

"I know."

"Am I supposed to just pack up and go? Leave him here alone?"

He sipped from his coffee without making a sound. Then, "Do you think he'll let you stay?"

She stopped to dab her weepy eyes with the wadded tissue in her fist. "I don't know, but can he really stop me?"

Danny slipped his arm around her shoulder, and Jessie leaned into him. "No. He probably can't. But at some point, you're going to have to figure out how to honor his right to make decisions for himself."

"Even when they're ridiculous decisions?"

"Even then." He kissed the top of her head, which somehow soothed her nerves. "It's a matter of respect. And what little I know about your grandfather, I feel fairly certain that respect is supremely important to him."

"But . . . I still can't . . . I mean, how can I *leave him* and—what?—go back to California and live my stupid life while he's here alone and sick? I don't think I can do it, Danny."

"You can, and you will," Grampy said from the doorway, and Jessie jerked toward the sound of his voice, nearly spilling her coffee all over Danny.

"Grampy, don't do that," she said after saving it.

He shook his head as he passed them and settled into the easy chair.

"Coffee?" Danny asked, pointing toward the pot full of chicory coffee in the kitchen.

"Not quite yet."

"I'll just go refill my cup then. Jessie?"

"No, thanks. I'm good."

She waited for Danny to exit before she set her cup on the floor next to the glider and folded her arms over her thighs and leaned on them.

"Grampy, listen. I can work it out to stay here for however long you need me."

"You got a life to untangle," he reminded her.

"But it's not as important as making sure you—"

"Jessie," he snapped without raising his voice. "I been prayin' for you fer a while now. The good Lord gimme what I asked Him. Been askin' to see you got your life on straight—"

"Well, you certainly can't think *that's* taken care of," she cut in.

"Hush now. You got some loose threads, but ain't nothin' hangin' thatcha can't trim up. Now you go on and git back there. I ain't droppin' tomorrah, Jessie-girl."

Salty tears rose and stung her eyes. "Are you sure?"

"As sure as a body kin be in this world. S'all up to the good Lord from here, Jessie-girl. But you gotta go be whatcher gonna be."

"Grampy . . ."

"Don't wanna hear no more outta you 'bout this. You got a plane to LaLa Land you gotta catch."

". . . I can't."

"You kin 'n you will, girl. The end. Next story."

⸺∞⸺

The good-bye between Jessie and her grandfather had been heartrending to Danny, and the residue from the moment stuck with him like an inescapable stench. His unexpected emotional investment in Jessie had clearly grown over the months at such a rate of speed and intensity that it had extended out to encompass her family of one . . . because the thought of losing the man she called "Grampy" tore through him like a bullet shot into him at close range.

Danny couldn't shake that final conversation he'd had with Grampy out on the sun porch while Jessie finished packing. His heart squeezed slightly as he replayed all ten or so minutes of it. He looked forward to recounting it for Jessie one day. When the time was right.

He glanced over at her, curled into a ball in the airplane seat next to his, so soundly asleep that her stillness seemed almost eerie. He gingerly adjusted the dial built into the armrest to change the music piped into his headset to avoid disturbing Jessie's much-needed rest.

Blues.

Elevator jazz.

Country hits.

Classic oldies.

Sweet Baby James called his name, and he withdrew, leaning back into the cement-like seat to allow the music to lull him back in time. To an open Jeep—Jessie at his side then too—the rush of air tossing her spun-silk hair. He opened his eyes a couple of songs later, half expecting to see the Santa Monica coastline speeding by. Instead, an ocean of blue heaven stretched beyond

275

the oval window, and fluffy cloud pillows cushioned the space beneath the Airbus.

He wondered what awaited them upon landing at LAX. Maybe he should have texted Piper to let her know they'd headed back as scheduled. Would Jessie rather go home and sink into familiar surroundings alone, or detour to Tuscan Son for sustenance out of that "life-changing" bread basket she loved so much?

When Danny glanced over at her once again, her crystal blue eyes had opened, and she peered up at him with a contented, sleepy smile. She moaned softly and yawned as she squirmed closer and nestled her head against him.

"Good morning," he teased.

"Mmmm. Are we almost there?"

"Another twenty minutes or so."

Just as the song changed on the program, Jessie asked, "What are you listening to?"

"Classic hits of the seventies," he answered, and he sang along with Neil Diamond so she could hear.

"September Morn?" She pushed upright and lifted one side of the headset. "Can I listen?"

"I can get you your own, you know."

She giggled. "I don't mind sharing with you." Their heads plastered together beneath one set of headphones, Jessie hummed along for a moment. "My mama used to love this song."

"It's a good one," he commented. "Stands the test of time."

Jessie tilted her head and looked up at him, smiling. Danny almost couldn't help himself and he leaned in for a soft kiss just as the headset slipped off and smacked the side of his nose.

"Oops," she said with a giggle, tucking it back into place.

When the song concluded, Jessie removed the headset and gently moved it into position on his head again. He pulled it off and asked, "Do you want to stop and grab some dinner before heading back to your place? Maybe Tuscan Son?"

"I don't think so. I'm so tired. I'd love to grab a couple of burgers or something and just head home with them." She considered his reaction for a moment. "Are you disappointed?"

"Not at all."

"Let's just sit on the floor and watch some mindless television. Can we?"

"Whatever you want."

It took no time at all to make their way to long-term parking, load the Jeep, and head out toward the beach. They picked up fast food burgers and fries, which they consumed from opposite sides of the sofa. Ten minutes later, Jessie was sound asleep again.

After cleaning up the trash and covering her with a blanket from the closet, Danny scribbled a note that he left on the coffee table.

"Lock the deadbolts. I'll call you in the morning. D."

With the intention of driving home, he mindlessly redirected toward Newport and turned up at his folks' place where Frank nearly knocked him over the minute he opened the front door.

"Danny, you're back. How was your trip, honey?" his mother exclaimed as she greeted him with a kiss to the cheek.

"Long."

"Are you hungry? I've just made your father a sandwich."

"No, thanks," he replied, kneeling down to playfully smack Frank's jowls a few times. "I ate with Jessie."

"Oh, how is she? Did you meet her grandfather?"

"I did."

"And?" she pressed, leading the way into the kitchen. "What's he like?"

"He's pretty spectacular, actually." Danny's gut wrenched again, like so many other times since they'd left Slidell.

"But?" Leave it to his mother with that maternal sixth sense of hers.

"He's sick."

"Oh? A bug?"

"Cancer," he said, and his mother turned around in front of the gaping refrigerator door, her startled expression frozen.

"No," she finally said. "Honey, I'm so sorry. Is Jessie all right?"

"Not at all. She's pretty heartbroken over it. It was all we could both do to convince her to come back and tend to business. She wanted to stay there with him."

"Of course she did!" Without missing a beat, she asked, "Honey, did you want a chicken sandwich?"

"No. I ate."

"That's right. So what can I do for Jessie? Anything?"

Danny sat on one of the tall stools at the counter and smiled at her. "I don't think so. But thank you for asking."

"What about you? Is there anything I can do for my son?"

He sighed. "Actually."

"What is it?"

He swallowed in a sort of gulp. "Well. Remember a couple years ago how you said I could have Grandma's ring if I ever decided to get engaged again?"

The butter knife in her hand dropped straight into the stainless steel sink and bounced around with a clatter.

"What in the world?" his dad said as he padded into the great room. Smacking Danny's shoulder, he greeted him. "Welcome back, son."

"Paddy," she muttered. "Danny plans to propose to Jessie."

Several beats of silence ticked past as the three of them exchanged meaningful glances filled with questions, unspoken excitement, and awkward trepidation.

Finally, Danny's father chuckled. "Well, that's the best idea you've had in a while, son."

His mother, on the other hand, bolted suddenly from the kitchen and raced around the corner. Danny rounded the counter and topped his dad's sandwich roll and slid the paper plate toward him. When his mother appeared again, she held a small black velvet box in the palm of her hand.

As she opened it, she said, "Your grandmother used to say this ring would cover all the bases for the girl who got it. It's *something old*, and *something new* for the girl who gets to wear it. It's *something blue* because there are sapphires set on both sides of the diamond, and it's *something borrowed* because she only gets to wear it until she passes it on to her daughter or son one day."

Danny thought Jessie might really like that sentiment. Assuming she accepted the ring, of course. It was modest in comparison to the one she'd been sporting when they met the first time. But at the same time, she wasn't quite the same woman she'd been back then.

"How are you planning to ask her?"

He grinned at his mother and shook his head. "I haven't really gotten that far. This only settled on me recently."

"Well, make it romantic," his father stated over a mouth full of chicken sandwich. "Chicks like the romance."

"Paddy, really."

He shrugged before shooting Danny a wink and a nod. "Trust me."

Danny used two fingers to gingerly remove the ring box from his mother's hand, and he carried it with him into the great room and flopped onto the sofa with a groan. He placed the open box on his knee and stared at it. His mother sat next to him without making a sound.

After a minute or two, she finally touched his arm. "Is it the ring, Danny? Is it not what you remembered it to be?"

"It's beautiful," he replied. "I just don't know if it's Jessie's style. . . . Would you try it on, Mom? So I can see it on a small hand like hers?"

She smiled and plucked the ring from the box. She slipped it down the ring finger on her right hand and modeled it with an amusing flair, wiggling all her fingers and flexing her wrist dramatically.

"When we met at Stephanie's wedding, I remember she mentioned having a special fondness for vintage clothing," she said. "Do you think she likes it in jewelry as well?"

"I have no clue," he admitted.

"We had the ring appraised years ago, and I think the jeweler said the center princess cut diamond is just under a carat, and the two trillion-cut stones on the sides are sapphires. I forget if the band is white gold or platinum—I can look for the appraisal paperwork this week. But I recall he wrote it up as an . . . engraved art-deco-inspired . . . filigree setting."

He placed her hand into the palm of his and admired it. "It isn't just any old ring, is it?" he observed. "I don't think I've ever seen anything like it."

"And I think Jessie is just unique enough to appreciate a beautiful, uncommon engagement ring like this one, Danny."

"Yeah?"

"Absolutely. This is Jessie's ring, honey. I just know it."

He sure hoped Jessie would prove her right on that.

"I was so surprised to get your call," Piper said as the waitress set two cups of coffee on the table between them. "Is everything all right?"

"Oh. Yeah, sorry." Danny shook his head. He should have realized. "I didn't mean to sound so cryptic on the phone."

"No worries," she said with a bright grin as she doctored her coffee with cream. "It's always good to see you. I wanted to hear more about your time in Slidell anyway. How did Jessie's grandpa seem? She said he's pretty sick."

"Yeah, that was a rough conversation for him to have with her. They're both pretty strong-willed."

"Said the diplomat stuck in the middle of them."

Danny laughed, admiring the light in Piper as she joined in. Something about her levity just seemed to brighten the whole place.

"I know Jessie's so appreciative that you were there with her, Danny. And I think it's a relief to her that you got to meet him before anything happens. What did you think? He's a doll, right?"

"A doll," he repeated with a grin. "Not the word that I would have chosen. But I really did feel a connection to him. And meeting him made me see why Jessie is so extraordinary."

Piper nodded and sipped from her cup. "They have a very special relationship, and he had a huge impact on her growing up."

"He still has an impact on her," Danny remarked. "And on me, in fact. I'm really glad I got to meet him."

They fell quiet as the waitress delivered their meals. Eggs and bacon, toast and juice for Danny; an egg-white omelet with cheese for Piper.

"So I get the feeling you have something weighing on you," she said, her stellar green eyes bearing down on him. "What up, Danny?"

He pushed his breakfast plate forward a couple of inches and leaned hard against the chair. "Oh, you're good."

Piper grinned. "I try."

He cocked a brow and glared at her for a moment, trying to formulate the words he'd rehearsed on the way over.

"I think you know how I feel about your best friend."

She took a bite of her omelet and laid the fork to rest on the plate. "I think so, but why don't you articulate it for me."

He tried, but he couldn't avoid the overpowering sensation that lifted both corners of his mouth into a grin as if attached to marionette strings.

"Danny Callahan," she teased. "Have you gone ahead and fallen?"

He smiled. "I have."

Piper lifted both hands over her head in a muted celebration of triumph. "I am so happy to hear this."

"Then I hope you'll be equally enthusiastic about my . . . intent to . . ." He hesitated before continuing. ". . . propose."

For a few seconds, she reminded him of an image trapped on the screen when the cable broadcast froze. Her hands still suspended, she repeated, "Propose?"

"Yes."

"Really?"

"I thought I might."

"So you haven't yet."

"No."

"I see."

Did she? Danny wasn't sure. Even less sure when Piper lowered her hands to the table and gently rested them on the edge without speaking.

"Or not," he added.

She seemed to shake something sticky from her thoughts, and the various shades of strawberry blond and copper in her short haircut glistened as she did.

"So you think it's a bad idea," he surmised.

"No. Danny, no. I don't think it's a bad idea at all. I'm just . . . surprised?"

"Imagine how I feel."

She chuckled. "Are you sure? I mean, you've obviously given it a great deal of thought. Of course you have."

Danny leaned forward and smiled at her. "Piper, I didn't even know I had it in me to love a woman this much."

She seemed to gnaw on his words for a moment before she sighed and grinned at him. "Really?"

"She's the end of the line for me," he admitted. "I'm just not sure where she is on that page. Is she ready? Has everything that's happened with Stanton and her grandfather been too much for her? I don't want to overwhelm her. And this is where you come in."

"Me." She gazed out the window thoughtfully and sighed. After a significant silent pause, she turned her focus back on him.

"I don't think there's any question that she's in love with you, Danny. But . . . Well, maybe you could wait until after the court date tomorrow to decide about the timing of proposing."

He digested her words before nodding. That made good sense to him.

"Can I get your thoughts on one other thing?" he asked.

"Of course."

He leaned to the side and pulled the velvet ring box from the pocket of his jeans. It opened with a soft creak, and he turned it toward her and set it—facing her—in the middle of the table. The moment she saw it, she gasped.

"*Ohhh, Danny.*" She touched it with one finger. "May I?"

"Yeah."

Piper lifted the box with wonder and a certain sort of reverence in her green eyes, peering down at it with a sigh. "It's . . . exquisite."

"It was my grandmother's."

"Oh, she'll love that even more than the ring itself."

Danny leaned forward and looked at the ring with fresh eyes. "I mean, after that mountain peak she had on her hand when I met her, this will probably seem like nothing much."

"No, Danny. That ring was more about Jack than it was about Jessie. It's not like she went with him to choose it. He picked it out for their anniversary."

"You don't think this will seem like a pretty big leap backward?"

"Not at all. And you know," she said, brightening, "she loves vintage jewelry. It's so unusual."

"Unusual, good?"

"Very good."

"Are you sure? Because I could buy something more traditional, with a bigger stone."

"No. This is your grandmother's ring, and it's filled with meaning. Not to mention how lovely it is. You have to give her *this ring*, Danny."

He exhaled a solid mound of relief. "After tomorrow."

"Yes. Once things with the store are clarified. I think her attorney has a good handle on things, and he was very encouraging when I spoke to him."

"You spoke to LaHayne?" he asked as he tucked the ring back into his pocket.

"Last week. He asked me to come to court."

"He did?" he stated, wondering why.

Danny thought he might call and talk to Steph on his way back to the beach to see what she knew.

Wanted to ring up Jessie to give 'er a pep talk 'fore she headed into court, but I just didn't have it in me. Came home from Tilley's tuckered out, and laid to rest a minute on the davenport. Didn't wake up again 'til Maizie let the screen door slam.

The woman plucks my last nerve. But her cookin' perks this fella right up, so I got high hopes fer later on.

I'll give Jessie a call after supper.

25

Jessie had tried on three different outfits before landing on the simple Michael Kors gray and black colorblock dress she'd bought at Nordstrom a while back.

"Don't dress too upscale or too trendy," her attorney had advised. "Instead, we're going for understated and professional."

."I can do that," she'd replied. But two hours in her closet that morning nearly proved otherwise.

The moment Piper knocked at the apartment door, Jessie yanked it open and spread her arms. "How does this look? Be honest."

"It looks just right. Let's go so we're not late."

She grabbed the quilted clutch she'd prepared that morning and left on the end of the sofa, stopped at the table for her keys, and followed Piper out the door.

Jessie couldn't help but notice that during the drive downtown, they seemed to choose safe, random topics of conversation—limited to the weather, the new menu Antonio planned to debut in a few weeks, and the work Amber had been doing with Going Places, the nonprofit Rochelle and Francesca put together.

When she ran out of polite steam, Jessie leaned on the passenger window and groaned. "Do you think Jack will be there?" she asked.

"Oh, I don't think so. What did Mr. LaHayne say?"

"I didn't ask him. It just occurred to me this morning."

"There's no purpose in his being there, sweetie."

"Or anywhere else," she cracked. "But he sure seems to show up a lot of places where he has no purpose."

"I wouldn't worry about that."

Jessie inhaled deeply and released the breath with a rumble. "I don't know why I ever married that man." When Piper didn't reply, she added, "I don't think I'll ever take that kind of leap again."

Piper glanced her way and lingered a moment before returning her attention to the road ahead. "What do you mean? You'll never get married again?"

"I don't think so."

"You're going to lump every great guy out there in with the one who is the definition of bad apple?"

"I just can't see taking that chance again. This has been such a nightmare."

"I know. But . . . well, think about it. How different would marriage be with someone like . . . say . . . *Danny*?"

Jessie chuckled. "It's not like he's going to propose. Besides, I think things are just right like they are. Marriage is just so . . . life-altering. You lose so much of who you are when someone else steps into your personal space that way."

"As it should be," she defended. "In a good way though. Look at Antonio and me, sweetie. My life would be absolutely incomplete without him. And I don't lose part of myself for him. *With* him, I become complete."

"I know. I'm not down on marriage for the rest of the world. But for me . . . right now . . . I just can't see it."

"No?" Piper seemed to be formulating a very personal argument. "I'm sad to hear you say that. I hate the thought that you could miss out on a life with someone like Danny just because of the evil that is *Jack*."

The seriousness of her friend's tone tickled Jessie a little.

"I'll tell you what, Piper. If Danny proposes to me today, I'll accept. Will that make you happy again?"

"Very." Her smile appeared somewhat . . . satisfied.

After parking the car, they hurried into the courthouse. Finding the correct courtroom proved somewhat difficult. So much so that, when they finally did, Jessie took her place next to Charles LaHayne with such eagerness she didn't notice the two rows of people seated behind him until Piper slid in beside Danny.

She skimmed each face smiling back at her.

Amber.

Aaron and Charlotte Riggs.

Steph.

She gasped when she landed on the face in the first chair in the back row. "Courtney!"

Courtney wiggled her fingers in a wave.

On the other side of her, Jessie saw . . . *Francesca Dutton?*

"What's going on here?" she whispered to LaHayne.

"We're going to present a solid picture for the judge about the way your life was turned upside down by Jack Stanton, a man pretending to be your husband, but to whom you are not legally bound."

"Do you think that will help get my store open again?"

"Well, we can hope, can't we?" he said with a friendly smile, and he jiggled her wrist. "Each of these people is willing to testify that you had no knowledge of Stanton's business dealings, that you were as shocked as the rest of the world when it came out, and that—aside from the ring you had to hock to put a roof over your head and start your business—you've received nothing of significant value from him. I think—"

"All rise," the bailiff announced, sounding like an old town crier. "The Honorable Victor Preston presiding."

Jessie managed to push to her feet and stand erect next to LaHayne as the stern-looking judge in the black robe took his place at the front of the room and rapped his gavel.

"Please be seated," the bailiff commanded.

The muffled sound of people returning to the rock-hard benches fell to silence.

"Good to see you, Mr. LaHayne," Judge Preston said without looking up. "Is this your client, Jessie Hart, sitting next to you?"

He stood as if commanded to do so. "It is, Your Honor."

"It seems like you're in quite a pickle, Miss Hart."

She gulped around the lump in her throat. "Yes, sir."

"And we have Uncle Sam's representatives here as well?"

She hadn't noticed the familiar Twin Suits seated at the back edge of the courtroom until the male half stood. "Yes, Your Honor. Special Agent Dale Glenn, Federal Bureau of Investigation."

"Good. We'll start with you, Agent Glenn. And then I see we have the corroborating witnesses you promised in the courtroom today as well, Mr. LaHayne."

"We do, Your Honor."

"I've studied the considerable amount of paperwork you presented to my bailiff, and I'm familiar with the basics of the situation, so let's get started."

The testimony of the Suit was direct and unfettered by emotion, opinion, or even an attempt to waylay the efforts to restore Jessie's life. In fact, after two hours of give-and-take conversation that never once required Jessie to speak, it seemed it was Courtney who carried the most weight with the judge when she debuted her testimony with one of those charming and electric Courtney smiles.

"It wasn't easy for me to be here, Your Honor. I've only recently adopted my first child and was spending some time with her at my family's home in London. We weren't due to return to the States for several more weeks."

"London," he exclaimed, and his entire expression softened. "My wife is from Lea, Lancashire."

"Oh," she cooed. "It's so beautiful there."

"And yet you returned early. Can you explain to the court why you did that?"

"I had to come back, if there was even a remote chance it could help Jessie sort out this mess. I mean, she didn't cause it. And she's done everything short of slinging hammer and nails to rebuild her life with hardly a thing outside of her sense of integrity. That's got to count for something." She smiled again. "Doesn't it?"

The judge turned toward Jessie. "You have some very dedicated people in your corner, Miss Hart."

Jessie's heart squeezed slightly. "I can see that. And I'm grateful beyond words."

"I'll tell you what, people. Let's adjourn while I give this some further consideration, and I'll give you my judgment when we reconvene at four o'clock."

Blessedly, after such a long time of struggling to breathe—or even imagine what her life might be like after that very day—at 4:05 p.m., Judge Victor Preston took out his giant sharp scissors and cut the cord appending Jessie's life to Jack's.

"And while we're here, Judge," LaHayne said, but Jessie could hardly hear him over the caterwauling celebration inside her head, "there's the matter of Miss Hart's name. Since she was never actually married to John Fitzgerald Stanton in the eyes of the law, we would like to have it stipulated here that she can return to her legal surname of Hart."

Jessie Hart.

Not Jessie Stanton. Or Hart-Stanton. Just plain and simple Jessie Hart.

Well. Not plain. And certainly not simple.

The overpowering joy bubbling inside her had all the power of a jet engine propelling her into Danny's arms the instant the gavel rapped for the last time.

"I wonder what the Suit would do if I went over there and kissed him right on the mouth," she exclaimed in his ear as he held her. But when her eyes landed elsewhere, Jessie gasped. "Oh, I have to thank Courtney."

And with that, she flew out of Danny's arms, stopping to hug Amber and Charlotte on her way toward Courtney.

"Today," she heard Piper softly exclaim to Danny as she moved away. "Not tomorrow or next week, okay? *To-day.*" But elation kept Jessie from stopping to ask what she meant.

Epilogue

Jessie couldn't stop to talk fer long when she rang me up from her phone in the car. Just long enough to tell her old Grampy that all was right with the world agin. Seems her people rallied 'round 'er and the good Lord did the rest.

Said a quick hi and bye to Danny, too. We had a private chat, that boy an' me, here in Slidell, and I ask 'im on the phone if he had the intent to follow through on it.

"Any minute now," he says to me.

I hung up right quick. Now I'm just a-waitin' fer the phone to ring agin so Jessie can tell me the news and I can act out the surprise she'll be expectin'.

Gotta spend some time thankin' God above for wrappin' things up nice with a big shiny ribbon. I kin go to sleep happy tonight. 'Cause my Jessie-girl kin. And that's what I been waitin' on.

Group Discussion Guide

1. If you read the first book in this series (*On a Ring and a Prayer*), how do you think Jessie has evolved throughout the two books?

2. How does Jessie evolve over the course of this book in particular?

3. What is significant about Danny's foray into Jessie's world and the wearing of a designer label?

4. How do Jessie's choices affect Danny, specifically his role as a private investigator?

5. In the first book in the series, Jessie's grandfather existed only as a secondary character. Now that you've "met" him in this book, what purpose does he serve to advance Jessie's story and her relationship with Danny?

6. Out of the circle of female friends surrounding Jessie (Piper, Amber, Courtney), what does each of them bring to her life in this book that aids her evolution?

7. How did you react to Jack's return? Is he redeemable in spite of his terrible behavior?

8. What would you say were the three key turning points for Jessie and Danny in this book?

9. Where do you see this relationship going in the third and final book of the series?

10. How did you feel about the cliffhanger at the end of the book?

11. If you could choose one Scripture that represents Jessie's life lessons in the book, what would it be?

Want to learn more about Sandra D. Bricker
and check out other great fiction from
Abingdon Press?

Check out our website at
www.AbingdonFiction.com
to read interviews with your favorite authors,
find tips for starting a reading group,
and stay posted on what new titles are on the horizon.

Be sure to visit Sandra online!

http://www.SandraDBricker.com

A Bonus for Readers from Author Sandra D. Bricker

How's that for another cliffhanger, huh?

Jessie's certainly seen her share of obstacles toward her happy ending. But there's still one more novel in this series, so you know there's more to her story from here. How about a little glimpse into what the future holds for Jessie and Danny? Just for you, sweet readers . . . the proposal you've been waiting for.

Excerpt from
From Bags to Riches
Book 3 of the Jessie Stanton series

Jessie hummed along with James Taylor as Danny drove along in silence. She glanced over at him and smiled. She loved the way he always removed the elastic band from around the gear shift and pulled his shaggy, long hair back into a ponytail before they set out anywhere in his open Jeep . . . and the way he always reached into the box behind the driver's seat and produced a cloth band for her hair. Even the music serenading their drive embraced her with a comfortable, predictable lull. She'd had so much instability in her life that the calculability of Danny's behavior had become a welcome warm blanket on a chilly night.

"Hey," she said suddenly as a thought struck her, a memory of her best friend speaking to Danny in a whisper. "What was Piper talking about?"

Danny's dimples deepened as he grinned. "What do you mean?"

"Before we left the courthouse. She told you something like, 'Today. Not tomorrow, but today.' What did she mean? And where are we going, by the way?"

"To celebrate," he stated. "You have just been set free from a barnacle by the name of Jack Stanton. You're free. Your store can reopen, and you can write your name with confidence again. You, my friend, are Jessie Hart."

Not that she'd ever actually been Jessie Stanton, but for a dozen years or so, she'd been duped into believing it while living in a world of utter make-believe, a world Jack had fabricated for the benefit of just about everyone he knew—including her, his fairy-tale wife. Instead, Jack had been a handsome cancer making his silent and diabolical way into every available cell of her life, con-ning her into believing their world—his business, the home they made, and the dreams they'd been dreaming—had been built on a solid foundation of rock. But when the sand was discovered, that life crumbled so quickly she'd barely had time to escape with anything more than the clothes in her closet and the rock on her hand . . . both of which became the stuff new foundations were made of. In her case, Jessie's non-sand bedrock came from the sale of nearly four carats of perfect Neil Lane clarity dropped into a platinum setting, and the proceeds had funded a marginally acceptable apartment. The infrastructure of her brand-new life, combined with the designer labels left behind in her closet, had been built: ADORNMENTS. Designer labels for rent to wannabes with champagne dreams living on ginger ale budgets.

"Hey, wait a minute," she blurted as she noticed the familiar surroundings. "Where are we, exactly?"

"Somewhere we can celebrate."

"But where?"

She hadn't meant to let him off the other hook about Piper's cryptic comments at the courthouse, but new curiosity trumped old.

"Oh, wait a minute," she remarked. "Isn't this the beach where we parked our jet ski that day we went boating with Steph and Vince?"

Danny lifted one shoulder in a partial shrug that revealed nothing.

"Danny?"

He parked and shot her a quick smile before hopping out of the Jeep. "Let's go for a walk." He'd made the same suggestion the afternoon they parked their jet ski in the sand.

Jessie stepped out of her shoes and looped them over two fingers before quickly following his lead. As they headed across the shoreline, her memory confirmed the first—and only—time they'd strolled this particular beach together. And she remembered it now like it just happened the Tuesday prior.

Danny had taught her all about tide pools that day and the sea life surrounding them. And then he'd kissed her half senseless. He'd kissed her in a way that washed away all of her fears and insecurities about making another mistake. At least in that one enchanted, extraordinary moment . . . Jessie's doubts had drifted away.

"I haven't been kissed in such a long time before you," she'd admitted to him. "In fact, I'm not sure I've ever been kissed the way you kiss me."

She could almost feel his fingers tangled into her hair again as she walked with him across the sand now.

"Again, Danny," she'd muttered to him then. "Kiss me again."

"What are you grinning about?" he asked, dragging her back to the moment so rapidly that she nearly heard the thud.

"Just remembering the last time we were here." She slipped her hand into his. "That was such a special day."

"What was so special about it?" he prodded in a playful tone.

Jessie smacked his arm, and a pop of laughter spouted out of him.

"Something happened to me that day that had never happened before," she said as seriously as she could manage. "Don't you remember?"

"Oh, I remember."

"Good. Because a girl doesn't see her first tide pool every day. I've never forgotten that moment."

Danny deflated slightly, so she ribbed his side with her elbow.

"And then of course there was that kiss."

He shot her a sideways glance. "Oh, did we kiss that day?"

Danny led her with caution as they climbed to the ledge of flat rock where they'd perched that afternoon. A lifetime ago, and yet just a moment ago. He helped Jessie settle into place before sitting beside her.

She leaned forward, inspecting the foamy surf below. "No sign of the tide pool," she commented. "I guess they float away?"

"The tide's just higher than it was that day."

"Oh. Do you think—"

His warm touch on her arm stopped her words in mid-air between them, and she jerked her head toward him. Without a word, he lifted her hand to his face, kissing her knuckles tenderly.

A warm, unexpected grin wound its way upward and she asked, "What was that for?"

"For love's sake," he replied.

Jessie giggled. "You love me?"

"Is that really a question?"

She shrugged before leaning forward and giving him a sweet little kiss. "No. I guess not."

"Good," he said, "because I have a question for you now."

"Okie dokie."

He reached into the pocket of his jeans and produced his cell phone. "Hold this?"

"Sure."

He placed it into her hand before digging back into the pocket again. This time, he came up with keys, a few random coins and the stub from the parking spot. "These too," he said, placing them into her open hands in one lump.

"Umm, okay." With a clumsy chuckle, he dug into his other pocket, and Jessie cocked a brow. "What on earth are you looking for?"

Danny smiled as he produced a small black velvet box and displayed it in his open palm.

"What's that?" she asked him.

"Well, here," he said. "First . . ."

Leaving Jessie with a glaze of cold perspiration on both palms, the back of her neck, and all down her chest, Danny slowly—with painful deliberation—replaced his cell phone . . . his keys . . . the change . . .

"Danny," she finally exclaimed. "What's in the box?"

"Oh. This?" he teased, glaring down at the velvet box. "This is just something I wanted to show you."

Show me. Undefined disappointment curdled the words.

"Yeah. Okay. What is it?" The lid creaked as he opened it, and she stared down at an exquisite diamond and sapphire ring. "It's beautiful. Whose is it?"

"It was my grandmother's. Then my mom's."

His mom's ring. Of course. He wants me to consign it.

Jessie swallowed around the lump she hadn't noticed forming at the base of her throat. "Oh. And you're showing it to me because—?"

"Well, I remembered that you're into vintage jewelry, and I thought you might give me an opinion."

"An opinion. What kind of opinion?"

"Just one in general. What do you think?"

"Well," she started, then her lips closed tight.

"It's nothing like the rings you're used to, I realize," he said. "But I thought it was kind of pretty. Mom said the diamond's just under a carat, plus the two triangular—"

"Trillion," she interrupted. "The cut of the sapphires is called trillion. And the band is really intricate."

"Art deco inspired," he told her. "Engraved art deco, I think she said."

Realization dawned. "Oh," Jessie said. "So you were thinking of placing it at the store. I could do that for you."

"You really think a woman would want to wear it?"

"Of course," she exclaimed. "It's exquisite."

"Try it on," he suggested. "Let's see it on your finger." She grinned as she plucked the beauty from the box and slipped it on her right ring finger.

"Danny, it's superb."

"You think so?" Just before she pushed it all the way into place, Danny reached out and stopped her, removing it. "Not that finger," he said. "This one."

The exquisite ring had barely touched the ring finger of her left hand when Jessie's pulse kicked into overdrive. She looked up at him and their gazes locked as he pushed the band all the way into place.

"My grandmother said you have everything you need in this ring. All the somethings."

"The somethings," she repeated. "What are the somethings?"

"I don't know," he admitted with a shake of his head. "But one of them is a something blue, which is where the sapphires come in."

"Oh." She couldn't help chuckling. "Something old, something new. Something borrowed? The woman who wears it . . . She has to give it back?"

"No. But she does have to pass it on to her firstborn son when he falls in love."

"Ah. I see," she said with a slow nod.

"So you really like it?"

Jessie smiled. "I love it."

"It wouldn't be a disappointment after the boulder you had before this one?"

"Not at all," she said, still not entirely sure what they were talking about. "It's unique and it has vintage style of its own."

"Yeah," he said, inspecting it on her finger. "I guess it does." After a moment, he added, "Hey. You want to wear it for a while?"

"Me?"

"Yeah. Break it in or something."

"Rings don't really need to—"

"Just until you decide."

"Decide what?"

"Whether or not you want to marry me."

Jessie nearly choked, and it took a solid minute to recover. "Are you proposing?"

"That depends. Are you going to freak out, or say yes?"

"I'm not sure," she admitted.

"Then I'll get back to you on that."

So much for Danny's predictability. Of all the unpredictable things he'd ever said or done, this was the most unpredictable of them all.

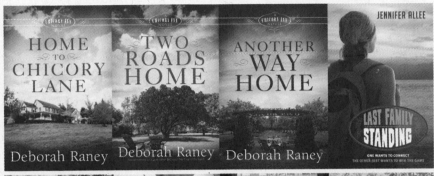

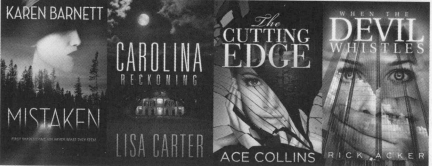

LP604   130